The Craving
Kiss me Deadly series

Anjalee Scott

Dedicated to my beta readers: Alicia and Tony. When the going got tough, your enthusiasm kept me going.

Prologue

Many centuries ago, Anubis, the god of the dead, fell in love with a soul he was transporting to the other life, and surrendering to her pleas, he placed her back upon the earth. Unable to restore her life, since that was only Isis's power, he left her there undead for all eternity. He demanded that she repay his kindness by sacrificing human lives, in his honor, by drinking their mortal essence. Then, so she wouldn't have to be alone, he sent her others of her kind to be with her, and they eventually spread throughout Egypt and then the world.

The homage to him eventually stopped, though, and he grew angry. And so, with help from his father, Osiris, god of the underworld, he inflicted mortality followed by death on some of them. The remaining vampires feared for their new lives and began to honor him by reproducing. This led to the deaths of more humans, as they were turned into the living dead, and Anubis was once again happy. It became a rule, then, that each new vampire had to create their own mate by their five-hundredth vampire birthday, or Anubis would call them home. It wasn't easy, though, because the mate had to be willing. It was the one stipulation.

One
Friday

It was a crisp, early September evening when the leaves were just beginning to turn, and Aria was walking across campus to her dorm room. She struggled to balance her book bag with her purse, along with the load of library books she carried in her arms, and she was failing miserably. A breeze blew past, ruffling her long dark hair all around her face, and it carried a musky fragrance. Now, she's a woman who loves a great smelling cologne on a man, but this didn't smell good—it smelled *damn good*. Her eyes quickly darted around the quad, but she didn't see any guys around, not even the cute one who sat in front of her in Government 201 and always distracted her with the Eternity fragrance he wore. This didn't smell like Eternity, Polo, or any of the others she had become familiar with, though. It smelled powerful—a raw strength that she doubted could be captured in a bottle—and it elicited a response from her sensitive lady area.

Suddenly, a chill ran down her spine as she sensed someone watching her. The cloudy sky was quickly getting dark, so she picked up the pace. Campus crime rates were low, and she didn't want to be the reason that statistic changed. She got back to her dorm room at Hudson Hall and found a flyer left by her roommate and best friend, Catherine Winston, taped to the bathroom mirror. It was advertising a fall bash in the nearby park with lots of music, young men, and booze—three things she needed after a long week of studying.

Aria had moved to San Francisco at the end of May from her hometown in Boise, Idaho. She had specifically applied to UCSF because of their Criminology program headed up by Dr. Lane Martin, who had written several books, which Aria had spent countless hours studying. The woman was her hero. Her ideas of a criminal's psyche meshed well with Aria's own ideas, so, naturally, she wanted to learn from her.

Aria had always been more into books than people, except for when it came to studying them. That was the real reason she was considering going to the bash to find Catherine. Cat was cool—and she was teaching her to loosen up and enjoy college—but Aria was more interested in what the impulsive fraternity pledges would do to prove their worth. In fact, she'd promised Cat that she'd consider pledging the Kappas with her, but there was no way in hell she'd let the members haze her just to show that she belonged.

She had a lot of friends back in Idaho, but, here, her shyness kept her from making more than a couple of friends. She mostly just had Cat and Kyle, her on again-off again boyfriend. Kyle was a decent enough guy, but his ego sometimes came between them. She wondered if he'd be at the bash and whom he'd be bringing with him *this* time.

Her cell rang, and she had to scramble across the messy dorm room to dig through her purse for it. She answered on the last ring, knowing from the display that it was Cat.

"Hey you," she answered.

"Girl. Gur-rl. You have got to get your skinny ass down to this party. All your favorite hot guys are here," she taunted, referring to some of the athletes Aria had secret crushes on. They were in Alpha Beta Gamma and went by the nickname the Mokers.

"I'm thinking about it," she hesitantly replied. Cat could be pushy when she wanted to be, and Aria knew this would be one of those times.

"Look on my side of the closet and wear the little black dress I've got hanging up," Cat ordered.

Aria felt backed into a corner. Part of her wanted to stay away from the crowd and relax in their room, while the other part wanted to go out and see what the night would bring.

Aria suddenly jumped when she heard scratching at the window. She rushed over to it and peered outside into the coming darkness but saw nothing except for the old oak tree. She sometimes hated living on the third floor; however, knowing someone couldn't climb in through her window was a comfort.

"Well?" Cat asked impatiently.

Aria bit her lip. "Okay, you talked me into it. Do you have decent shoes to go with the dress? I know I don't."

Cat giggled. She was a shoeaholic and had a little bit of everything crammed into their tiny closet.

"I might have something in there that will fit you."

Luckily for Aria, they were close in shoe size. Cat's feet were just a little smaller, though, so Aria usually had to go with an open toe.

"All right, let me tidy up and change, and then I'll come find you," Aria told her before ending the call.

She entered the small bathroom and pulled off her pink T-shirt. Her white c-cup size bra followed, as did her white cotton panties. She frowned slightly at her reflection in the mirror above the sink before grabbing a clean washcloth out of the cabinet. The frown wasn't a reaction to her figure—she felt it was decent enough—it was directed specifically at the apex of her legs. She hadn't been involved with anyone since Kyle, and that was over two weeks ago, so she had neglected shaving herself. She ran her fingertips over the soft dark hairs curling up on her mound and wondered if she should even bother with it. She bit her lip and contemplated doing some quick landscaping because she hoped to get laid soon, and she desperately wanted oral sex if she did. With her mind made up, she grabbed her razor and shaving foam and proceeded to make herself presentable again. Kyle had preferred her hairless, so, this time, she left a thin landing strip instead. She preferred a little badge of womanhood.

When she was finished with shaving and washing up, she donned a black push-up bra, a black thong, and then the skimpy dress that she found on Cat's side of their shared closet. She had to rummage through several pairs of shoes to find

a pair that she both liked and would fit into
without too much shoving required. The pair she
settled on was a pair of black strapped stilettos
with an open toe and silver studs, and since she
was borrowing a complete outfit, she raided Cat's
jewelry box for some earrings and hit the jackpot
with some silver hoops. Satisfied with her attire,
she looked at her reflection and touched up her
makeup before wondering about what to do with
her hair. She considered putting it up, but Kyle
had preferred that, and this wasn't about him.
After a three-month stretch of dating this last
time, she needed to rediscover her single separate
self. She used her hands to tousle her loose curls
and left it tumbling over her shoulders. She
spritzed on some Obsession, grabbed her purse,
and headed out for the party full of anticipation.

As she walked across the vast campus
alone, she couldn't shake the sensation of being
watched. She looked around and saw a group of
giggling females in the distance, and it made her
long for her friends back home—she wished she
wasn't shy so she could have friends like that in
San Francisco, too. A movement in the shadows
between two buildings caught her attention, and
she felt all her muscles tense up. Instinctively, she
hugged her purse tighter to her body while
reaching into it for her can of pepper spray.

A shout pierced the air as two young men
came bursting into the light. They were
roughhousing with each other and paying no
attention to her.

Ugh, Aria, stop being such a fraidy cat.

Feeling relieved, she picked up the pace to
get   to   the   party   in   the   park.

Two

It took Aria five minutes to get to the park and another five minutes to find Cat, who was surrounded by a group of guys. She admired her friend's confidence around the opposite sex. Even though Aria knew she was attractive, she was often painstakingly shy.

"Aria!" Cat called out, "It's about time you got your ass down here."

Aria shrugged her slight shoulders. "Sorry," she mumbled while trying to avoid the stares of the three young men standing there.

"My dress looks great on you, doesn't it boys?" Cat raised her brows at them, and they nodded in agreement. "Aria, this is Jason, Todd and Chris." She pointed to each man as she said their name. A chorus of "hellos" rang out, and Chris extended his hand.

"Hi," she mumbled back and took Chris's hand.

"Can I get you a beer?" he asked and pointed toward the kegs.

"Um, I guess so." Aria wasn't twenty-one yet, and she wasn't big on drinking, but she thought it might loosen her up enough to enjoy the evening.

"Great, I will be right back with it."

As soon as he left, the man named Jason began to trash talk him. "You don't want to talk to him. He's not good with the ladies."

Cat laughed causing the beer she had just sipped to spew out of her mouth. "You should talk," she said with a giggle.

"Hey, I hold my own," he defended himself and gave her a playful nudge to the shoulder.

"They're both no good," Todd interjected, "so you don't want to waste your time with either of them. You should get to know me." He stepped closer and lightly touched her arm.

Aria felt her cheeks go up in flames. She wasn't used to this kind of attention, and now that she had it, she wasn't sure that she liked it.

"Hey," Cat's whine pierced her thoughts, "what am I, chopped liver?"

Both young men looked her up and down and smiled. "Not at all doll," Jason answered.

Chris suddenly reappeared and handed Aria a plastic cup almost overflowing with beer. She took it while being careful not to spill it on Cat's dress.

"Thank you."

He smiled a boyish grin. "Sure thing."

Cat suddenly shoved past Aria, causing the amber liquid to spill forth on her, when a hip-hop song came on.

"I want to dance," she hollered over her shoulder and quickly made her way to the makeshift dance floor.

Cat could dance well, but it was in a particularly sexy stripper fashion. She enjoyed being the center of attention, and this was one way she guaranteed it. The three young men turned their attention away from Aria to observe.

"There she goes," Jason mumbled with a smile, and the other two nodded. "I think I will go help her."

Aria finished her beer and joined her friend as well. She figured it had to be more comfortable than standing with Chris and Todd, trying to think of something to say.

While dancing, she scanned the pavilion for Kyle, and sure enough, he was dancing with a tall, leggy redhead. Aria wanted to look away from them, but it was like gawking at a car wreck. When they began kissing, though, she did finally look away with tears stinging her eyes. The cruel worm of jealousy had burrowed into her.

"Hey girl, what's wrong?" Cat asked while looking in the direction that Aria had been staring. "Oh, never mind. I see them." She put her hand on her friend's arm and squeezed. "Hey, it's his loss. He's a jerk."

Aria nodded while wiping at the first tear streaming down her cheek. "I know, but I'm going to head out, okay? I'm tired, and I still need to do some studying before bed."

"Okay, be careful heading back, and I will see you in a little while"—she glanced at Jason—"Or maybe not." Her wicked grin gave away her plans for the evening.

Aria gave her a little wave and started in the direction of the campus. She turned, though, and headed to the other side of the park instead. She wanted a quiet place to think, and her dorm was   anything   but   quiet.

Three

Aria lost her way. Some would say—especially her parents—that she had lost her way in life, but right now, she had lost her way walking around the park. She was in Lincoln Park to walk around and clear her head, but now her head was screaming at her. She shouldn't have come here at night.

Fog was swirling over the sections of playground equipment, and she swore she could see shapes other than that of the slides and swings. She also thought she could hear whispering, which put her instincts on high alert.

Gangs probably hang out here at night.

The only self-defense she knew is the training she received from a short college class, so her hand tightened around the small container of pepper spray she had in her pocket. She clung to it like it was a lifeline.

"Maybe it will be," she whispered so softly, it wasn't even audible to her.

A rush of wind blew past her shoulders and tousled her hair with its icy fingers. She paused and sniffed the air—there was a scent traveling on the breeze telling her she, indeed, wasn't alone. It was almost like a man's cologne but none she had ever smelled before. It smelled powerful, masculine, and dangerous. She rather enjoyed it.

"Aria, get a grip and run," she screamed in her head. She only made it two feet in the dense haze, though, because she ran into something—strike that—it was *someone.*

The musky scent surrounded her just as much as the fog was as she backed up and pulled the pepper spray out of her pocket. She hoped with all her heart that it was in the *on* position.

"Come to me," a sexy voice whispered on the fog. "Come to me, my angel."

Her legs felt heavy, as if the fog had a grip on them, as she tried to back up, hoping to bolt for it. She couldn't run. She even stopped walking backward because she felt like she was in quicksand.

The large shape approached, and she wondered if she'd pee her pants right where she was frozen solid.

The fog lifted just enough to outline the physique of a tall man with dark hair down to his massive broad shoulders. However, the thing that really caught her attention was his eyes. They seemed to glow a light blue in the darkness. Even through the mist, which still danced around them, she could clearly make out sky-blue eyes.

"Come to me," he whispered again, and this time, she noticed just how erotic his voice was. It was velvety-rich and deep, almost a purr. She could actually feel it pet her at the juncture of her thighs, and the vibrations caused her to grow damp.

Against all rhyme and reason, she took a step forward.

"Good," he approved and took her by the hand. "Now, this will sting." He pulled her into his massive embrace and leaned in to kiss her, or so she thought. He bypassed her lips and went to her neck.

Aria felt a piercing sensation, and a soft mew escaped her lips. Then she felt his tongue as he lapped at her skin and his hands as they roamed and squeezed her hips, then her waist, and finally the rigid peaks of her lush mounds. As ripples of desire coursed through her veins, she began to feel faint. Her knees began to give out and she felt herself slumping. Then she could feel the cold hard ground beneath her just before everything faded away.

He was the beginning and the end.

Four

Saturday

Aria woke up to the sound of children playing nearby. Without opening her eyes, she mumbled, "Turn the TV down, Cat."

The noise continued, though, and bright light from the window shone on her face. Then it dawned on her that her bed felt hard and cold, so her eyes flew open.

"Why am I here?" she questioned aloud. She recognized the park, but she couldn't remember why she was in it.

She slowly stood up and brushed the dirt off her backside while she looked around to see if anyone had noticed her. It didn't appear as if the mothers watching their little ones play knew she was there. She looked down and saw the black dress and high heels, which she knew belonged to Cat, and she started to remember the night before. She flashed back to the party, to Chris, Jason, and Todd, and of course, to Kyle and his date. After that, she drew a blank. She had no idea why she'd be in the park, but she knew she needed to get back to the dorm.

She took a step, but a wave of dizziness overcame her, so she hesitated. She felt weak all over.

Coffee. I just need some coffee.

Slowly, she made her way back to Hudson Hall ignoring the curious stares from the doting mothers, who were no doubt wondering where she was coming from dressed the way she was.

Her steps were awkward because of her fatigue and the heels she was wearing, but she finally made it to her room on the 3rd floor of the antiquated dorm. Cat was still sleeping soundly in nothing but a skimpy pair of panties and tank top. Aria thought about waking her to get some answers about the previous night, but she figured she got in late herself, so she let her sleep. Instead, she opted to take a shower before she had her coffee. With her plastic caddy full of products in tow, she padded off to the shower room.

There was a redhead bathing herself when Aria stepped into the community shower.

"Hi," the pretty woman immediately acknowledged her presence.

"Hey," Aria replied.

"I just started here, I'm Marissa."

"Nice to meet you, I'm Aria."

Marissa wrung out her long hair and gathered her belongings. As she passed by, she said in a low voice, "It was nice to meet someone who's not totally stuck on herself. A lot of the girls on this floor have been real bitches so far."

Aria just stood there with her mouth gaping open. She'd never thought of the girls in her dorm as being hard to get along with, and she hoped the girl wasn't referring to Cat.

She quickly bathed and headed back to her room, where she found her roommate awake and watching television.

"You finally decided to join the living, huh?" Aria asked in a playful, upbeat tone. "It's about time."

Cat slanted her eyes at her. "Someone's in a good mood and doing the walk of shame."

Aria grabbed a second towel from her laundry basket and gathered her hair up in it. "No I'm not"—she paused and focused her gaze on the wall instead of her roommate—"Well, at least I don't think so. I woke up in the—"

"Whoa, whoa, whoa," Cat interrupted her explanation with eyes as wide as saucers. "What is that on your neck? Is that a hickey?"

Aria's hand flew to her neck, and she realized it was a little tender to the touch. She ran to the bathroom mirror to look at it, and Cat was right behind her.

"Don't pretend like you don't know what I'm talking about? Now give me the dirty details. Was it Chris Woodson? I noticed him leave not long after you did."

Aria strained her neck toward the mirror to examine the sore spot, and she was surprised by what she saw—on her neck were two tiny holes.

"What is that? It's not a hickey," Cat stated the obvious.

Aria shrugged with a sigh. "I honestly don't know, but my guess is a spider bite. I was on the ground after all"—she touched the sore spot again—"still..."

"Still what? What aren't you telling me?" Cat put her hand on her hip and wagged a finger. "It *was* Chris, wasn't it? You guys got kinky, and he bit you."

"No. I mean I don't think so. It seems like something happened that I should remember, but I can't."

"You'll just have to retrace your steps then. Now, I'm starving, so let's go get breakfast."

"Yeah, okay." Aria hesitated at the mirror before going back into the bedroom. "Give me a minute to get dressed."

Aria dug through their small closet and settled on a black hoodie and blue jeans. Then she quickly pulled her hair up into a ponytail and put on some light makeup.

"Are you ready yet?" Patience was not one of Cat's traits.

"Yep, let's go."

They walked to the school cafeteria and stood in line behind a bunch of gossiping girls.

"She didn't even come home last night," one of them complained, and Aria felt a flush creep up her face.

She didn't think they could be talking about her because she didn't know any of them, and she didn't think Cat did either, not that she thought her friend would talk about her behind her back anyway. However, it still made her self-conscious.

"Sounds familiar," Cat whispered low.

Aria's face scrunched up. "Oh, hush now. I wasn't doing anything immoral."

Cat scowled at her friend. "Bummer then."

Aria had to laugh at her roommate's callousness. "You are terrible," she whispered back. Then she listened more to the other girls' conversation.

"I'm really worried," the whiny girl continued, "She's never done this before. It's not like her at all."

"Did she go to the party and maybe meet a guy?" one of the other girls asked.

"No, she was in the library studying for a big exam."

"The campus library?" the third girl inquired with concern in her voice now too.

"No, the public library downtown."

Just then, a boy rushed up to a group of males in the line ahead of the girls, and excitedly asked his friends, "Did you hear the news? A girl was found dead in the woods near the library."

"Oh no!" the first girl wailed. "I bet that's Trish. I have to go." She took off running, and her friends were close on her tail.

The boy that had spread the news jumped the line behind his friends and Aria considered saying something to him about it, but she thought better of it. She was too shy to confront people like that, and she hated it.

"That could have been you, you know?" Cat scolded her. "You could have been found dead this morning too."

Aria's mouth pulled down in a frown. "Don't be so dramatic. We don't even know what happened."

"Hmm. Let's find out"—she tapped the guy on the shoulder—"Excuse me, was the girl murdered?"

Surprise registered on his face, but then he smiled at both of them. "I don't know. Police are checking it out. Hey, how about I buy you two lovely ladies breakfast today?"

Cat grinned at Aria and replied, "Sure."

"All right," he said with a smug grin. *Leave it to Cat to pick up a guy in the cafeteria line.*

"Cat," Aria began, "I'm going to go find out more about the dead girl. I will see you back at the dorm."

"Uh! You can't leave now," her roommate whined.

"Sorry. The truth is, I've lost my appetite. I'll see you later."

With that she turned on her heel and walked off in the direction of the dorm. She was going to make some phone calls to try to get the scoop on the story. She felt she had to because, in her gut, she knew it had something to do with her.

Five

Kellan, shapeshifted into a crow, flew over the city looking for prey. He despised the daytime hours when he had to shift into an animal form because it took away the power he felt as a vampire. It was better than just lying in wait in the cavern where he slept, he supposed, and sometimes it helped him find his human prey for that evening. It did the day before—he had watched the girl go into the library at sunset and waited until dark when she had reemerged. She had been fun.

He swooped down into a tree as he recalled how much fun the girl had been. He had noticed the confident sway of her full hips first, and then he noticed her full luscious lips and perky mounds, which were hugged by the obviously tight sweater she wore. They were jiggling when she walked and begging to be caressed, he was sure of it. He had grown full and hard from the sight of her and the thought of her warm blood seeping slowly into his hungry mouth while he enjoyed the pleasures of her ample flesh. When she left the closing library, he had swooped in on her and led her to the nearby forest. With a few soft words whispered in the wind, she was his—body and soul. He had held her up against a tree while thrusting himself into her wet insides. He had felt her muscles tensing up all around him while he hammered into her and listened to her breath come in short bursts. She gasped a few times when he pushed into the deepest corners of her flesh, and that only fueled his passion, his hunger. His mouth trailed a blazing path down her neck and lingered over her pulse point. He licked her there before sinking his teeth deep inside her soft flesh. Her blood spilled forth in a red river just as his seed spilled forth in a thunderous climax all over the outer folds of her swollen satin lips.

"More," she had whispered, "I wan—" She sank to the ground as her last breath escaped her lips. To keep his existence hidden, he used a pocketknife to cut a deep slit over the puncture marks.

After that one, there had been the raven-haired beauty in the park. How fortunate he had been to find her. She tasted so sweet—like honey and vanilla—and smelled like wildflowers. He would have taken his time tasting her flesh and using her for his pleasures if he wasn't so expended from the woman at the library. Damn the luck that he hadn't found her first. He had been so mesmerized by the vixen that he had completely forgotten to slit her throat.

Oh well. Even if they suspected vampires are real, how would they prove it?

He took flight again and scanned the college campus for someone to have that night. That's when he saw her—another raven-haired goddess. He swooped in closer to imprint himself with her scent and almost flew right into another tree. She smelled of wildflowers just like the girl from the previous night—it was the exact same scent. He flew in a little closer to get a better look and nearly fainted away. It wasn't possible, but there she was—alive and well. Stranger still, it made him slightly happy.

He flew near her while she walked across the campus until she went into a building. He was stuck outside her dwelling until invited in by someone, and that, of course, would have to wait until he was in his vampire form.

Six

Aria had the feeling of being watched again, but she looked around at the other students sitting out on the grass and walking by, and no one was paying any attention to her. *Paranoid much?* She shook her head to remove the uneasy feeling, for all the good it did. She figured maybe it was just the crazy crow that kept flying in close to her, but she kept a watchful eye out.

Relieved to finally be inside her dorm, she bypassed some girls she knew at the lobby soda machine and went straight to her room. She ran a Google search on her phone for the number to the local police department. She thought that if she pretended to be on the campus newspaper staff, someone would give her some useful information pertaining to the recent murder. Unfortunately, she was stonewalled—they weren't willing to release any specifics in the case.

Frustrated, she drummed her fingers on the small student desk and thought about other ways to find out what she wanted to know. Then it came to her—Tabitha Reese. She was the police chief's daughter and a huge gossip. She was also in Aria's first class on Monday—Abnormal Psychology. Aria smiled to herself at her small success but then frowned as her fingers played across her neck where the mark was. She knew the two things were connected somehow, but it didn't add up for her yet.

On the way to study in the library, Aria ran into Kyle—literally. She was rounding the corner and bumped right into him. To make matters worse, he had his arm lazily draped around an unfamiliar girl's shoulders. Aria felt her face go up in flames.

"Um, sorry," she mumbled without making eye contact with him or the girl.

He laughed arrogantly and replied, "It's all right, babe."

Babe? As fast as she could get her feet to move, she sidestepped them and walked down the corridor to the library.

To her surprise, Tabitha was in there and surrounded by a group of chattering girls. Aria sat at the next table and strained to listen in. As she suspected, they were talking about the lady found dead in the woods behind the public library. Now was her chance to get information, so she slipped herself into the conversation.

She found out that the woman had been discovered with her throat slashed, and she had bled out from the inflicted wound. So far, the police had no suspects, but they had questioned her long-time boyfriend because evidence of recent consensual sex had been discovered.

"Did you know her?" Aria heard herself ask the group as they stood to leave.

Tabitha gave her a once over before answering, "No. Her name is Trish Rose. My dad said she is, well was, a student here though"—she turned toward the others and spoke a little faster—"Then he lectured me on campus safety yet again." She rolled her eyes while blowing a bubble from her chewing gum.

The librarian gave the females a stern look, so Tabitha and her friends left, while Aria took books out of her bag. Studying was almost useless, though, because she couldn't concentrate on what she was reading. Her mind kept going back to the morning when she had awakened in the park. She still had no recollection of how she got there, but she'd figure it out even if it took her days to do so. Deciding it was a waste of time to be there, she gathered her books and headed back toward the dorm.

She had plans to meet Cat for lunch, but her appetite still evaded her, so she called her roommate and begged off by complaining of a stomach ache.

"You aren't pregnant, are you?" Cat teased.

Aria scoffed, "You have to get laid to get pregnant."

"Well, if that's a suggestion, I hear Chris was really into you last night."

"No, Cat, it's not a suggestion. I mean, he's cute and was nice too, but I'm not looking for anyone right now."

"Shit girl, your finger will go numb before you find someone as nice as Chris. You should snatch him up."

"I will pretend I didn't hear that," Aria replied with a light giggle. "I'm going back to the crib for a nap. Catch ya later."

As she hung the phone up, Aria felt the hairs on the back of her neck stand on end. She sensed someone watching her, again, but the only other students around were minding their own business. Then she saw it—the crow. The bird was only four feet away, and its beady eyes watched every step she took.

When she reached her room a few minutes later, she lay on the twin-size bed and closed her eyes while focusing on her breathing. She attempted self-hypnosis to recall the events of the previous night.

She was walking through the park and then stopped when she could smell something fragrant. Flowers? No, it was a man's cologne. It was intoxicating and spellbinding. She saw him in the fog. He was tall, broad shouldered, and from what she could see, heart stopping gorgeous. He called out to her with the most wonderful voice. It was deep and soothing, and there was no way to deny his request. What was it again? Oh, yes, he wanted her to walk to him, but her feet had felt so heavy. And the fog…it held onto her. Then she felt a sting.

Aria's eyes flew open. She remembered everything.

Seven

When she came out of her trance, her hand instinctively flew to her neck. *Was I really bitten?* She ran to the bathroom mirror and examined the area. It wasn't as visible now, but she could still make out two tiny puncture marks. *Well, what does that mean then? Why would someone bite me?* She didn't have the answers, but she knew where to start looking for them. She grabbed her purse and keys and headed for the parking lot. She'd go to the public library first and then the park.

The sun was already setting, casting shadows on the building walls all around her as she located her 2012 blue Camry in the parking lot. The car had been a high school graduation gift from her parents, who had been trying to compensate for the fact that she was adopted ever since she found out in the eighth grade.

The crispness in the air sent shivers down her spine as she climbed in behind the steering wheel. She didn't mind the cooler temperature, but she hated the shorter days. She glanced down at her pale arms—she hadn't even gotten a tan over the summer. As she started the engine, a sudden thud startled her. She looked up from the ignition and found a black cat on the hood of her car. It was staring at her through the windshield, and it gave her even more chills. It wasn't a dislike for cats—it was just the intensity of its gaze. She got out of her car and tried to shoo it away, but it didn't want to budge. Then, when her hand got too close, it nipped her and ran off.

"Ouch! Bad kitty," she called out after the feline.

With a deep sigh, she got back behind the wheel and pulled out of her parking space. She wanted to get to the library before the last bit of daylight turned dark.

Kellan had run off behind some shrubbery to hide while licking her blood from his fangs. He just needed a taste to be sure, and now he was—it was the taste of honey and vanilla. He glanced toward the setting sun and smiled on the inside—it wouldn't be much longer before he could find her and taste her again. He thought about shifting back into a hawk and following her, but another beauty nearby spotted him and scooped him up into her embrace.

"Aw, what a cute kitty," the girl cooed as her delicate hand stroked between his ears.

Kellan breathed in the mixture of her perfume and pheromones and decided she'd make a delicious snack.

"I'm going to sneak you into my room. Shh"—she held a finger up to her lips—"don't tell anybody."

Don't worry, my pretty, neither of us will be telling   anyone   anything.

Eight

Aria pulled into the parking lot of the library and parked where she found yellow crime scene tape hung at the edge of the woods. As soon as she stepped out of the car, the pungent metallic smell of blood stung her nostrils. Moisture pooled in her eyes, and she couldn't tell if it was from the odor or if it was from her sympathy for the girl.

Slowly, she approached the closed-off area while having second thoughts about being there. She checked to make sure no one was watching before stepping past the yellow tape and approaching where blood had stained the grass. It was dark out now, but the moonlight struck down upon the discoloration. She took a deep breath and knelt to touch the grass. The area was much larger than she had anticipated, and when she pulled her fingers away, they were sticky. She pulled them toward her face because there was something besides the smell of blood. There was the smell of a man's cologne in the air. She could definitely smell a heavy, although pleasant, musk—and it smelled familiar. She felt an alarming reaction between her thighs. Given where she was, and what had happened there, she shouldn't feel hints of desire, yet dampness clung to her.

Gathering her wits, she jogged back to her car and drove the short distance to the park all the while wondering if going there was the right move. *What do I really expect to find there?*

She slowly walked around the deserted playground, breathing in the heady scent of the same musk. It was a lot stronger there, and so was her body's reaction—she immediately grew wet, and a tingling sensation erupted between her velvety lips. Her fingers went to her neck and traced where the bite was while her mind tried to sort   everything   out.

Nine

The young coed had placed Kellan on the floor and stripped down before stepping into her bathroom just as the last bit of daylight had slipped away. He had control over shapeshifting, so he waited until he heard the shower water running before changing back into his vampire self. He picked her blouse up off the floor and breathed in deeply. She didn't smell like wildflowers, like the other beauty, but she smelled good like a woman should. He picked her panties up and sniffed them as well. Her scent beckoned to him, and his rod grew hot and heavy. There were two things that made his body cling to the human world: his heart racing when he drank blood and the pleasure he attained from sex. In a matter of mere minutes, he would enjoy both.

By the time the water shut off, he was lying down on her bed. She emerged from the bathroom in nothing but a towel and gasped. Her eyes flew to the door and then back to him while she weighed her options. One hand reached for the bathroom doorknob while she considered backing up into the small room.

Kellan wasn't worried. No matter what, he would have her—completely. He crooked his finger, while she was frozen in fear, and called out to her in slow soothing tones.

"Come to me, my beauty. Drop the towel and come here."

With wobbling knees, she did as he requested and let the towel fall to the floor. Her body looked delectable in the spray of moonlight shining through the window, and he became even more aware of his throbbing. When she got to the bed, he stood up, towering over her, and took her left hand into his right. He slowly drew it to his lips and gave it a seductive kiss. It wasn't necessary—he already had her under his spell—but it was something he liked to do. When he had been human, in the sixteen hundreds, it had been a common practice for aristocratic men to treat their women with gentility, and he liked keeping that piece of humanity with him.

Her free hand roamed up his bare broad chest, and she made soft mewing sounds when his muscles rippled in response beneath the graze of her fingertips. She pressed her own bared chest against him, while her hands made their way around his trim waist, and her rose-tipped nipples tingled as their skin made contact.

He leaned down to capture her soft, pink lips to suckle them before his tongue found its way into her mouth to dance with hers. He felt her body tense up when her tongue brushed against his fangs, so he broke the kiss and moved his mouth along her jaw line to her neck. He planted seductive kisses along her neckline and lingered over her pulse as one hand cupped her perky breast. It was tender and swollen beneath his rough hand as he teased its protrusion, and it beckoned his mouth. He flicked the erect nipple first before drawing it deep inside to claim it while his other hand slid down her torso to her triangle of curls. He pushed past her downy mound and over her velvet soft lips while his mouth continued to torment her peaks.

The girl moaned and ran her hands through his hair and then over his massive shoulders. Her claws dug into them when his finger slipped between her lips to tease the entrance to her fiery furnace.

"Oh, God, put it in. Please stop teasing me," she begged on a pant.

Kellan chuckled and gently pushed on her shoulder to make her fall back onto the bed. He would have taken his time with her, but he still needed to find the other woman before she made it safely home, and he had every intention of taking that slow.

He grabbed the girl by her calves and pulled her to the edge of the bed before draping her legs over his arms. He looked down at her womanhood, splayed open before him, before driving his hard shaft inside her heated tunnel. His flesh filled her completely, and he began to grind his hips into hers. She bucked wildly beneath him and screamed her pleasure into the darkness of the room. With each hard thrust, her cries became louder until he finally put a hand over her mouth to quiet her. Then he leaned in and bit into the breast that he had lovingly licked just moments before. She screamed into his palm while her heart rate quickened to an unbelievable pace.

He continued to drain her until her raspy breaths, coming out of her nostrils, ceased. Then he took his knife out of his pants pocket and slit her throat, but there was hardly any blood remaining to run out. He laughed silently to himself.

They'll have a hard time solving this case.

By the time her body was discovered, the puncture marks would be barely noticeable, and the police would be left to wonder where all her blood had gone.

Satiated for now, he left the crude dormitory to locate the mystery woman. He found a private area outside of the building to shift into a hawk to make his search faster. He would just have to follow his nose, or in this case beak, until he found her.

He swirled the night sky over the campus, the town, and then the park where he had first met her. He couldn't see much through the dense fog that had settled over the area, but he could vividly smell wildflowers in the air.

Ten

Aria passed by the seesaw and sat on one of the swings. She came there searching for answers, but she still didn't have any—at least none that made sense. The only thing that connected the dead girl's attack and her own was a scent, and that wasn't much to go on. It certainly wouldn't do the police any good.

After the swing stopped its sway, she stood up to leave, but she had only taken one step before freezing in her tracks—a soft thud nearby caught her attention and put her on alert. She quickly patted her pocket for her can of pepper spray, but it was in the car. The only thing she could do was run, but as the musky scent grew stronger, she knew that wasn't happening—her feet felt like lead weights.

The fog that had been swirling around the park parted like the Red Sea as a shape emerged. She didn't have to be any closer to him to know he was the source of the musky scent. She didn't have to be any closer to him to know he was dangerous. But he got closer.

Kellan chuckled softly before purring, "I've been waiting for you; although, I'm still not sure how this happened"—he reached out and took some strands of her hair, which he brought to his nose before letting it slip through his fingers—"but here we are. The Fates have brought us together again." He chuckled once more.

Aria was completely mesmerized by the sexy man. She couldn't see his face, because it was dark and cloudy out, but she knew he must be gorgeous. His light laughter stoked the heat of her already warm, dark haven while his voice brought it to a rolling boil. Tingles, like shockwaves, ran down her arms, which he now gently grazed with his fingertips—or was it his fingernails? Either way, she found it incredibly erotic.

Her voice cracked as she managed to choke out, "Again?"

"Why yes," his sultry deep voice hummed, "But I think you already knew that. However, just to be sure I'm not forgotten, let me give you a sample of what's to come." He leaned down and captured her lips with a bittersweet fervor while his hand moved from her arm to search for the soft fullness of her bottom.

Aria's mind screamed at her to run, while her body accepted his voracious invitation. She knew whole heartedly that she should be attempting to fend him off, but she lost all control over her senses while he searched the corners of her mouth and squeezed her ass, forcing her to nestle against his groin, which, she could tell, was full and hard. The fire inside her reached new heights as the stranger's hand moved up to cup her breast and torment her nipple.

When his mouth gave her some reprieve, she moaned, "Why?"

His lips stopped their trail down her neck, and in an amused tone, he answered, "Because it feels good," before going back along his path.

Aria didn't quite know what to say. No matter how much her brain screamed at her to shout, "Stop," she just couldn't form the word. However, a sharp stinging sensation suddenly arose from where his mouth was, and she did scream. She screamed and struggled to get away—she didn't have a fetish of biting or being bitten. She turned her hip as sharply as she could and brought her knee up to contact his crotch, and it worked.

Under a wave of agony, Kellan released the feisty wench who then bolted. Being kneed in the nuts was already excruciating, but having it done to him while he was hard was an unbearable amount of pain that no man should have to endure.

Overcoming his suffering, he righted himself, licked the remaining droplet of blood from his lips, and stared off into the darkness. Her taste was exquisite and unlike any he had ever savored before. It gave him the warmest glow he had ever basked in, and before he knew it, his sore manhood was erect again.

It   was   time   to   go   hunting.

Eleven

Aria fought back her tears as she ran toward the parking lot. It was still foggy out, so finding her vehicle was a challenge. As she dredged through the mist, images of the crime scene from the library and of her parents' house coursed through her mind. She was so focused on her mother's face that she didn't realize she had found her car until she ran into it and landed flat on her ass. Scrambling to her feet, she fumbled in her pocket for her keys and pressed the button on the fob to unlock the doors. Once safely inside, she pressed the lock button and made the engine come to life. She put the car in gear just as she heard the click of the doors unlocking. She pressed the gas pedal hard, but the tires just spun while an unseen force held the vehicle firmly in place. Burnt rubber filled the air and her nostrils causing her eyes to burn. She released the gas pedal and reached for the gear shifter to put the car into reverse when she heard it—the unmistakable sound of the door being opened.

Kellan opened the unlocked passenger door and climbed inside. The overhead light came on bringing her wide-eyed face into full view. Even when she was scared, she was radiant, and it gave him pause. Her sharp intake of breath jutted her full breasts forward, and it instantly made him hard. His first instinct was to drain her and be on his way but seeing her again and smelling her blood stirred another thirst—the kind only the velvety depths of her body could quench.

Aria snapped out of her trance and reached between the seats for the can of pepper spray, which she then squirted liberally into the man's face—into his extraordinarily handsome face. While he cried out in pain and wiped at his burning eyes, she scrambled for the door handle. She swung the door open and put one foot on the ground when a massive hand grabbed hold of her arm in a vice-like grip. She thought her bone might break in his grasp as he yanked her closer. He stared hard at her through watery eyes while he used the back of his free hand to wipe the remaining droplets of pepper spray off his cheek. She swallowed hard in anticipation of what would happen next.

Kellan's immediate thought was to slap the girl, but once again, his upbringing stopped him. He grabbed her shoulders and shook her while hissing, "You are becoming quite the handful, my beauty"—he yanked her closer to the point of their lips almost touching—"and I don't think you want to test my patience any further."

Aria tried to maintain a grip on her senses while the man spoke in a velvety seductive voice and moved his hand from her shoulder to run his fingers through her hair, but it was difficult. His mouth was so close she could feel his breath on her lips. She understood the direness of the situation, but it was as if she was watching herself in a dream. She was helpless as his mouth moved over hers and engulfed her in a probing kiss. His tongue slipped between her lips, which were parted in surprise, and made sweeping, swirling motions inside her mouth. Regaining some of her sanity, she tried to bite it, but he just responded with a guttural moan and plunged deeper and harder.

Kellan relished the flavor of her as he explored her mouth, and he tried to imagine what the rest of her would taste like. He decided he would need to find out. He would take her life, indeed, but he would enjoy her womanly charms first—luckily for her, he wasn't a selfish lover.

Aria felt herself slipping within the folds of passion as the assailant held her mouth hostage. Then his agenda became even clearer as one of his massive hands moved over her breast and squeezed. He splayed his fingers over her mound before capturing her nipple in between them and pinching. An electric current coursed through her veins, and something began to replace her fear—desire. Before she had time to think about what that implied, and before she could protest, his hand slid lower on her body and slipped itself snuggly between her clenched thighs while his mouth moved itself to her neck and began to gently suckle.

Aria felt herself swelling beneath his fingertips, and without even realizing what she was doing, her hand pressed on top of his as her legs parted.

Kellan chuckled to himself while he suckled her neck and used his hand to manipulate her most sensitive area through her clothing. She was succumbing to her passion as he'd intended. If they weren't in the tiny car, her clothes would be crumpled on the ground by now. The painful swelling between his legs told him to quickly remedy the situation.

So that she couldn't try escaping while he got out of the car, he looked hypnotically into her half-closed eyes and murmured in Romani, the old world tongue of vampires, "Va rămâne în cazul în care vă aflați, și va ceda la controlul meu total." *You will remain where you are, and you will yield to my total control.* He gave her another passion-filled kiss and exited the car while she sat there in a haze.

Kellan opened her car door for her and leaned down to pick her up in his arms. He carried her to a soft patch of grass and gently lay her down. He paused, standing over her, and admired how beautiful she was with her dark hair falling softly off her shoulders. Her eyes slowly fluttered open to look at him, and he noticed their beauty. Even with only the moon illuminating the night sky, he could see that they were green with flecks of grey. He sighed with pleasure as he drank up her exquisiteness. Everything about her was beautiful, and he grew tired of having her body concealed from his hungry gaze. His throbbing member agreed with him and urged him to kneel beside her and remove her clothes. Normally he didn't play with his prey this much. The process was typically a quick one, but he had every intention of taking his sweet time with her. Something about this woman called to him and awoke every cell in his body—especially the ones in his erection. He quickly unbuttoned her blouse and smiled when he saw that her bra clasped in the front. While his right hand moved to the button on her jeans, his left deftly flicked the clasp open, and her ample breasts sprung forth. He grabbed her right mound and squeezed until her nipple grew hard against his palm. Then he leaned down to capture it between his lips, and he began to flick it with his tongue until soft mewing sounds escaped from her. His hand continued to work her pants open, while he enjoyed his feast, and when it reached her velvety soft mound and lips, and the moistness within, his hunger grew—he needed a taste.

Aria, wrapped in a haze of pleasure, moaned softly from the man's exquisite touch. His mouth had been sucking on her puckered bud, and she even thought she had felt him nibble. It was an indescribable sensation, and she only hoped it would last, but, yet, she knew she shouldn't be feeling that way. She should be scared out of her mind. She should be trying to escape. Then there was the onslaught of his hand. It had slipped intimately between the petal-soft folds of her womanhood, and she felt herself go up in flames. Her eyes rolled back as he released her wet nipple, which grew harder when the cool night air hit it, and began kissing his way down her abdomen. She knew where he was headed, and anticipation made every part of her tingle. Still, she knew this was wrong, but she couldn't find the strength to stop it.

Aria felt her pants and panties being yanked down before she felt his mouth closing in on her while a thick finger probed her passion-moistened depths and caused her head to spin. Then his tongue was upon her, spreading her lips and seeking out her treasured pearl. He moved it around expertly, causing it to harden beneath the moist heat of his mouth and tongue, and she cried out.

"Does that feel good? Do you like this?" he murmured seductively.

"God, I'm on fire," she whispered in the cool air, causing her breath to mist and swirl about her. "I-I can't," she cried as her body tightened up before releasing in a shattering climax beneath the expertise of his suckling.

Kellan chuckled softly while licking up the moisture seeping from her fiery furnace. "Mmm," he moaned, "you taste nice and sweet." Then he raised himself up and released his rock-hard rod from its confines. "You are ready for me," he growled and then slid his thick head inside her heat. "Ah-h." She was snugly wrapped around him, and he felt her tighten up even more so while he gave her inch after inch of himself until he was fully embedded.

"Oh fuck," Aria screamed into the moonlit night while raking her claws down his massive chest. The pleasure she received with each stroke was immeasurable. "God, you are killing me. I can't take it," she howled as another orgasm wracked her body on a tidal wave of desire.

"Mmm, no, I'm not killing you, my pet." *At least not yet.* He thrusted harder into her wetness. "You can take it. You can take all of it," he growled sensuously while pulling her legs over his arms to go deeper inside her. He leaned down to capture her pouting nipple once more and suckled harder this time. Her body was stroking him with pleasure, and every time it clenched around him, it brought his own culmination closer. When it finally took hold of him, he released her nipple and sank his teeth into the softness of her bosom while his seed flooded her. Her warm crimson essence spilled forth into his mouth and was unlike any he had tasted before. Again, it was sweet like a mixture of honey and vanilla. It was perfection. She had cried out at the puncture, but she was still under the drugging force of his spell, so she didn't try to fight him— not that it would have done her any good if she had. Nevertheless, he used one meaty hand to pin her wrists while he drank from her. And, even though he had already come, he continued to move inside her—he intended to take every pleasure he could get.

Once he felt full and was sure she had been drained, he reached for his knife. He hesitated when he felt the cold wooden handle, though. Her skin was too perfect to mar, other than his puncture marks, of course, and a light hickey on her neck, so he left her as she was. He left her naked and lifeless.

So he thought.

Twelve
Sunday

Aria's eyes fluttered open to the first rays of sunlight, and she shivered in the cold morning air. It only took a second for her to realize she was naked and not in her bed. *Why? Where the hell am I?* Her mind panicked to recall the past few hours while she rushed to gather her clothes and get dressed. She noticed a couple of aches during the process—one was between her legs, and the other was coming from her breast. She looked down and saw two small puncture marks on her right bosom, and more dread filled her. Her chest tightened, and her breath came in shallow gasps as she finished dressing and scrambled to her feet. Her eyes darted left then right to figure out where she was, and she recognized the outskirts of the park. Yes, she recalled, she had gone to the park last night. She had gone there to think, to figure out the mysterious events of the previous night.

What did I find out though? That was where she was drawing a blank.

She spotted her car through the trees and felt some relief—at least she hadn't been carjacked. She involuntarily reached between her legs. *But was I raped, or did I just have random sex with some guy?* Her mind wandered back to Chris, but then she recalled that the party had been the night before, and she hadn't seen him since. *Kyle?* No, they hadn't been together in weeks.

She opened the car door, and it hit her—a wave of delicious musky cologne and testosterone. Her hand flew to her breast. It had been the same man from the night before, and she was sure this time that he had bitten her, and even though she couldn't remember everything, she was sure they had had slept together. With tears flooding her eyes, she drove back to the campus like a bat out of hell.

Cat wasn't in their room when Aria got back to the dorm. At first, she thought her friend was in class, but then she remembered it was Sunday, which was good because otherwise she'd have been late for her own class.

Aria threw her purse down and ran to the bathroom. She pulled off her blouse and unhooked her bra to look at the puncture marks while fingering the tender area. As she stared into the mirror, her face grew hot and her chest tightened. She spun around, dropped to her knees, and began to violently retch.

She cleaned her face, brushed her teeth, and with a shudder, hooked her bra and buttoned up her blouse. She was fastening the last button when Cat's voice rang out from behind her and caused her to jump out of her skin.

"You know, if you are only going to live here part-time, I could rent out your bed," Cat teased. When she saw the look on Aria's ashen face, though, she immediately quit smiling and became concerned. "My gosh, sweetie, what's wrong with you? You are paler than usual." She reached out and brushed the hair out of Aria's troubled face.

"Nothing," Aria mumbled and looked away.

"Okay, well, where were you? Who's the guy?" She crossed her arms and tapped her foot.

Aria felt her cheeks go red, and her fingers twitched nervously while she fidgeted with the buttons on her blouse. She didn't want to tell Cat the truth—she didn't even know the whole truth.

"Umm"—she looked down at the floor— "there isn't any guy. I was out late studying with another friend, and I didn't want to wake you, so I stayed in her room."

"Really?" Cat's voice was laced with skepticism, "And what's her name?"

"Tabitha Reese," she lied.

"Hmm, okay. Call the next time, though. I was worried about you."

Aria hated lying to her friend, but she didn't want to admit to having hooked up with a random stranger—and she knew that she did.

"Sure, but it won't happen again. Now let's get some breakfast because I'm famished," she said and hoped she sounded upbeat.

Cat eyed her suspiciously. "I just ate, but you go ahead, and I will catch up to you later."

"Sure, sounds good." Aria was somewhat relieved—she didn't want to be asked any more questions about last night.

She dug in the closet and put on a clean shirt and then grabbed her purse to go. She felt grimy and needed to shower, but the breakfast bar would soon close, so she needed to hurry. Also, she wanted to bathe when no one else was in there—she didn't want anyone to see the bite mark. She didn't want any more questions—especially when she didn't have the answers. She was just glad her hair had hidden the hickey on her neck from Cat.

Thirteen

Kellan was shapeshifted into a hawk and soared the sky over the small town. He felt elated today. The woman's blood from last night had felt extra nourishing as he drank from her, and the glow he normally felt afterward lasted much longer than it usually did. The glow from the sex had also lasted a long time—she had satisfied that hunger nicely too. Even now, he could clearly recall how wonderful her body had felt, and it made him hungry again. He tried to envision his prey for the coming evening. Maybe tonight he would try a redhead or a buxom blonde. He turned himself around to fly toward the campus. He had already had two luscious treats from there, so it was reasonable to assume he would find a third.

Kellan reached the school, perched himself in a tall tree, and fixed his eyes on a cute blonde surrounded by boys. She was giggling about something, and they were eating it up. She wasn't nearly as attractive as the brunette from the night before, but she'd suffice. He continued to ogle her until another feminine form caught his eye. The sway of the girl's hips was hypnotic, and so was the soft sensuous curve of her ass. Her back was to him, so he got to watch it in action while she walked across the campus. He could picture his hands cupping it while he sank his teeth into her neck, and it made him shiver.

He flew from his perch to follow the mesmerizing lass and almost flew right into a flagpole when the fragrant smell of wildflowers wafted past him. He zoomed in closer, thinking it had to be a coincidence, but then she turned to look at someone behind her who was shouting the name Aria, and he saw that it wasn't. It was definitely *her.*

What the fuck is going on here? There is no possible way she could be alive.

His thoughts raced through his brain while he soared in circles above her. He had never heard of this before. He had drained her dry—he was sure of it. He didn't even leave enough blood to turn her into one of his kind, but even if he had, he would still need to bite her a third time for the change to take place. Somehow, he knew, she was going to plague his existence.

Fourteen

Aria turned when she heard her name called out. Then she regretted it.

"What do you need, Kyle?" she asked in a clipped tone.

Her ex-boyfriend looked at her with surprise on his face, and she figured it was because she wasn't fawning all over him. Instead, she placed a hand impatiently on her hip, and her head was tilted.

He put his hands up in defense and replied, "Whoa, babe. I was just going to ask you how it's going, and to tell you that I hope it wasn't uncomfortable for you yesterday."

His arrogance always grated her nerves. "Oh, I'm just fine. I'm fine and dandy," she said with the biggest smile she could force.

"Aria," someone else called out to her, and she turned to see Chris headed in her direction.

She looked up at Kyle and said, "If you'll excuse me, there's someone I would rather be talking to. Bye now." She turned in Chris's direction without looking back.

"Hey," he said with an easy smile, "How's it going?"

She smiled back, feeling more confident than she did at the party, and replied, "I'm great. How are things with you?"

"Good. Things are pretty good." He nodded slowly to affirm his words. "Did you hear about that girl who was murdered at the library? She was in my Algebra class."

Aria fidgeted uncomfortably as flashbacks of the previous night hit her. She recalled going to the library to look around, and her stomach turned when she also recalled the scent of blood. Her chest began to tighten again, so she excused herself.

"Chris, I'm not feeling well, so I'm going to have to get going." She grimaced as another wave of nausea hit.

"You are looking a little green around the gills, but can I get your number before you go?"

"Um, sure. Hold out your hand," she told him while quickly fishing a pen out of her purse. Then she wrote her phone number on his palm. "Call whenever, but I do need to go now." She took off at a brisk pace toward her dorm. Her stomach finally began to settle, but she wanted to get to her room anyway so she could concentrate on the bits and pieces of her memories from last night.

Kellan watched the woman, named Aria, he now knew, as she talked with the young men, and something bubbled up inside him—jealousy. He didn't like the way she smiled at the second fellow, and he hated the way both men had been looking at her. He was feeling territorial, and he needed to do something about it. He needed to change her.

He followed her in the sky as she practically ran to her dwelling, and then he perched on the gargoyle above the entrance. The ornament moved its eyes to look right up at him, but he didn't care. He would sit there all day if he needed to, and then, after dusk, he would hunt her.

Fifteen

Aria had been back in her room for only a few minutes when Chris called and asked her if she wanted to hang out later that night. She still claimed not to feel well, though, and told him that maybe during the week they could do something if he wanted to. He sounded disappointed but promised to call in a day or two.

When they hung up, she stared at the phone for a minute, thinking about how nice he seemed. If only he had been her lover instead of the mysterious stranger she couldn't even remember. At least then she'd have an excuse for her promiscuous behavior. While she still couldn't remember all that had happened, or how it went down, she had the strong suspicion that she hadn't been raped because she didn't feel injured at all—except, of course, for the bite mark. *But was that just foreplay?* She didn't know. She got up off her bed and went into the bathroom to look at it in the mirror. She pulled off her sweatshirt, unhooked her bra, and cupped her right breast. The chilly air made her nipple grow instantly hard with little bumps all around the areola, and a pleasant shudder ran down her spine as she flashed back to the sensation of a hot mouth on it. She knew it wasn't Kyle's mouth she was remembering because breasts weren't a big deal to him, so he didn't pay them much attention. In fact, he was a selfish lover by all counts.

Aria searched all over her honey soft mound, but she couldn't find the puncture marks. *What in the hell?* Tears welled up in her eyes as she explored the possibility that she had imagined the whole thing. *But it was so real, and it was the second time it had happened.* Surely, she didn't imagine it twice.

She redressed and went back to her bed where she opened her laptop. She ran a search on Trish Rose to see if the police had updated their records, but she didn't find anything. Trying to think like a detective, she ran a search in public records to see if there were any reports of attacks in the area that involved biting. She was once again disappointed, though, because nothing came up except for some random links for information on vampire movies, books, and legends.

"Pfft, right," she exclaimed just as Cat entered the room.

"What are you scoffing at?"

Aria felt foolish, and she didn't want to explain what she had been looking for. Instead, she opted for, "Just stuff about vampires." She would've made something up, but Cat was already looking over her shoulder.

"Are you getting ready for Halloween?" she teased.

"Um"—Aria's eyes darted right then left—"something like that." It was kind of truthful—she felt like she was in a horror film. It was a bad movie where she couldn't explain her behavior because she couldn't remember it.

"Hey, while I'm thinking about it, I ran into Chris, and he said you ran away from talking to him. What's up with that? You like him, don't you?" She stared at Aria with her arms crossed as if she was scolding a small child.

Aria sighed before quietly responding, "I didn't 'run away' from him per se, but I did rush off because I felt sick to my stomach."

"Oh. Well do you feel better now, sweetie?" Her stance relaxed, and she reached out to clasp Aria's shoulder.

Aria nodded. "Yeah, a little, but I'm going to turn in early. I have a test in the morning, so I want to get plenty of rest," she lied. The truth was she wanted to try self-hypnosis again.

Cat looked at the clock on the nightstand and yawned with a big stretch. "You know, I'm still beat from the party last night, which you didn't show up at"—she shot Aria a scathing look—"so I think I will hit the hay too."

"Great. I'm going to go take a shower first." Aria climbed out of bed and gathered some clean underwear, pajamas, and her shower caddy.

"Don't take mine," Cat joked, "See you in a bit then. What should I tell Chris if he calls?"

Aria rolled her pretty hazel eyes. "Tell him I will call him back tomorrow."

"Okay, but take my advice and don't blow him off. Unlike Kyle, he's genuinely a nice guy."

Aria spun on her heel to face her friend. "I thought you liked Kyle."

"I played nice for your sake, but, no, I never liked him. I've always thought he was a womanizer, and I think your situation proved me right," she replied while putting toothpaste on her toothbrush. "You are much better off without him," she said in a garbled voice because she had already put the toothbrush in her mouth.

"Yeah, I know," Aria replied with slumped shoulders.

She knew breaking up with him had been the right decision, but it didn't make it any easier for her. She had wasted too much time and energy trying to shape him into the guy she wanted. Maybe she should settle for a nice guy like Chris.

But what about passion? She found Chris attractive, but she couldn't picture him being sexy. Suddenly, she had another flash back. She was being touched intimately, and her heart was pounding its way out of her chest. Big strong hands made their way over her naked flesh and were followed by a hot mouth—a talented mouth.

Aria shuddered, and her eyes grew wide. She was glad that Cat was in the bathroom, so she didn't see her reaction to the vivid memory. She had been wondering if maybe she was drugged the night before, causing the memory loss, but now she knew that must not have been the case, and it bothered her. She had given herself willingly to the stranger, and it was frightening. She could have been killed last night—just like Trish Rose was. Then her mind turned in the direction of the musky scent she had picked up at the crime scene, and she connected the dots. She had smelled it at the crime scene and at the park, both last night and the night before, and she had smelled it in her car on the way back to school this morning.

It   is   the   same   man.   It   must   be.

Sixteen

Kellan kept himself in the shadows by Aria's building while he waited for the vixen to come out. Hours went by, though, without her making an appearance, and he began to lose hope that she would. Only a couple of stragglers were wandering the campus at the present hour. He fought hard against the temptation to feed because he wanted to be ready at a moment's notice if she walked out the front door.

At one point, out of pure frustration, he had shapeshifted into a cat to see if he could get invited into the building when he saw a group of girls walking that way. They had fussed over him and petted him but ended up leaving him outside.

Anguished and needing to satiate his carnal appetite, he left her campus in search of prey elsewhere. It wasn't long before he found a lone woman pulling into a driveway, presumably hers, and he swooped in for the kill as soon as she climbed out of her car. It was quickly over, and he made his way back to the cavern.

Aria tossed and turned in her sleep. She was back in the park, caught up in a swirl of fog, and a dark shape was coming her way. Then she heard Cat call out to her, *Aria, run. Run away from*

him. Aria tried to move her feet, but they were being held in place by the fog. Suddenly, the shape was upon her, and she didn't feel afraid anymore. Instead, she felt aroused. She was aroused by his massive frame, his musky scent, and when he finally spoke, his voice.

Don't be afraid, my pet. I'm going to bring you more pleasure than you can handle.

His hands were soon scalding her flesh as the flames of passion licked her nerve endings, and an electric tingle ran up her spine. He lifted her off the ground, and she wrapped her naked legs around his waist. She felt him enter her wetness with a powerful thrust, and her body shook as she instantly released all over his thick flesh. He pumped her up and down on his tumescence, and it wasn't long before she was once again brought to the brink of sanity. Her body convulsed around him, and she screamed into the foggy night while digging her nails into his massive shoulders.

You are mine now, my pet.

She didn't protest his declaration. Instead, she kept moaning in delight as he rocked her body and shook her to the core. She felt the blood swelling inside her jewel and braced herself for another tidal wave of ecstasy when something took its place—a sharp stinging sensation in her breast. She looked down and saw her blood running into his mouth.

No! she heard herself scream.

Aria's eyes flew open, and she shot up in bed, covered in a cold sweat.

"What? What's wrong?" Cat hollered at her.

Aria panted on jagged breaths, "Nothing. It was just a dream."

"Oy vey, you scared the shit out of me."

"Sorry," Aria mumbled to her friend while her hand flew to her breast. She felt her heart pounding beneath her fingertips, and then she felt sick. She jumped out of bed and ran to the bathroom   to   retch   again.

Aria, who normally hit the snooze button a couple of times, jumped right out of bed as soon as the alarm went off. She had spent the entire night in fitful nightmares, so she was relieved to be pulled out of them. No matter how the dreams began, they always ended the same—with being bitten.

On the way to her abnormal psychology class, she saw Chris in the hallway and gave him a little wave.

"Hey, do you feel better?" he inquired with a kind smile.

She tilted her head and shifted her bookbag to maintain her balance beneath the heavy load. "Yes, I'm feeling better. Thanks for your concern"—she looked nervously at her watch. She was hoping to catch Tabitha before the lecture started to see if she had overheard anything about the open murder case—"Um, I need to speak to someone before class, so I will catch you later, okay?"

Disappointment shadowed his handsome face, but he forced a smile. Then a blush crept up his neck before he asked, "Would you like to see a movie tomorrow night? There's a new comedy out that is getting great reviews."

Aria took a deep breath and was prepared to say "No," but the genuine look of interest on his face was a welcomed change of pace from her experience with Kyle, so she heard herself saying, "Sure, give me a call."

A corner of his mouth turned up, and he gave her a wink. "All right then, I'll call you tomorrow." He raised his hand in a slight wave before turning on his heel and heading down the corridor.

By the time Aria entered the classroom, all the seats around Tabitha were occupied by other students, and the instructor was approaching the podium.

I will just have to go about this another way.

The lecture was on frontal lobe damage as a common trait in serial killers, and it interested her, but she still found it difficult to focus on what the professor was saying. Instead, she found herself checking her watch every five minutes and doodling in her notes. Without even thinking about it, she was drawing fangs.

After class, she had an hour to study before her next class. She rushed across campus to the administrative building where the professors had their offices. She was hoping to find Dr. Martin between her lectures, and she did.

"Aria"—she looked up from the papers she was grading—"what can I do for you? Do we have an appointment?"

Aria shook her head. "No, I'm just wanting to pick your brain on something if that's okay."

"Sure"—Dr. Martin motioned to the chair in front of her desk—"have a seat and tell me what you want to know."

"Thank you. I'm curious about gathering information on the recent murder case—the one involving Trish Rose."

Surprise registered on the distinguished woman's face. "Oh? What is your interest in the case? Are you using it for an assignment in one of your other classes?"

Aria bit her bottom lip. There wasn't a way to describe the connection she felt to the victim without her instructor and course advisor thinking she was crazy. So she went with a half-truth.

"It just interests me. We're studying how to process crime scenes in my forensics class, and I want to use it as a reference."

She seemed to buy it. She tilted her head and straightened the papers she had been looking at. "Well, the investigators use the NCIC database for one thing, but civilians don't have access to it for obvious reasons"—she looked at her wall clock—"Look, I have got to get to a meeting with Dean Paul, but if you want to, read this." She handed Aria a book from the shelf titled *How to Think Like a Detective,* which she had written.

"This is your first book, right?" Aria asked while turning it over in her hands to read the description on the back.

Dr. Martin smiled at her while she gathered some file folders. "Yes, you are correct, and it will be used in my lectures, so you'll have a leg up on the rest of the class. Take it for as long as you need, and good luck with your assignment."

Aria followed her out the door and then found a quiet spot in the courtyard to look at the book. She skipped to chapter three, which was on collecting evidence and making conclusions from it. With determination to find the truth etched in her frown lines, she pulled a notebook and pencil out of her bookbag and began taking notes. She was half of a page in when her phone chimed from a text. It was a silly message from Cat, who was bored in her history class. She typed back a quick response, and then she located the news app on the phone. She was going to dig around for anything related to Trish Rose's case, but she stopped in her tracks when she read the front-page headline. *Local woman found dead in her driveway while another student from UCSF is found dead in her dorm room.* Aria's eyes widened in shock as she used her fingertip to scroll through the stories. She skimmed over the first section, hunting specific details, but she didn't find anything useful. There weren't any suspects in either death; however, it did say that the police thought the cases were related to the one involving Trish Rose. Aria's body went numb, and she almost blacked out. According to the story, the girl from school was also in Hudson Hall. The killer was in her building, and she had to wonder if he was there looking for her.

Glancing at her watch, she saw that it was time to get to her English class, so she gathered her belongings and stood up on wobbly legs. The stress of the murders was affecting her, and she had the sickening feeling it was going to get worse. She also had the feeling that she was part of the solution, somehow, and that she was on her own in finding out the reason.

   Kellan had shapeshifted into a cat and was lurking about the campus looking for Aria. When he found her sitting on the grass in the middle of the courtyard, he sat under a tree and admired her extraordinary features. She grew more beautiful with the passing of each day. The sun was casting highlights in her dark hair, and the gentle breeze was moving it around her shoulders. The feminine gesture of tucking it behind her ear tugged at his heartstrings and gave him the urge to run his hands through its thick waves. Her fragrant aroma of wildflowers tickled his nose every time the wind blew, and it drugged him with lust. He had to find a way to get to her at nightfall. He needed her body, and he needed to possess her soul by blessing her with immortality. It amazed him that it took four hundred years to want to claim a mate.

Eighteen

After her English class, Aria walked back to her dorm room to check on Cat and to find out about the girl murdered the night before—including her name since it hadn't been released in the news article.

Police still occupied the building, and one officer, who introduced himself as Officer Jessup, wanted to interview Aria. He asked her if she knew the victim, Tracy Jennings, if she saw anyone suspicious, or had she heard anything out of the ordinary.

"No, I don't—didn't—know her, and I didn't see or hear anything," she explained.

"All right, well here's my card in case you think of anything later," he said and handed her a slightly bent business card.

"Okay, I will," she agreed and then turned to go upstairs to her room. She felt exhausted.

She normally didn't need to nap during the day, so the sudden fatigue made her think she might be coming down with something, but then she recalled how she hadn't slept well the night before and decided to blame it on that.

Cat wasn't in the room, but Aria knew she had a class at that time, so she wasn't worried. Tucked in bed, she closed her droopy eyes, and it only took a couple of minutes for slumber to whisk her away to lucid dreams.

She was in her macroeconomics class taking a surprise pop quiz when she heard her name being whispered from the hallway. She rose from her desk and slowly approached the doorway where she hesitated when the pungent aroma of a man's musk hit her. She tried to back away from the exit, but invisible ropes wrapped around her waist and pulled her forward. As she inhaled the carnal scent, she felt her heart rate quicken, and her panties became damp and clingy. She tried to turn in the opposite direction, but the magnetic pull was too strong to fight. She heard heavy breathing, and it was eerily close by. Then a large shadow fell upon her while a meaty hand clasped her shoulder and spun her around. She found her face pressed into the hard, warm muscles of a broad chest—a chest that smelled so masculine, it made her insides flame—while the hand on her shoulder slid down her slender arm to clasp her hand with a tight squeeze.

"Come," the man said in a husky whisper that left no room for a rebuttal. He tugged on her hand and led her back into the classroom—only it wasn't her classroom anymore.

The room was a bedroom unlike any she had ever seen before, and she gawked in amazement. The room was draped in sangria tapestries and filmy curtains. Even the canopy bed in the middle was decorated in the burnt red color and was overflowing with pillows. He led her to it and surprised her by scooping her up into his arms in one fluid movement before tossing her upon it, unexpectedly in the nude. Languidly, he followed and climbed atop her, bracing his weight on his brawny arms.

Aria seized the opportunity to look up into the face of her seducer for the first time, and

she gulped. He was incredibly handsome with a
mane full of long dark hair falling around a
chiseled jaw adorned with full lips. His piercing
eyes bore right into her soul as his manhood bore
into her tight body and made her cry out in
pleasure.

"Kiss me," she moaned as he thrust
repetitiously, each time harder than the last.

He chuckled softly and answered her plea
by saying, "I fully intend to and so much more."
He leaned in and kissed her neck, which stoked
the embers of desire within her until she felt like
she was in Dante's inferno.

"Oh, bite me," she breathed while feeling
herself climaxing.

"Again, I fully intend to," he growled, and
she suddenly noticed how razor sharp his teeth
were.

Aria's eyes flew open, and she shot up and
out of bed with her hand flying to her neck.
Whew! It was just a dream. She took in several deep
breaths to calm the pounding of her racing heart
while her eyes darted around the room to make
sure she was alone—the dream had felt incredibly
real. It had been so realistic that she pinched
herself just to make sure she was awake.

She leaned over her bedside table to turn
off her alarm clock and then straightened her
clothes and hair up. She had algebra II in twenty
minutes, but she decided to blow it off. She had
an important errand to run in town.

She grabbed her purse and took off for
the public library.

Aria made sure no one was around when she grabbed a few books from the dusty shelf. She hugged them tightly to her chest and ducked around the corner so other patrons wouldn't see her escape to a corner table in the reading room. She turned on the table lamp, which buzzed while it warmed up, and under the flickering splash of light, she cracked open the first book from the stack to chapter one—*The Legend of the Vampire*.

With the usual intensity she used when she studied, Aria read stories about Vlad the Impaler, Countess Elizabeth Bathory, and the legend of the Ka, which originated in Egypt. She got so involved with her reading, though, that she missed her other classes for the day as well. However, she needed to find something that made sense of everything happening in her life. She needed to find proof.

Nineteen

The sun was hanging low in the sky when Aria got up to leave the library. She wasn't planning on checking out the books, for fear of what the librarian would think, but she hadn't gotten to the second or third book in the pile, so she decided to take them with her. The librarian indeed looked up at her over her reading glasses.

"Interesting reading," she commented.

Aria felt a blush creep up her cheeks. "Oh, I'm doing research for school," she lied.

The librarian looked around to make sure no one was listening before whispering, "You know, if you want to do some in-depth research, you should visit Madame Gabor. She's a local Gypsy fortune teller, and my sister swears by her. I think she's in her nineties, so she's seen a lot. If anyone would know about the subject, it would be her. Gypsies carry legends with them from the Old World." She slowly nodded and gave Aria a knowing wink.

Aria accepted her library card and books from the woman and shrugged. "Um, okay. Thank you, I will keep that in mind." She slowly backed away from the desk and turned toward the exit.

"She is on 3rd and Market Street," the woman called after her. "Look her up."

Aria just nodded again and gave a little wave with her free hand before pushing the door open. When she made the short walk to her car, she glanced over to where the crime scene was. The police must have finished processing the scene because the yellow crime scene barricade tape was gone. For a moment, she considered walking back over to it, but she could still remember tasting the metallic smell of blood and didn't care to taste it again. She turned left at the stoplight and headed in the opposite direction of the campus. She drove, instead, into town and found the Gypsy's shop on 3rd and Market Street just as the librarian had said. The lights were dim in the storefront, though, and when she squinted, she could make out a closed sign hanging on the door.

Well, there's always tomorrow I suppose. She turned around in the parking lot and headed back to campus.

After a groundskeeper shooed him away, Kellan ducked behind some bushes and skulked while he waited for the sun to go down and for Aria to show herself. Unfortunately, she never did.

He wasn't sure if she was even home, so he crept through the parking lot, taking deep whiffs of air. Soon, as his vampire self, he was standing before a car that smelled like wildflowers, and he smiled as he enjoyed the titillating scent. It sparked all his senses and made him come alive. He stood there with an erection that could take down a mighty sequoia, and the only thing he could think about was burying it inside her. However, since she never showed her pretty face, and he had no way into the building, it remained that way as he wandered the city in search of prey.

His frustration was bubbling up inside him like a volcano when he came across two young women walking through a mini mall parking lot littered with trash from the day's patrons. The women were talking and laughing and had no idea he was near until it was too late for them. He chose the brunette and pulled her into his vice-like grip, where she had no chance of escape, and he sank his teeth into her carotid.

"No! Oh my god!" The other woman shrieked and turned to run, but he was too fast for her. He grabbed her by the neck with one hand and snapped it before she could draw attention to them.

Several hundred feet away, people were exiting the stores and heading toward the parking lot, so he had to be careful. He took one more pull of the brunette's blood before whipping out his knife and cutting her across the fang marks. He let her body fall to the ground next to her friend's and then made his way back to Aria's dorm. He still hoped to see her before dawn, which was seven hours away.

Aria lay on her bed with her library books and only looked up from them when Cat entered the room.

"Hey," her roommate greeted her, "what are you doing?"

Aria slightly shrugged. "Not much. I'm just reading."

Wanting to snoop, Cat reached out and snatched up the book Aria wasn't holding. "*The Reign of the Vampire?* You're really getting into this kind of thing, aren't you?" She raised her brows and scrunched up her mouth.

"It's research," Aria replied with a sigh. She figured if she made it sound like homework, Cat wouldn't ask too many questions. She figured wrong.

"Research?" she asked skeptically, "What class is it for?"

Aria fiddled with the corner of her comforter and looked at the messy closet while she thought of a lie. "It's for my literature class."

Cat looked at her sideways. "I've had that class, and I don't remember anything like that being on the syllabus." She set the book down and stood over Aria with her arms crossed.

Aria knew her cheeks were red. "Well, we're studying folklores."

"Humph. Well, that's interesting. I'm glad to see old Dr. Jones is mixing things up." She spun on her heel and walked toward the bathroom. She stopped short, though, and looked over her shoulder. "You don't believe in that crap do you?" she scoffed.

In truth, Aria didn't know what to believe, but she responded, "No, of course I don't."

Cat drew the back of her hand across her forehead in a dramatic fashion. "Whew! I thought maybe you had gone mad."

Aria giggled. "Check again around finals."

She laughed too. "I hear that." She ducked into the bathroom and turned on the faucet. "Have you talked to Chris lately?" she called out over the running water.

Here we go. "Yeah, I talked to him yesterday."

Cat popped around the corner with her toothbrush in her mouth. "Oh?" she questioned with frothy spittle running down her chin.

Aria wasn't in the mood to talk—she wanted to keep reading—but she answered, "He asked me out to the movies for tomorrow night."

"Yes!" Cat jumped up and down while clapping—it was the eternal cheerleader in her. She darted back into the bathroom to rinse, but she returned in a flash. "Give me details."

Aria shrugged, and her mouth turned down. "That's it. We're going to the movies."

"Oh. Well"—her face fell, and she began wringing her hands—"I think a distraction from what happened here last night will do you good."

"Yeah," Aria agreed softly, "I could use a distraction."

"Do you want to talk about it? Did you know her?"

Aria shook her head, "No, I didn't know Tracy. Did you?"

"Huh-uh, but it's so sad and scary too." She grimaced and popped her knuckles.

Aria nervously tapped the library book pages. "Yes, indeed it is." When she looked up from the book, Cat was standing there completely naked. "What are you doing?"

Cat tipped her head to the left. "Um, getting ready to shower, duh. Do you want to grab dinner after your last class?"

Aria bit her lower lip. "I'm not going to class. I'm not feeling well."

"It's not like you to miss your classes. Are you coming down with something?" she asked while wrapping a towel around her slender form.

Aria closed her eyes for a moment. "No, I'm just worn out. I didn't get enough sleep last night."

"Hmm, well take a nap then. I'll see you in a bit." She left with her shower caddy in hand.

Aria went back to reading the book in her hands, *Werewolves, Vampires, and the Unexplained,* but a knock on the door interrupted her. Marissa was on the other side, and she was holding a single red rose. Aria could tell from her puffy eyes that she had been crying.

"Hi, Aria," she managed to get out on a shaky breath.

"Hi, Marissa. What's wrong?"

Fresh tears rolled down the redhead's flushed cheeks. "We're having a candlelight vigil tonight for Trish Rose an-an-and Tracy Jen-Jen-Jennings," she sobbed.

Aria stared wide-eyed at the shattered girl. "Um, that sounds like a good idea. What time is it?"

"Sev-sev-seven o'clock," Marissa got out on fresh sobs.

Aria gently squeezed her arm. "I'll let Cat know, and I'm sure we'll be there."

The broken girl nodded and went on her way to the next door with her sobs echoing in the hallway.

Aria turned around and leaned against the doorframe. Marissa must have been friends with one or both girls, or it could just be she was terrified for her life. And maybe she should be—there was some kind of monster on the loose. She headed toward her bed, but she caught a movement by the window out of the corner of her eye and stopped in her tracks.

Relax Aria, it was just a bird.

She walked to the window while her hand clutched the bottom of her oversized shirt so tightly that her knuckles turned white. When she peered out into the night, she gasped. She could clearly make out a man standing in the yard. The biggest cause of her concern, though, was the fact that the man was staring back at her, and his long, dark hair was familiar.

Kellan looked up at Aria staring out her window. He was fairly certain she recognized him, but it was fine. Maybe she'd come to him—he could always make her.

In Romani, he chanted, "Vin la mine şi să îmbrăţişeze destinul tău nou. Nu vă fie teamă." *Come to me and embrace your new destiny. Do not be afraid.* He smiled his vampire grin when he saw her step away from the window.

Twenty

It had been a long day and an even longer evening. Aria and Cat went to the candlelight vigil and cried with the other young women, and then, upon returning to their room, Aria dove back into her library books. She read and re-read until the pages became blurry, but she didn't find herself any closer to a plausible answer.

Then it occurred to her that maybe she was being irrational about the entire thing, so she cracked open Dr. Martin's book. She was only a couple of pages in, though, before exhaustion settled in from head to toe. She looked over at Cat, who was already sleeping soundly based on the snoring coming from her side of the small room, and turned out her lamp.

It took twenty minutes of tossing and turning before Aria fell asleep, but once she did, she was in REM sleep in no time.

She dreamt she was in the local morgue, and Trish Rose and Tracy Jennings were laid out on slabs—or at least that is what the toe tags said. Crisp white sheets covered the bodies, and she could smell the bleach on them to the point of becoming nauseated. She walked around the two tables and stopped near Trish Rose's head. Her hand quivered as she held it over the edge of the sheet. She was bitterly cold, but she couldn't tell if it was because of the room temperature or because of what she was about to do—she needed to look at the bodies. She needed to see if there were bite marks.

Kellan anxiously walked around Aria's building. He had been certain that she'd come outside to him, after he had chanted the spell, but she had yet to show her lovely face. He had no idea what had gone wrong, but it shook him to the core.

He had just turned away his third flirtatious co-ed for the evening. Sure, he was hungry, but he had no time for that now. He needed to be ready to spring to action when she showed—if she showed.

As the night drug on, he knew he needed to do something or miss his opportunity, so he changed himself into an owl and flew to the ledge outside her window. He peered through her filmy curtains and saw her tossing and turning in her bed, and the overwhelming desire to be with her grew even stronger. That was his mate in there.

Kellan walked toward the building entrance and lucked out when a tipsy blonde was stumbling her way inside. He shapeshifted into a cat and ran in on her heels with her oblivious to his presence. He ran up the staircase to the third floor where he prowled the hallway and sniffed each doorway until her scent of wildflowers filled his nostrils. This was it—his chance to turn her.

Making sure no one was watching, he changed back into his vampire form and tried the doorknob. It was locked.

"Elimina toate barierele din calea mea." *Remove all barriers from my way.* He waved his hand as he chanted, and he heard the metallic click of the lock tumblers. Anticipation filled every fiber of his being as he slowly turned the knob—the door opened with ease.

Silent like fog, he crept through the darkened room to the bed where Aria's roommate was softly snoring. At first, he was going to dispatch her, but he thought better of it—he'd save her for Aria just in case there was female rivalry between the two of them. Thus, instead, he chanted a spell to make sure she'd stay asleep.

"Somn profund." *Slumber deep.*

He moved with quiet steps over to Aria, who was tossing and turning in her sleep. He watched her for several minutes, simply admiring her beauty in the moonlight which was streaming in through the tiny window. He reached out and stroked a lock of her hair, and her eyes flew open.

"Doar visezi." *You are only dreaming.*

Her breathing became faster and more jagged while her pupils dilated to the size of saucers. When her bottom lip quivered, without any words spilling forth, he reached out and touched it gently with the tip of his index finger.

"Shh," he whispered. "We don't need words for what we're about to do." He used the same hand as before to stroke her from her neck down to the V-neck of her T-shirt before leaning in and whispering in a husky seductive voice, "Moans, on the other hand, are optional."

Aria's lips slightly parted, and her pale pink tongue darted out to moisten them. Kellan took that as an unspoken invitation and captured their sweetness between his own. He nibbled on her bottom lip while his tongue fought its way inside to tangle with hers. Her kisses were almost toxic, he thought, while he drank their drugging nectar. He could already feel the tight swelling of his burgeoning erection as it strained against his clothing. With one hand, he deftly unfastened his pants to let it spring forth like a tumescent fleshy sword, and it was aimed at her.

He pulled back her covers, slipped his hand down the cotton shorts she was wearing, and traced the thin strip of hair on her soft mound. While she swallowed hard, he extended his fingertip to her private satin flesh where he began to massage in slow deliberate circles.

Aria broke the kiss with a gasp. Her dream lover was tormenting her with his hand, and she couldn't find the words to beg him for more, so she settled for digging her claws into his massive muscular shoulder. He used his free hand to pull her T-shirt up over her swollen breasts, and then he took a dusky ripened peak in between his full lips and suckled.

With her moan of pleasure still on her lips, Kellan sank his finger between her fleshy folds and found her dewy center. She was incredibly hot and wet, and he felt her clench around him as he moved in a circular motion.

Aria's eyes rolled back into her skull when his tongue traced the path his finger had taken, and a cry escaped her throat. His clever tongue set off a blinding heat inside her, and every lash of it kept her prisoner to the flames of desire engulfing her.

"Yes," she finally spoke as her release flooded her, "right there." She drew her knees toward her while her hips bucked off the bed.

Kellan decided it was time to give her what she truly craved, so he rose over her, pulled her to the edge of the bed, and plunged himself inside her slippery depths. He watched her breasts bounce in the moonlight as he worked her into a passionate frenzy with his deep thrusts.

Aria clutched at the bedding until she was certain she'd tear it. Her lover was so deep inside her, that she thought she might collapse all around him. She could distinctly feel his thick swollen head probing her engorged womanly center, and the intensity was overwhelming.

"Mmm," he growled, "you are so ripe for me, my beauty."

He grabbed her thighs, pushed her further back onto the small bed, then climbed on top of her with her legs pushed to her chest.

His moans of ecstasy mixed with hers and filled the stifling room—the air was thick with lust and body heat much like the park had been thick with fog. Kellan leaned in by her ear and nibbled on the lobe before planting kisses below it. She climaxed again, and this time, it brought him to his own. As she screamed and clawed him, he hesitated his trail of kisses and grunted while filling her full of hot seed.

"It's time, angel of the night," he growled sensuously and sank his teeth into her neck. The flavor of honey and vanilla flooded his hungry mouth once more while a warm glow flowed through his veins and into his cells. He felt intoxicated.

He kissed her quiet lips passionately and stared into her glassy eyes. The transformation would finish taking place while the moon still hung in the sky, and she'd remain in a deep sleep. He wanted to carry her back to the cavern, but there wasn't time—the sun would be rising all too soon, and he was going to barely make it in time by himself. He'd simply have to return for her tomorrow night. He gave her one more kiss and made haste back to the cavern just as a pink glow lit   up   the   horizon.

Twenty-one
Tuesday

Aria's eyes refused to open at the screech of her alarm clock when it went off at 6:00 a.m. She could hear it, but she couldn't get her body to respond. It took a vigorous shaking from Cat to do the trick.

"Aria, wake up! What the hell is the matter with you?" she hollered with concern. "Are you okay?"

"Wha-what?" she mumbled while her eyelids slowly fluttered.

She smacked her lips and thrust her tongue to bring moisture to her parched mouth. She couldn't remember ever feeling so tired, but oddly, something in her felt wide awake. The turmoil of moods was making her nauseous.

"Girl, you are looking paler than ever. Are you okay?" Cat repeated.

Aria drew her hand up to her forehead and cheeks—she didn't feel warm. In fact, she felt quite cool to the touch. "Um, yeah, I'm okay. I'm just a little tired."

"Just a *little* tired? You slept through the damn alarm clock, Aria."

Aria nervously laughed and popped her knuckles. "Yeah, that was weird." She put her feet on the cold floor and forced herself out of the bed. Dizziness hit her hard, though, and she almost plopped back down, but Cat caught her by the arm and steadied her. She looked sheepishly at her friend, who probably assumed she had been out drinking last night, and forced a smile.

"Whoa, head rush," she said with another light laugh.

Cat was staring at her with a quirked brow, and her mouth was pulled down. "Are you wearing colored contacts?"

"What? No, I don't wear contacts at all. Why?" Her free hand instinctively flew up to touch just below her right eye.

"Your eyes look blue today is all."

"Oh, maybe it's this color." Aria looked down at her T-shirt, which was white. "Okay, maybe it's the light. Anyway, I need to get cleaned up before my first class."

"Me too." Cat ran a hand through her tangled blonde waves.

Before Aria got two steps away from her, though, Cat reached out and brushed Aria's hair away from her face.

"Hey, have you been sucking face again? You've got another mark on your neck. Please don't tell me you got back together with Kyle."

Aria's eyes widened as she bolted for the bathroom while calling out over her shoulder, "No, of course not."

"Ooh, was it Chris then?" Cat's enthusiasm rang out loud and clear from the main room.

Aria stared into the mirror at the red spot on her neck. There was something there just like before, and even though they were miniscule, she could see puncture marks.

Just like on the bodies from the morgue in my dream last night.

"Aria?"—Cat popped around the corner—"Was it Chris?" she asked again with a Cheshire grin while stripping down to nothing.

Aria continued to stare into the mirror, and she fingered the area. "Um, no, it must be acne or a rash. I've not been kissing anyone."

Cat put her left hand on her hip and cocked her head. "Yeah, sure." She put both hands up in front of her and back away from the doorframe. "But you'd better put some make-up on it, so Chris doesn't see it."

Aria ran both hands through her hair. Cat's obsession with her dating life was starting to get on her nerves. She opened her mouth to retort but then closed it—she was too tired to argue. Cat was already out the door anyway.

She prepared her toothbrush, and while brushing, she pondered her fatigue. She had gone to bed early enough, and she couldn't recall waking up during the night, so there was no rational reason to feel so physically drained. While her mind was fully alert, her body felt like it could sleep for days.

After her final rinse, she undressed and put her dirty clothes in the overflowing hamper she shared with Cat. She reached for a clean pair of panties, folded neatly in the small dresser they also shared, but stopped mid-grab. Instead, her hand snaked down to her nether region, and she gently petted herself. She wasn't going to masturbate—she was just recalling her dream lover. Sighing, while her eyes closed and her hand began to move in slow circles, she remembered how attentive he had been. His mouth had moved perfectly within her womanly folds, and he had thrusted into her body with raw strength bringing her to orgasm multiple times.

"Mmm," she moaned and increased the pressure of her fingers. *Now* she was masturbating. She could, with clarity, recall every touch, every thrust, and every flick of his tongue. She could also remember how she had felt at the time—as if she was in a state of hypnosis. He had entranced her, worked her up into a frenzy of desire, and played her body like a concert pianist. Every touch created a new note only the two of them could hear. And then, when she couldn't withstand the intensity of the pleasure any longer, he had bitten her. She couldn't remember feeling afraid, though. She could only recollect how he had taught her the true joys of being a woman. Even now, as her fingers moved deftly over her swollen nub, he was the one in control of her pleasure, and that, she realized, was a frightening thing.

The black cat sat protectively on the stoop to Aria's building. Kellan wished he could make his way inside to check on her, but even if he got into the building, he wouldn't have a way into her room. He felt pure excitement in the thought of showing her all the joys of the new life waiting for her. He'd help her pick her first prey tonight, and he had some ideas in that department. The young men he had seen her talking to on more than one occasion came to mind. They already knew and trusted her, so it would be easy for her to dispatch either of them. Thinking about her feeding made him want to feed, so he trotted off to look for a mouse or small bird.

Kellan prowled through the flowerbeds, which had dried out since the coming of autumn, and found a juicy mole to dine on. His meal was interrupted, though, when he saw something that made him choke on his food—he saw Aria. He quickly dropped the prey and ran closer to the woman to make sure she wasn't a mirage. She looked like Aria, smelled like her, and when he eavesdropped on the conversation she was having with another young woman, he recognized her voice.

How the hell can this be?

He stared with his tiny mouth hanging open and his tail twitching. There was no plausible reason for her to be walking around. He was certain he had taken enough blood, it was her third bite, and he had put a spell on her to keep her in slumber. By all counts, she should burst into flames from being exposed to the sun while in her vampire body. However, here she was chattering and laughing with a friend as if nothing had changed within her, but something, he could tell, had changed about her. He scrutinized her body—she was slightly paler, her hair was shinier, and she was radiating a special glow.

He admired the ravishing beauty from a few feet away from where she stood in line for the cafeteria while his mind raced. He had never heard of his kind surviving the sun—no vampire was that gifted. She had a mysterious aura, and he needed to figure out exactly what it was. He decided to seek the guidance of an oracle.

Twenty-two

Aria took a ravenous bite of her sloppy joe sandwich and tried to concentrate on what her friend was saying. She felt starved and had insisted they go to lunch earlier than usual.

"So, what are you going to wear tonight for your big date?" Cat asked while stirring the ice in her glass of tea.

Aria held up a finger so she could finish chewing while she shot her roommate a scathing look. "I wouldn't call it a *big* date, so keep the hype down, and I haven't decided yet."

Cat flashed a coy smile. "There's always an L.B.D."

"I don't think a little black dress is appropriate for the movies," Aria replied while rolling his eyes. "I'll probably go with jeans and a light sweater."

"Okay, well then I suggest you wear that dark blue one I love. It will go with your eyes. And you can wear my black boots if you want. In fact, since you're the only one who wears them, you can just have them."

"Thanks," Aria said with a smile, "I'll take you up on that offer." She cleaned her tray and then started on Cat's since she was just picking at her food.

Cat cocked her head and quirked a brow. "Are you storing up for winter or hoping you can avoid eating in front of Chris tonight?"

Aria chuckled at her own expense. "I'm just really hungry. I don't know why."

Cat wrinkled her nose. "You're not preggers, are you?"

"Hell no," Aria said, but then worry shot through her as she realized it was a possibility— she'd been having sex with *someone* the last couple of nights, and she wasn't on the pill. In any case, she wouldn't find out for another couple of weeks.

She looked down at her watch and sighed. "It's time for history class, so I'll catch up to you later." She gathered her purse and bookbag and dropped her tray off on the way out.

On the way to class, her phone chimed from a text message. It was from Chris and said that he was looking forward to their date. She sighed, and her mouth twitched to the side. She wasn't sure if she was looking forward to it or not. Sure, he was attractive and good on paper, but she wanted some excitement too. She desired something hot, and she couldn't picture him as a core shaker—now her mystery man, on the other hand, rattled the whole planet. If only she could figure out the mystery…She had a scary suspicion the answer was in her library books, but that was too insane to believe. She felt the need to consult an expert—she'd go see the Gypsy fortune teller after class, even though that felt insane too.

Aria parked her Camry on Market Street and made the short walk to the juncture with 3rd Street where the fortune teller's shop sat. A set of bells on the door jingled when she opened it, and an elderly woman's head snapped up, while the customer sitting in front of her turned around for a look. Aria gave them a weak and shaky smile.

"Have a look around, dear. It'll be just a moment," the Gypsy, who must be Madame Gabor, informed her before getting up and closing a heavy curtain that spanned the width of the room.

Aria walked around the quaint shop taking in its old-world charm. The dusty hardwood floors were painted with colorful circular rugs, and vintage wall tapestries portrayed the scenic charm of Italy. A plank of wood had the palm of a hand painted on it and contained a large eye in its center. She reached out and traced the lines on the wood with her fingertip, noticing how smooth it was from the lacquer.

She looked to her left, and the glint of metal in the afternoon sunlight caught her attention. There was a rack of charm necklaces sitting on a small table, and she picked a silver one up to look closely at the talisman. It was a pentagram with the head of a wolf in its center. She was fingering the points on the star when the rustling of the curtain startled her. The customer gave her a knowing glance as she quietly left the shop, while Madame Gabor approached her.

"Do you like that piece?" she asked. "It is a popular item in Romania." Her wrinkled lips turned up in a half-smile.

"Um, it's interesting," Aria softly replied. "Does it mean anything special?"

"That all depends," the fortune teller answered with a low chuckle.

"On what?" Aria prodded while following her to the small table behind the curtain.

Madame Gabor shut the curtain behind her and, when she turned back around, winked. "If you believe," she said cryptically.

Aria opened her mouth to ask in what, but snapped it shut—she was afraid to hear the answer. Then she wondered if she was brave enough to hear the answers to the questions that brought her there.

"Come, sit, sit." Madame Gabor sat down in her chair and gestured to the one across from her.

Aria looked down at the yellow wooden stool and pulled it out. The sound of wood scraping against wood permeated the room and made the hairs on her neck stand up. She chastised herself for being so creeped out—she had come there for help, after all, although she began to feel foolish for it.

"So, my dear, you have questions about your future. For twenty dollars, I will tell you all that you wish to know," Madame Gabor said while shuffling a deck of ornately decorated tarot cards.

"Okay, sure." Aria dug through her purse and pulled out a twenty-dollar bill, which she handed to the fortune teller, but the woman held her hand up to stop her.

"Put it on the offering plate and cover it with that cloth." She nodded toward a bright blue scarf lying on the tabletop.

Aria's brows furrowed, but she did as she was instructed.

"So," the woman began, "would you like to know about the man you'll marry, how many children you'll bear, or what kind of career you'll have?"

Aria gulped hard, and she was certain Madame Gabor could hear it. Then she wondered if the woman was a true psychic. Wouldn't she know why she was there? Nonetheless, she tucked her hair behind her ear and was prepared to answer when the elderly woman gasped and startled her.

"You have the mark," she said on a shaky breath. Her eyes bulged as she stared, and her hand resting on the table began to tremble.

Aria's hands flew to her chest. "What? I have what?" she shrieked. She hadn't meant for her voice to sound as shrill as it did, but the woman's expression terrified her.

The Gypsy looked deeply into her widened eyes, and she repeated on a whisper, "You have the mark."

Aria shook her head in confusion. "What mark? What are you talking about?" Her eyes looked at her hands and arms to find a flaw in her alabaster skin while her mind raced.

Madame Gabor didn't respond, though. Instead, she stood up and went to the other side of the curtain. Aria then heard the distinct metallic click of the lock on the entrance door followed by the shuffling of the woman's feet as she returned and closed the curtain.

"Please tell me what you are talking about. What mark?" In the back of her mind, something nagged her. She wasn't sure how it could be, since it had disappeared, but she wondered if the woman was referring to her neck.

Madame Gabor reached out and took one of Aria's clammy hands while her free hand pointed to Aria's neck. "You have the mark"— she hesitated and turned Aria's hand over to search   her   palm—"of   the   vampire."

Twenty-three

Kellan soared high, in the body of a bald eagle, over the Santa Cruz Mountains in search of the oracle he believed he'd find there—Gaia. Hundreds of years ago, while in Egypt, he had heard stories from others of his kind that the oracle, who had served Anubis, had been banished from the land by Isis after misguiding her. Gaia retreated to the North American continent and eventually ended up in the mountain range known to the Americans as the Santa Cruz Mountains. He only hoped that she was still there.

Once he got close enough to her, she'd be able to sense his presence because of his ties to Anubis—vampires are his children—and she'd show herself. Kellan knew she'd do so because the oracle had spent centuries trying to get back in the god's good graces; therefore, she remained a servant of his children.

Kellan flew over a peak and spotted a cavern in the side of the mountain about four hundred yards away. It was a good place to search, so he landed near it, sought out some prey, and then entered it to take his rest until nightfall. He'd been losing out on sleep lately, because he was always watching Aria during the day, and he was starting to feel weak. He was surely going to need his strength to deal with whatever secrets Gaia revealed when she unraveled the mystery surrounding Aria.

Twenty-four

Aria gasped and quickly pulled her hand back, tucking it into her chest. She'd taken books out on the subject, true, but to hear it aloud was almost more than she could bear.

Madame Gabor eyed her carefully before speaking again. "You believe, don't you? I can read it on your face."

Aria struggled to find her words. "I-I-I don't know what I believe, that's why I came here"—her fingers went to her neck—"How did you know? I can't even see it anymore."

Her knee began to twitch wildly and knocked against the table, so she placed her hand on her thigh to steady the trembling. There was nothing she could do, though, about the bile rising in her throat like a volcano. She swallowed hard to force it down and stared down at her hands in her lap.

The Gypsy clutched the amulet she wore and spoke in hushed tones. "I possess the evil eye which allows me to see things that have a sinister aura around them, and you, my darling girl, definitely have such a presence."

She shuffled the deck of tarot cards three more times while she talked and then broke them up into three piles, flipping the top card over on each stack. She slowly studied them while playing with the talisman hanging around her neck and mumbling something incoherent under her breath.

Aria fidgeted in her chair, and a whoosh of air escaped her lips. "Well, what do you see?"

Madame Gabor placed both of her wrinkled hands on the table and pursed her lips into a thin line.

Aria felt her chest tighten up from the glum expression on the fortune teller's face. Her ears began to ring, and she felt her heart skip a beat as it pounded against her ribs.

"Please tell me," she pleaded.

Madame Gabor raised one hand up to silence her and bowed her head for a couple of seconds while her eyes closed. Aria was worried the woman had fallen asleep, or worse, but then her eyes flew open.

"These cards represent your past, present, and future. Each card has more than one meaning, but when put together, they define each other to tell a story"—she pointed to each pile and continued—"The lovers represents your past, death fills your present, and judgement is in your future." She caught the look of terror and confusion on Aria's face and held her hand up once again. "What this means is your past is filled with internal conflict as you have tried to determine your identity"—she cocked her head in thought—"Are you adopted by chance?"

Aria felt the color drain from her face, and her hand began to tremble. "Why, yes, I was adopted as an infant. Now you said death fills my present. Is that because of the murders happening around town, because that's why I ca—" She broke off because Madame Gabor had placed one finger to her pale pink lips to silence her.

"Death doesn't always mean its literal translation. In your case, it means a transformation. I see a new cycle of your life developing, which leads us to the judgement card. There is an awakening taking place within you that may lead to changes for the better." Her mouth looked like it was trying to smile but twitched instead. Then her hand went to her amulet once more, and she squeezed it until her knuckles turned white. She studied Aria's face and asked, "May I see your palm, please?"

Aria hesitated before placing her hand in the Gypsy's. Madame Gabor then traced the etched lines with her fingertip, which would normally have tickled Aria, but she was petrified and didn't even feel it. The woman's head slowly bobbed while she studied Aria's flesh. Then she looked up with a slight smile.

"I see that you are very strong—a warrior. You are resilient and will be able to handle what is happening to you right now."

Aria was confused. "But I don't understand what that means. What is happening to me? A vampire is after me? How can I 'handle' that?" she fired off while blinking rapidly. "You said I have the mark of the vampire, right?"

Madame Gabor nodded. "Yes, I did say that, and you do. The undead is moving about in your life circle, but take heart that something is protecting you from it. You have your own aura, which is protecting you. Perhaps you are Gypsy and have your own evil eye," she said with a wink. "Don't worry about it too much. Your destiny will reveal itself to you in pieces, and you will have the strength to handle it. Now, it is getting late in the afternoon, and I must close my shop before the sun sets."

Aria scrunched her brows together and frowned. "Is that because of the vampire? Aren't you afraid since they apparently exist?"

The woman surprised Aria when she laughed. It was a cackle filled with the wisdom that comes from great age. "My dear, vampires have always existed, and my people have always known it. Many cultures believe in the undead, while some, like yours, traditionally do not. The evil eye will protect me, so I am not afraid"—she opened her hands up in a gentle shrug—"Now werewolves, on the other hand, are a different story," she said and laughed again.

"Werewolves?" Aria shrieked. "Are you being serious?"

The Gypsy frowned slightly, and her eyes looked downward. "Well, that is a story for another day, free of charge." She gave Aria another wink and a pat on her shoulder. "I'll walk out with you if you give me a minute to gather my knitting materials and purse."

Aria stubbed the tip of her sneaker against the chair leg and chewed her lip. "Um, that's okay. I'm all right." Then her eyes shot up, and she asked in a rush, "Do I need one of those talisman things for, you know, protection?"

Madame Gabor looked at her as if she had asked something unreasonable. "No, dear, as I mentioned before, you have all that you need. It is unusual, I must admit, but you have an inner amulet of your own. You did confirm being adopted, so I think you may have some Romani in you." She reached out and took a handful of

Aria's dark hair. "Yes, it is possible. Do you know anything about your biological parents?"

Aria frowned again. "No, I've never asked." She had never had a reason to inquire about them before. Her adoptive parents were very much real parents to her.

"Well, maybe now is the time that you do. You need to find out who you are," Madame Gabor advised. She was about to say something else, but her phone rang, and she quickly answered it.

Aria slipped out the front door and made a fast-paced walk to her car. The sun was dipped low in the sky, and despite what the woman had told her, she had no desire to be outside after dark.

Twenty-five

Aria thought about everything Madame Gabor had said while she drove back to school, blowing through stop signs and at least one red light. She felt as if she hadn't received the answers she had been seeking. True, the Gypsy confirmed that vampires really existed, but Aria still didn't know why one would be after her or seducing her. She also couldn't comprehend why she'd be considered a warrior—she had been meek all her life. And what did that mean exactly anyway—was she expected to fight the mythical creature? How could she when every time she had been around him, he had managed to seduce her into unspeakable acts?

You need to find out who you are rang through her mind. She dug into her purse for her phone and dialed her parents. She got their answering machine, though, so she left a message for them to call back when they had the chance. The first shadows of nightfall blanketed the area and prompted her to make another call. This time she dialed Cat's number.

"Hey, what's up?" Cat answered after the third ring.

"Um, where are you?" Aria rushed.

"I'm in the room studying for a change. Why?"

Aria sighed with relief. "Please just stay there. Don't go anywhere, okay?"

"Um, okay, but why? Where are you? Are you out with Chris?"

Shit! I forgot about him. "I'm on the way back to campus, and I'll explain when I get there. Bye."

She looked down at the speedometer and saw that she was over the limit by twelve miles per hour, so she tapped the brakes. She didn't need to get pulled over now. She wasn't supposed to be on her phone either, which stopped her from calling Chris to cancel their plans.

When she pulled into the parking lot a few minutes later, she hopped out of her car and darted to her dorm room, where she locked the door behind her. Of course, she had to wonder, would a lock stop the monster? If what she dreamed last night was in fact not a dream, then she supposed not.

"What or who has gotten into you?" Cat asked from her bed where she was reading. "Are you fighting with Kyle again?"

Aria had no idea how to tell her friend about her visit with the fortune teller. She wondered if she even should. She wanted to protect Cat, but she didn't want to end up in a mental hospital because of her revelation. She had no idea how open her roommate would be to such things, so she decided to keep it on the down low for the time being.

"No one has gotten to me, including Kyle," she answered. "I'm just on edge because of the murders around here. I wanted to be sure you were safe."

Cat put her hand over her heart and batted her lashes. "Aw," she teased, "you care.

You really do care." Then she broke out into a fit of giggles.

Aria shook her head and groaned. "Be serious for once, eh? Someone is out there killing young women, and the last time I checked, we fall into that category."

Cat reached for something on her nightstand and produced a small canister, which she thrust in Aria's direction. "That's why I have this pepper spray. I keep it with me wherever I go," she stated proudly.

Aria's shoulders slumped. "Does it come in garlic?" she mumbled.

"What?"

She looked at the floor and curled her hands up. "Nothing. Don't mind me." Her phone rang then and startled her. She hoped it was her mom or dad calling her back, but it was Chris.

"Hi, Chris," she answered.

"Hi. Weren't we supposed to meet twenty minutes ago outside the cafeteria?" he inquired with a hint of frustration in his voice.

She scuffed the toe of her shoe against a black mark on the floor to erase it. "Yeah, sorry about that. Look, something has come up, and I'm not going to be able to make it tonight after all."

"Oh," he said in an octave lower than before. "You know, if it's just too early, we can hit the next show at 7:00."

Aria's mind raced as she tried to figure out a nice way to let him down, but she couldn't think of any. She wondered, too, how she was supposed to spend the rest of her life hiding away every time the sun went down. Obviously, based on the night before, if the vampire wanted to get to her, he would no matter where she was. She doubted, though, that he'd attack in a crowded movie theatre, so maybe she'd be safer there.

*But what about Cat? What if he comes here for me and finds her instead? What if he attacks me when I'm with Chris…*Her head spun and made her groan.

"Aria? Are you still there?" Chris's voice brought her back to the present, and she knew she couldn't put off giving him an answer.

"Yes, I'm still here. I guess the 7:00 movie will work, but can we grab a coffee first? I don't want to fall asleep during it, and I'm a little tired," she lied. The truth was, she wanted to stay up all night if she could. If the movies were right, vampires didn't come out in the daytime.

"Yeah, sure," he replied with enthusiasm. "Actually, would you like to grab dinner first? I heard there's a new Italian place in town that's pretty decent."

"Okay, that sounds good. I'll meet you downstairs in a half-hour, okay?"

"I'll be there," he said. "Bye for now." The line went still.

Cat clapped her hands like a happy child. "Yay! I'm so glad you're going out with him."

Aria simply smiled before rummaging through the overstuffed closet. She grabbed a dark purple sweater, black jeans, and the boots Cat said she could have and quickly changed into them. Then she touched up her make-up and dug around in her jewelry box for some purple hoops. Her fingers came across a silver crucifix necklace, and her heart began to race as the reality of the situation hit her like a tidal wave. She stared at the jewelry while she tried to imagine what the rest of her life would be like.

How do you even survive something like this?

The Gypsy had promised her that she'd be able to handle everything that was going on, but she felt like she was spinning out of control, so how could she handle it? How was she supposed to be a warrior when she was terrified out of her mind?

She pulled the necklace out of the jewelry box and started to put it around her neck but stopped. She walked over to Cat and handed it to her instead.

"Here. I'd like you to have this," she said.

Cat eyed her suspiciously. "Um, why?"

"You like silver jewelry, and I think it will look good on you. Besides, you gave me your boots, so it's only fair if I return the gesture."

Cat chuckled. "Okay, if you say so. My parents will get a kick out of it. They'll think I'm finally being a good girl," she mocked and rolled her blue eyes. Then she eyed Aria from head to toe and nodded in approval. "You look good for Chris," she cooed with a Cheshire grin. "That purple really brings out your new blue eyes—they almost look like a silvery-blue tonight."

Aria's fingers flew up to her face to the corners of her eyes. "Huh, I wonder how that's possible," she mumbled.

"You'd better get going. He's probably downstairs by now scratching at the door like a sad puppy," Cat teased.

Aria ran her hands through her hair to tousle her waves before grabbing her purse and heading out for her date. She just hoped that going wouldn't be a mistake.

Twenty-six

Kellan took on his vampire form just as soon as the sun went down. He expected Gaia to immediately show herself, but when she didn't, he assumed he had the wrong cavern. When he turned to leave, though, a powerful voice rang out behind him.

"Why have you come here?"

Kellan turned to see a stunningly beautiful woman surrounded by bright light, and it was difficult for him to form an answer. He knelt before her and bowed his head.

"I seek your wisdom, Oracle," he finally replied. "I need guidance that only you can provide."

She slowly approached him, and he noticed the gray wolf by her side for the first time. She chuckled softly and said, "You are a child of Anubis, who banished me from Egypt, and yet you seek my council?"

He continued to bow before her, which put him at eye level with the wolf, and humbly answered, "Yes, I am what you say, and I have heard stories that you will help my kind, which is why I'm here. I am in search of answers I know only you can provide, my Oracle."

The beautiful seer looked down at Kellan and told him to rise. Then she examined him from head to toe with appreciation in her eyes, which appeared to glow a light purple.

"It is true that I sometimes help the children of Anubis. But if I help you, you must do something for me. You must carry word to Anubis of my good deeds, so he will once again welcome me in his court. Do you agree?"

"Yes, Gaia, prophet to the gods, I will do your bidding."

The oracle's full lips curved up into a smile. "Good. Now what is it you desire to know?"

Kellan held his hands together loosely before him and maintained strong eye contact with her. "I have bitten one who defies the laws of both the mortal realm and the immortal one. She isn't dead, but she doesn't behave like a vampire either—she walks freely in the sun."

Gaia slightly tilted her head and made a soft mewing sound. Then she turned to her left and gestured for him to follow her. She led him to a stone well filled with water that had a peculiar vapor hanging over it and a curtain of light behind it. She looked at the wolf and motioned to the glowing portal. The creature first bowed to her and then jumped into the light where it disappeared. While Kellan watched in amazement, she turned to the well and waved her hand over it in a slow circular motion. Light splashed up from the water and broke up the mist to splay on her lovely face while a sudden breeze caught her hair and rippled it in a hundred amber waves.

She stared into the light, with her eyes glowing, and told him, "You must beware the evil eye, or it will be your end. I see that the mortal, whom you desire, is caught between the living and the dead, but that is all I can see"—she looked up from the well, and the glow disappeared from her violet   eyes—"There   are   magical   forces surrounding this mortal that I've never seen before. There is a protection on her that even my vision can't penetrate."

Kellan's eyes widened in astonishment. "What do I do then? How do I completely transform her into my mate?"

The oracle shook her head. "For the first time in thousands of years, my vision is unclear. For any other answers, you must go before Isis and beg of her council."

Kellan could hear the finality in her voice, so he knew it was time to leave. He bowed once more in her honor and spun around to go.

"Are you certain this human is worth it?" she called after him.

He turned back to face her, out of respect, and answered, "Aye. I'm certain."

"So be it."

Once outside the cavern entrance, he changed back into an eagle and flew to San Francisco as quickly as he could. He needed to see his obsession again before he built up the courage to go before Isis, the god above all gods, and asked for a favor.

Twenty-seven

Aria looked over her menu at Rigoberto's while their waitress fetched their colas. Normally, she loved Italian food, but, presently, she couldn't work up the appetite for it.

"What sounds good?" Chris asked while scrutinizing each item on the menu.

"I'm not sure yet," she informed him. "I might just have the spaghetti special."

"Cool. I'm thinking about having the sirloin steak."

"Oh, that sounds good," she said and located it on the menu to see what side dishes came with it.

The waitress returned then and set down their drinks. "So, what have you decided on?" she asked while eyeing Chris.

Chris looked at Aria to allow her to go first with her order.

"I'll have the steak cooked medium-well with the potato and house salad," Aria told the young woman.

Chris closed his menu and said, "And I'll have the same, except that I want it well-done, and bring us some garlic bread, please."

"With extra garlic," Aria added with a grin and handed the waitress her menu.

"You got it," she told them and left to put in their orders.

"So," Chris began, "how are your classes going so far?"

Aria looked up from the napkin she'd been folding and unfolding and replied, "They're all fine, but I wish we could get involved in the recent cases. I learn better by getting my hands dirty—a book can only give you so much information, you know?"

He nodded in agreement. "I get that, but of course, it doesn't really apply to my accounting studies," he said with a smile. "Did you know any of the victims?"

"No, I didn't know any of them," she softly replied. *But I know who is responsible.*

Aria wished she hadn't brought it up—it was a subject she couldn't discuss with him. If she told him a vampire was involved, he'd disappear and stick her with the check. Luckily, her mother interrupted with a phone call.

"Hi, Mom, thanks for calling me back, but I can't talk right now. I'll call you later," she answered.

"Um, okay. I guess we'll talk later then. Love you," Maria Sandoval replied.

"Me too, bye."

For the next several minutes, they chit-chatted about school and their hometowns, and then the waitress reappeared with their dinner. Chris watched Aria while she cut her juicy steak up.

"I don't know how you can eat meat that isn't cooked all the way," he said with a grimace. "It's gross, and this is coming from a guy."

At first, she laughed, but then she looked down at her plate, and it made her pause. She normally ordered all her meat well-done, and she had no idea why she didn't in this instance.

However, it looked appealing to her, so she dug in with a shrug. She tore off a big chunk of the garlic bread and took a healthy bite.

Garlic thwarts vampires, right?

"It's nice to see a girl who doesn't pick at her food," Chris observed. "Usually, you all are too *dainty*." His voice changed to a feminine octave, and he batted his lashes.

Aria would have laughed, but she was choking on a bite of bread. Her violent coughs burned her throat while tears pooled in her eyes, which were squeezed tight.

"Are you okay?" Chris wondered. "Here, take a sip." He handed her a small glass of water, which she eagerly accepted.

"Wow, I guess the garlic was too strong for me," she mumbled with a red face after her hacking subsided.

"I was worried I might have to give you the Heimlich maneuver," he teased with a boyish grin, and she laughed with him. His chuckles stopped when he looked at his watch, though. "Uh-oh, we'd better wrap this up soon, or we'll be late for the movies."

They quickly finished their meals, and he took care of the bill. "I'll go bring the car around for you," he told her before stepping outside and taking off in a run.

Aria stepped out into the night air, and a breeze kicked up around her heels. At first, she enjoyed the tickling sensation of it tousling her hair, but then every muscle in her body tensed when she smelled musk. She looked left, then right, but she didn't see anyone aside from patrons entering and leaving the restaurant. She wrapped her arms tightly around herself in a protective hug and tried to map out an escape route.

Can I outrun a vampire? She doubted it.

A car suddenly honked its horn and scared the wits out of her—in her panic, she had forgotten all about Chris. *Shit! I've put him in danger.* Her mind raced as she quickly climbed into the black Mustang and pushed the door lock button, which received an inquisitive look from Chris.

"Rough neighborhood," she muttered with a nervous laugh.

"Don't worry, I'll protect you," he mocked and gave her a pat on the leg. Then he shifted the car into first gear and pulled away from the curb.

Aria sat with her hands in her lap and quietly listened to the sound of the gears shifting as the car propelled down the highway. As they got closer to the theatre, she knew she had to say something to get out of the movie. Earlier, she had thought that a public place would be safest, but now she wasn't so sure—she pictured the two of them as sitting ducks. Even worse, she was picturing Cat in their room as an easy target. She needed to get back and...*and what? Protect her?* Madame Gabor did call her a warrior—maybe that actually meant something.

"Chris," she hesitated, "I'm not feeling so great. I think my dinner is disagreeing with me." For effect, she rubbed her stomach and scowled.

"Oh, so you don't want to go to the movie then?" he asked, and she heard his disappointment.

"I'm sorry, but I just want to go to bed. Do you mind?"

"No, no, of course not. If you don't feel well, you should get some rest."

"Thank you," she replied meekly. *Now that I've taken care of that, what's next?* A shiver ran through her as she considered the possibilities.

Twenty-eight

Kellan could now find Aria whenever he wanted to because of the immortal bond formed after the third kiss of death, and he didn't like where he found her. He had located her at a restaurant, and it appeared as if she was on a date with the same man he had seen her talking to before. He watched them through a window as they ate their meal and enjoyed each other's company, and jealousy bubbled up inside him as well as confusion—she was eating human food. It was just one more indication that his attacks on her weren't working, and there was no logical reason.

He replayed the oracle's advice, especially the part about going before Isis for help. While he wasn't fond of the idea, it was probably his best chance at solving the magical mystery of the beautiful woman. Gaia had also told him to beware the evil eye, and he knew to take the advice seriously—Gypsy magic was a proven threat against his kind, and if it was a part of Aria, he needed to know about it as soon as possible.

He watched Aria stand outside the restaurant while she waited on her date to get his car, and he felt his manhood begin to swell. She was a vision of beauty in the purple sweater she wore that hugged her in all the right places, and he pictured himself taking it off her. There was something different about her, but he wasn't sure what it was until she moved—her movements were more lithe than usual. Also, her scent had changed from fresh wildflowers to heady orchids.

Maybe my immortal kisses are affecting her after all. If so, she'll be hungry soon.

He considered following the black car and dealing with the young man inside, but then he decided against it. When she did become hungry, the punk would make a good first meal. Kellan's lip turned up in a snarl—he hoped that she wouldn't want to seduce the young man first. He had no intentions of sharing the vixen, so her meals would have to be fast food.

Kellan changed into a peregrine falcon, the fastest flying bird, so he could get to Egypt as soon as possible.

Twenty-nine
Wednesday

Aria awoke with a stir, shooting up in her bed and flinging the covers while her heart pounded in her ears. Once she realized she was alone in her room, her breathing and pulse slowed down, but she still felt ill at ease. Cat was gone, but she had left a note on Aria's alarm clock, saying that she was having an early breakfast with Jason Marquette. Aria smiled as she reread the note—Jason was Cat's major conquest.

She climbed out of bed and trotted to the bathroom mirror where she checked her neck for bite marks. Nothing. She pulled her nightgown down to check her breasts. Still nothing. Relief washed over her as she realized she hadn't had a visitor last night. Her dreams of ravenous beasts had been just that—dreams.

She took a quick shower and dressed in the pink sweater her mother had given her the last time she went back home for a visit, and it reminded her to call her back. She dialed home and fiddled with her left earring nervously while she waited for someone to answer, but the machine picked up again.

"Hi, I wanted to let you guys know that I changed my mind about coming home for the four-day weekend. I'll book a flight today and let you know what time to pick me up at the airport. I love you. Bye."

She hung up and went online to book a flight to Idaho—asking about her birth parents was something she couldn't do over the phone. She knew her adoptive parents were going to be hurt by her questions, so it was best to handle it in person.

Her flight was in two hours, so she quickly packed and left a note for Cat before driving to the airport. She added in the letter, "Please wear the necklace I gave you. I'll explain why later."

Aria fell asleep not long after take-off, and she immediately slipped into the dream realm.

It was nighttime, and she was walking through the woods when she heard the leaves crunching behind her. She walked faster, but so did whatever it was that was following her, so she broke out into a run. Tree limbs whipped her skin as she dodged as much of the brush as she could, and she stumbled several times. She could hear snarling over her own furious panting and the pounding in her ears. She tripped and fell this time, and when she tried to get up, vines wrapped around her ankles and held her in place. The growling grew closer, and she saw the glow of yellow eyes through the brush. She screamed at the top of her lungs.

Aria jerked and yelled, "No!"

About forty pairs of eyes turned to stare at her, and she felt a blush creep up her neck and into her face.

"Oops, sorry," she mumbled and smiled sheepishly.

She looked down and played with the zipper on her jacket to avoid the uncomfortable stares aimed in her direction.

"Bad dream?" the middle-aged woman next to her asked.

Aria answered in a hushed voice, "Yes," and then went back to playing with the zipper.

The woman chuckled softly and gave Aria a pat on her arm before going back to her puzzle book.

Aria pulled her library book out of her carry-on bag—she had brought one of the books on vampire legends. She opened it up to the index in the back and searched under the G's for Gypsy. Then she flipped to page 211 and began to read about the Romani and their beliefs in Kali, the Indian deity associated with drinking blood. She went on to discover beliefs about the evil eye and Gypsy curses. When it was time to land, she had learned quite a bit about the Romani people. Her mind wandered back to what the fortune teller had said about her—she might be a Gypsy and have her own evil eye. It was a small thrill to think that it could be true. She had no idea where or whom she came from, so the possibility was there. She couldn't wait to get some answers about her real family.

Aria's parents met her at the gate with a ton of hugs and kisses, and then they made the twenty-minute drive home to their yellow ranch house.

"What made you change your mind about coming home over your little break?" her mother asked. Then she scrutinized her face and added, "Something is different about you"—she reached out and touched her daughter's hair—"Wait; it's your eyes. Are you wearing blue contact lenses?"

Aria forced her mouth to turn up in a half-smile. "Yes," she lied, "they are a trial pair from the eye doctor. I just wanted to try them out." Her tongue shot out to wet her dry lips.

"Oh, well they're very pretty, but so are your hazel eyes," her mother observed. "Now, not that I'm complaining, but what brings you home?"

Aria wasn't sure if she wanted to get into things right then, so she hesitated and looked at the floor while cracking her knuckles—a habit that her mother had scolded her for on more than one occasion.

"Aria, what is it? Is something wrong?" David Sandoval inquired. His concern was etched into the lines on his forehead, and his eyes were narrowed in on her.

She wasn't sure how to begin—this was going to be a touchy subject to discuss with them. "Um, we are studying genealogy in one of my classes, and it has raised some questions for me," she said rapidly while her eyes darted between her parents.

"Questions"—her mother repeated while getting up from the sofa and walking across the small living room—"What kind of questions?"

Aria swallowed hard and looked into her mother's worried face. "This is difficult to say. I would like to know who I came from"—she folded and unfolded her hands in her lap—"but I don't want to hurt you. I'm just curious is all."

Her father uncrossed his legs and leaned forward. "Aria, we knew this day would come. We have always thought of ourselves as your parents, but we know there is more to the story of you than that"—tears brimmed his brown eyes—"so you aren't hurting us." His facial expression belied his words.

Aria looked at her mother who was dabbing her eyes with the handkerchief she always carried. "Mom?"

Maria Sandoval forced a half-smile. "Your father is correct—you deserve to know everything. To be honest with you, though, we really don't know that much. I mean you were found in St. Joseph's church by Father O'Hara. He didn't see who left you." She sat down by Aria and took her hand.

"There was that letter, though, hon. Do we still have it?" her father chimed in.

Her mother genuinely smiled this time. "That's right. I forgot about the letter found inside your bassinet. Yes, we still have it—it's with your baby things. I'll go up to the attic and look for it. Do you want to help me?"

Aria nodded with the first bit of enthusiasm she had felt since her arrival—she was getting somewhere. To imagine reading her biological mother or father's last words to her was exciting. Nostalgia hit, too, at the thought of looking at her baby things.

"Yes, I'm happy to help," she answered while standing up to follow her mother.

"I'm going to fix an early dinner while you girls do that," her father stated and rubbed his hands together. "I'm going to start a fire first, though. How does that sound?"

Aria hugged herself and rubbed her arms. "Sounds good to me. It's a little chilly in here."

"I think so too. Now, you go ahead and catch up to your mom before she starts piling up my memorabilia for a garage sale."

Aria smiled at her dad before walking to the pull-down ladder and climbing it to where she could hear her mother frantically digging through several years' worth of odds and ends. She sighed with some relief at the possibility of finally getting some answers, but then she frowned with worry as she thought of Cat being alone and unprotected.

But then how would I be able to protect her anyway? I didn't stop him from biting me...

Thirty

Kellan had made it as far as Las Vegas before he decided to stop and rest. *This isn't the way to go,* he decided. *It will take way too long, and time is of the essence.*

As soon as the sun went down, he'd find a way to get on a flight to Cairo. Of course, it would take more than one nightfall to get there, so he'd have to stow away in the luggage area to protect himself from the sun. He'd need help to do this, so he'd have to create a minion. He'd also need to feed before the journey to keep his vitality up.

He perched on a ledge near the top of Harrah's Hotel and Casino and watched the multitude of patrons eager to risk everything for the slim chance of winning a buck. This wasn't his first time to Sin City, and the culture always amazed him, especially how open the frigid Americans were about sex here—it reminded him of Paris. Of course, his first visit to Las Vegas had almost overloaded his senses—the noise and lights were a little too much. The crowd, on the other hand, had been delicious. Yes, he had fed well on that visit, and he intended to do so again tonight.

He watched the ladies of the evening mulling around the street corners and in front of an adult toy store. He had never tried to screw one because he wanted conquests—he liked the thrill of seduction. He enjoyed tearing down the walls women put up in a false pretense to protect their innocence—it reminded him of his youth when he was a young dandy in Paris. Even then, he could always get them to succumb. His looks, his debonair charm, and his family's money had turned more than one virgin into a wanton hellcat. Unfortunately, it all caught up to him the night he met Gabriella in 1616. He could vividly recall how the moonlight had illuminated her flawless alabaster skin and made her green eyes sparkle like emeralds. Even her delicate voice was absolute perfection, and it had drawn him in like a puppy to a babe. The tides had turned for him, and he had become putty in her delicate aristocratic hands. It was the first and only time a woman had seduced him, and the sex was unlike any he had ever experienced during his life. She had taken him to the brinks of sanity as the insurmountable pleasure wracked his young body, and when he had reached the highest point of euphoria—just between life and death—she bit him. That had been the beginning of what would become his new immortal life. She'd seduced him for three nights, and while he fell hopelessly in love, he felt his body changing.

On the third night, she whispered, "Stay hidden from the sun. I'll never forget you." Then, with one last kiss, she disappeared from his sight, leaving him to discover his new life on his own.

He could have been angry at having had his life ended on that fateful night, but instead, he embraced his new life with vivaciousness.

Kellan snapped back into the present when he saw an odd little man at the newspaper stand across the street. He decided the fellow would be perfect as his minion, and he began to follow him with a smile on the inside—he hadn't had a crony in hundreds of years.

Thirty-one

When Aria reached the attic, her mother was going through a pile of baby clothes with a nostalgic grin. She looked at Aria and held up a tiny blue dress with red bows.

"Look at what I found. This was your outfit for your first birthday party," she cooed. "And look at these little shoes. I can't believe your feet were ever this small." She handed the items to Aria to look at while she dug around in the old leather trunk some more. "Here are some onesies, and this was your favorite dress when you were four—she held up a red polka-dotted dress. It was your favorite because I made it to match one of mine," she said with tears rolling down her cheeks in a slow stream. She reached out and touched Aria's hair, which had tumbled over her shoulder. "See? I'm your mom." Her voice cracked, and her hand was trembling. Aria could tell she was trying her best to contain her emotions, and it made her feel guilty.

"I know you are," she said with a sigh while tears pooled in her eyes too. "I have never doubted that either"—she looked down at the terrycloth onesies she held—"I'm sorry I'm putting you through this, Mom." She wiped away her tears and used the inside of her sweater to dab at her runny nose.

"Aria, sweetheart," her mother began softly after a shuddering breath, "you have the right to know about who created you. There is no shame at all in wondering where you came from"—she put down the romper she was holding and took Aria's hands in her own warm ones—"I'm actually surprised you didn't ask sooner."

Aria looked down at their locked hands. "I just never really cared to know until now. My mother"—she looked up at the woman before her and corrected herself—"I mean my birth mother didn't want me for some reason, so I never cared. To me, *you* are my mother in every way that matters, despite not having given birth to me."

Maria Sandoval beamed from ear to ear. "I don't know what to say," she whispered and squeezed Aria's hand before focusing her attention on a cardboard box marked *baby stuff.* Aria could hear her mother's fingernails scratching the cardboard as she rummaged in the makeshift storage container. She was smiling the entire time, and Aria, once again, wondered why her parents hadn't adopted any more children. She had asked once, and they both agreed that she had been enough for them. Still, she thought, it would have been nice to have had someone else to play with besides the neighborhood children.

"Are there any other boxes I could start looking through?" she asked, trying to be helpful. "I hate just sitting here while you do all the work."

Her mother shook her head. "It's fine, sweetie. I don't mind. I'm enjoying looking at your things. Here, look at this teeny tiny spoon"—she cooed and held up the baby spoon—"Oh, look, here's the little fork too." She handed both items to Aria and returned to her treasure hunt.

Aria tried to imagine herself eating with the utensils, which were decorated with little lambs, and then she wondered if she should save them for any children she may have one day.

Probably not since a vampire is after me.

A single tear made its path down her pale cheek as the glumness of the situation hit her once more, and she cracked her knuckles again. This time, her mother noticed and shot her a knowing scowl, so she immediately stopped.

"Wait! I think I found it."

Aria felt her heart thud in her chest as anticipation coursed through her. In a matter of minutes, she might be reading words from her birth mom, and that was big—especially if it helped to unravel the weird things going on in her life right now. She leaned in to get a look inside the box just as her mother pulled out an envelope, which had turned a yellowish color over time. The paper made a loud crinkling sound as she pulled the letter out and opened it up. It, too, had turned yellow over the course of twenty years.

"Let's see"—her mother began while she opened the antiquated letter—"Yes, this is it. The adoption agency told us it was found in your bassinet." She handed the note over to Aria with a trembling hand.

Aria's hands trembled, too, as she took the letter. Her lips moved, without a sound, as she read it to herself.

"My dearest child, it is with a heavy heart that we must part ways. I'm sorry that I brought you into this world, only to abandon you, but I do it with good reason—it is for your safety. I hope that when you read this, you're an adult so that you can possibly comprehend my reasons. Your life is in danger from those who dwell in the shadows. Your father came to me, under the cover of darkness, and brought the kiss of death. He would have forced you into the shadows as well, if I hadn't hidden you from him and his kind. This is the only way I can protect you from that life. I hope that the church finds you a loving home, and I hope that you can forgive me for bringing you into the world with a shroud of darkness over your head. By the time you read this, I will surely be gone. Perhaps that is my destiny, but with all my heart, I hope that I am changing yours.

"I hope that you will never need this, but if he or one of his kind finds you, you must use it.

"Io sono la luce, dove abitano le ombre. Io combatterò quelli portati dall'inferno. Nel buio della notte, io sono uno di troppo forte per combattere. Sangue di Romani, mi rende liberi. Ayres nome mi protegge da te. Sono al sicuro dalla situazione che deriva dal tuo morso immortale. Your mother, Nadya."

I am light, where the darkness dwells. I will fight those brought from hell. In the gloom of the night, I am too strong for you to fight. Romani blood sets me free. Ayres name protects me from thee. I am safe from the plight that comes from your immortal bite.

Aria reread the letter except for the last part, which she'd have to translate later. She focused her attention on the words and what they meant. Her mother spoke of her father coming in the darkness and having a "kiss of death."

Does that mean what I think it means?

Her mother cleared her throat before she spoke softly. "Your father and I found the letter to be odd. We think that maybe she had a mental condition and was babbling nonsense. What do you think?"

Aria's eyes went wide. "Yeah, that makes sense. She must have been crazy." She carefully folded the letter back up and put it in the tattered envelope. "I'm going to go back down and see if Dad needs help with dinner. Thanks, Mom." She forced her smile but not because she was ungrateful—she was just extremely concerned.

"Aria," her mother spoke softly, "are you okay, hon?"

Aria used the back of her hand to wipe away a stray tear. Her voice shook a little when she answered, "Yeah, I'm okay." Her smile was crooked, she knew, but she tried to mask her true feelings—she was scared for herself and everyone she loved.

Thirty-two

Darkness came and so did the 6'3" inch shadow lurking outside the minimart for the small man. While he waited impatiently, Kellan made quick work of a hurried Latina who crossed his path and disposed of her body in a nearby Dumpster. The people walking by on the busy sidewalk probably assumed he was seducing the woman, whom he had pressed up against the concrete building. To the naked eye, it would have looked like he was simply kissing her neck. She was petite, so he'd have to have a more satisfying meal after he took care of urgent matters.

Right on cue, the short man came out of the store and began his walk down the sidewalk with a sack of groceries in each arm. Kellan followed him around the corner and quickly shortened the distance between them until he was breathing down the man's neck. The man abruptly turned around, dropping one of the bags, and looked up. Even though it was dark out, and the streetlights nearby were broken, Kellan could see him trembling.

"What do you want?" the man asked with a sharp but shaky intake of breath. He stooped and picked up his sack full of food.

Kellan chuckled a low throaty laugh. "I want to give you a new life."

The man scoffed and waved him away. "Shit. You're a Jehovah Witness, aren't you? Well,

I'm not interested, buddy. I've already found Christ."

Kellan laughed again. "No, I assure you I do not represent a church. I want to offer you an opportunity for employment."

The man puffed up his chest and jabbed a finger in the air. "Who sent you—my ex? Is this about her damn alimony? Tell the bitch she'll get it at the first of the month!"

He turned his back to Kellan and fumbled with his set of keys. He took two steps toward a door a few feet in front of him, but a strong hand on his shoulder stopped him.

Kellan grasped the short man by both his shoulders and spun him around, causing both bags to drop this time.

"Fuck! You broke my eggs, asshole!" He threw an impulsive punch, but Kellan stopped it in time, not that it would have done him any harm if the fist had contacted his granite-like chest.

"That wasn't very nice," he growled and picked the dumpy man up by his collar with his arms flailing.

"I-I-I'm sorry, but uh, you know, I can only afford so much to eat each week, and this is it."

Kellan tilted his head to the side and popped his neck. "You're not going to have to worry about that anymore. Now, let's try this again. What's your name?" The man didn't answer, so Kellan gave him a shake. "Speak!"

"It-it's Ray. I'm Ray." His voice cracked and sounded garbled as Kellan's knuckles continued to dig into his neck.

"All right, Ray"—he let the man down but maintained a clasp on his shoulder—"I've selected you to be my minion."

Ray's eyes went wide with confusion. "Your what? Whatever that is, I don't want to do it."

Kellan leaned in, with his eyes glowing, and snarled, "Do you think you have a choice?"

He sunk his teeth into the unsuspecting man's neck and took one pull of the pungent fluid—men didn't taste good to male vampires, which is why Kellan didn't replace his last minion three hundred years ago. The man cried out from the pain and tried to jerk away, but the vice-like grip on him held him in place.

A neighbor, who must have heard the commotion, turned on the little porch light nearby at the same time Kellan locked eyes with Ray.

"There now. Don't you feel better already?" Kellan asked with fake concern dripping from his voice while blood dripped from his fangs.

"I—" He stopped and searched in the darkness, examining his hands and arms. "Yes, Master," he mumbled and bowed his head subserviently.

Kellan smiled, fully exposing his fangs, and praised, "Very good. I think you will prove to be very useful to me. Now, the first thing I want you to do is to find a flight heading to Cairo. You'll book one ticket."

Ray dug around in his pocket and pulled out a pack of smokes and a lighter. After he lit his cigarette, he replied, "But won't we need two tickets, Master?"

"No, you'll be traveling with your pet," Kellan answered with a sly grin. The man still looked confused, so he shifted into a Doberman and then shifted back.

Ray jumped up and down clapping his chubby hands. "Oh, Master, what a wonderful gift you have!" He pulled his cell phone out of his pocket and ran a Google search for flights. "I found one leaving in one hour from here."

"Book it and pack a bag."

Thirty-three

"Are you going to eat your food or play with it, honey?"

Aria looked up at her father with a dazed expression. "What? Oh, yeah, I'm not that hungry. May I be excused?"

The lines in his forehead deepened with worry, and he exhaled loudly. "Do you want to talk about it?" Before she could answer, though, he looked at his wife with a scowl and asked, "Was this a mistake?"

Aria's head snapped up before her mother had time to answer, and she said, "No! It wasn't a mistake, but I need time to absorb it all, okay? I need to figure out what it means."

Her father didn't let it go, though. "It's the ramblings of an upset and likely unstable woman, Aria. Nothing more, nothing less."

"David, let's let her deal with it the way she needs too," her mother said sternly. She didn't argue or disagree with her husband often, but when it came to Aria, she had always been defensive.

He nodded and threw his hands up in the air. "Fine, but just talk to us if it's overwhelming you. Fair enough?"

Aria gave him a weak smile to reassure him. "I will. Now, I'm going to go take a bath and get ready for bed." She cleaned up her dishes and loaded them in the dishwasher before giving him a kiss on the cheek. "Good night, Daddy."

"I'll come to your room in a bit to brush your hair," her mother told her. It was a customary bedtime ritual of theirs to give them a chance to chat about their day or anything else that they wanted to.

"Okay, I'll see you in a little while."

Aria made her way to the small bathroom off her bedroom and started the water. While the tub filled, she reread the letter which had been neatly folded in her pocket. A pang of concern for her birth mother tightened her chest as she sank into the hot water. She wanted the bubbles from the lavender bubble bath to whisk away her anxiety, but it wasn't working. She knew her mother had gone through the terror she was going through now, and she had a glum feeling about how it must've turned out. *How could she have survived a vampire?* Aria's fingertips traced her neck and breast where she had been bitten. *How am I surviving? Am I going to turn into one like in the movies?*

Warm tears ran down her cheek and mixed with the hot bath water. She pulled both hands together in front of her and said a heartfelt prayer. She prayed for her soul and for the safety of her loved ones. Then she added one in for the rest of the San Francisco community, which caused a frightening thought—what if he followed her home to Idaho? *Can vampires do that?* If so, how would she protect her parents? Madame Gabor's words flitted through her.

"I see that you are very strong—a warrior," she had said. But, Aria didn't feel like one...

She quickly finished her bath and dressed in a warm flannel nightgown. Her mother must have heard the tub draining, because she rapped on Aria's bedroom door shortly afterward.

"Come in," Aria called out softly and pulled her vanity chair close to the bed.

Her mother entered the room, picked up the lacquered hair brush, and sat on the bed behind her.

"So," she began, "tell me about Cat. How is Catherine doing? Are you two still getting along as roommates? I know you are used to having a room to yourself."

Aria smiled before answering, "Cat's great. She's the sister I never had."

"Ah, then I'm sure there will be fights," her mother, who had four sisters, teased. "Girls are more competitive than boys. I remember always being mad at one of your aunts." Aria saw her mother's reflection in the vanity mirror, and she was shaking her head.

"Yeah, but they say it was always *your* fault," she jabbed playfully.

"Ha! I'm sure they do. Now what about boys? Did you ever make up with that one fella? What was his name again?"

Aria cleared her throat, which had suddenly tightened at the thought of boys and her recent experience with them. "Kyle. His name is Kyle, and, no, we aren't getting back together *ever*. He's a jerk."

"Aria Jane Sandoval, that's not very nice." Her mother wagged a finger at her in the mirror.

"Well, it's true, Momma. He thinks too highly of himself. He's a bad seed."

Her mother continued to run the brush through her silken strands. "Fine. Is there anyone else?"

Aria hesitated—she certainly couldn't describe her mystery lover to her mother. Then Chris popped into her thoughts, so she finally answered, "There is someone who's interested in me. His name is Chris, and he seems nice. We went to dinner last night, but that's all so far."

"Hmm, okay. Is he handsome?"

Aria smiled at her mother's searching gaze in the mirror as a blush crept up her neck. "Yes, he's cute."

Her mother flashed a wicked grin at her. "Is he sexy?"

"Mother! I can't talk about that with you," Aria whined. She assumed her mother had figured out that she was no longer a virgin, but she didn't want to discuss it.

Her mother laughed warmly. "Aria, you are a grown woman away at college, and I'm no fool. Woman to woman, we can certainly talk about such things. I'm not going to ask for details."

Aria looked at her mother's reflection with skepticism. "Well, anyway, I haven't thought about him in that way. He's just polite and nice," she answered honestly.

"So more like a friend then," her mother theorized.

"I suppose so, at least for now."

Her mother stroked the back of her head before kissing the top of it and setting the brush down on her vanity. "There is nothing wrong with being just friends. If the sparks are there, you will feel them."

Aria thought about the sparks she had felt while being seduced by her mystery lover—her vampire—and shivered. Fortunately, her mother didn't seem to notice the ripple.

"Good night, sweetheart. Have pleasant dreams," her mother told her with a squeeze on the shoulder while she rose from the bed.

"Good night, Mom. I love you guys." Aria often expressed her love for her parents, but it seemed more important to do so tonight—*just in case.*

"We love you too, Aria." Her mom turned out the light and shut the door.

Aria pulled the blankets up to her neck and stared at the ceiling in the darkened room. There was a little nightlight on in the corner, and she took comfort in its beam. It felt protective, somehow, as did her grandmother's quilt tucked in around her.

Thirty-four
Thursday

Aria awoke to the early rays of sunlight streaming in on her face. Her sleepy eyes searched the room to establish her whereabouts, and she heaved a sigh of relief when she realized she was back home in her bedroom, and she had survived another night. She could faintly smell bacon, and it made her smile—her parents must be okay too. She dressed, brushed her hair and teeth, and went into the kitchen where she found her dad reading the newspaper at the table and her mother at the stove.

They exchanged pleasantries, and she took a seat at the table with her father after grabbing a cup of coffee. As was custom, he handed her the Style section of the newspaper. She scowled at the outfit the front-page model was wearing just as her mother began setting food on the table.

Her father's laughter startled her. "Do you see something you don't like?"

Aria held the paper up for him to see. "Yeah, check her out. That outfit is crazy." She wrinkled her nose up in distaste.

"Well, that's a shame because I think your mom grabbed you that same outfit for your birthday," he teased.

Aria smiled at her father. She liked being away at school, which gave her a chance to spread her wings, but she missed being home with them.

Then she grew sad as she wondered how they would manage their grief if they lost her.

This might be the last time I see them.

"Aria," her mother interrupted her thoughts, "why are there tears in your eyes? What's wrong, sweetie?" Her father looked at her now, too.

Aria wiped away the moisture collected in her eyes and answered with a shaky smile, "Nothing's wrong. I just miss you guys. I miss this." She gestured toward the table.

"Home-cooked meals or our company?" her father inquired with a mischievous grin.

She laughed at his silliness. "Both."

"You can always go to school here, honey. If that fancy school isn't what you want it to be, just come home," her mother said, and Aria knew she was being serious. Even if they lost tuition money from her transferring, she knew they wouldn't complain if it meant she'd come home.

"No, no, school is great. Everything is fine—I'm just feeling sentimental," she lied.

"Okay, well, what's on the agenda for today? Are you going to go visit with your old friends?" her mother asked.

Aria had been so focused on other things, that the idea never occurred to her. "Yeah, I'm going to see if they can get together. They're probably in classes now, but maybe I can see them tonight." *Visiting with them might get my mind off other things.* She excused herself after eating a few slices of bacon and sent a text out to her two best friends. Within the hour, she had dinner plans with them.

Aria met up with her friends, Claire and Julie, at their favorite pizza joint. Mario's was their hangout while in high school, and it had changed very little over the years.

"So, tell us about the big city," Claire prodded. Her eyes were wide from expectation of juicy details. She had never been anywhere special, so Aria's journey was a big deal to her.

"She means tell us about the boys," Julie interjected before Aria could say anything. Of the three of them, she had always been the most into the opposite sex.

"Well, I'm sorry to disappoint you, but I don't have any good stories in that department," Aria explained. "There was one guy, but that didn't work out, and I'm not looking to replace him any time soon." She saw the disappointed looks on their faces, so she added, "Well, there is one other guy, but that's new, and I'm not sure how far it will go. We've just been out once."

"Did you sleep with him that one time?" Julie probed. She was no stranger to one-night stands.

Aria's eyebrows furrowed together. "No! We just had dinner, and you know I'm not like that." Julie and Claire both nodded in agreement with her statement.

They spent the rest of the visit talking about old times and the sights Aria had seen in California so far. It was all too soon that Aria had gone back home and was heading to bed after talking to Cat and then telling her mother about her visit.

She had fitful dreams of vampire bats all night, and when she woke up at 3:00, she decided to go back to school Friday. If the vampire was going to attack again, she didn't want to be anywhere near her parents. If she was to be a warrior and go to battle, she wanted to be where it   had   all   started.

Thirty-five

After the plane was filled with darkness, the quiet Doberman changed back into a vampire. Kellan crouched in the aisle of the aircraft at first, and then he stealthily made his way down it toward the last row of seats. He had already scoped the situation out, as the dog, and knew that the row was vacant except for one passenger—a lone woman.

The woman was mumbling incoherently in her sleep as Kellan slid into the seat next to her. He reached out and stroked her creamy dark brown skin. Her eyes flew open in surprise and then, he could see through the darkness, fear.

"Essere perfettamente immobile." *Be perfectly still.*

Her open mouth snapped shut, and she didn't budge. Her breathing was rapid though—that hadn't changed—and her nostrils flared. He could hear her heartbeat in the stillness of the cabin, and it made him smile. It was sweet like the song of a siren—it beckoned him to feel it pulsing against his lips while he drank her precious nectar. There was a sharp intake of breath when he sank his teeth into the soft flesh of her smooth neck. She tasted sweet like a ripened nectarine, and he took long drugging swallows until her heart ceased to beat, and he was satiated. Then he slipped back to where Ray was asleep, with his blanket pulled up to his thick neck, and changed back into the pooch. He closed his eyes and eventually fell asleep to the loud sound of Ray's snoring. It would be several hours until they reached Cairo, and then with the time difference, it would be Friday evening there.

Aria's decision to return to school early made her parents sad, but they didn't give her a hard time about it. She thought that they knew she needed time to mull over what she had read in her birth mother's letter, but they didn't bring it up again, and that made her relieved—she hated lying to them.

The only flight to San Francisco was an early one, so she had to leave their house by 8:00 to get through the security check in time to make the 9:00 flight. Her mother helped her pack, and then both of her parents drove her to the airport where they said a quick good-bye.

She stayed awake during the flight to avoid making a spectacle of herself again. She read her library books and dog-eared the pages of most interest. There was a section on Gypsy spells that warranted her attention the most. She read it three times and then pulled out her mother's letter to examine the part written in another language. She compared it to some of the spells from the book, which were written in Old World Italian, and noticed that some of the words were the same. The discovery caused a renewed energy to shoot through her—her mother spoke the old-world language, which possibly meant she was Italian. Aria read her words again. She had said, "I hope that you will never need this, but if he or one of his kind finds you, you must use it."

It must be a curse, and if that's true, maybe my mother was a Gypsy. Maybe Madame Gabor is right—I come from Gypsies.

With the revelation came a new strength. She felt hope for the first time that maybe she'd be strong enough to survive what was happening to her—maybe she was born to be a warrior after all. Of course, she'd have to decipher that section of the letter before she knew anything for certain. She bit her lip as she considered all the possibilities, but then a deep scowl crossed her pretty features as something else crossed her mind. Based on her mother's words, she could assume that a vampire fathered her.

So, what does that make me then?

She decided to pay another visit to Madame Gabor when she got back to San Francisco. She had more questions for the woman.

Aria was going to stop by the Gypsy's shop before heading back to campus, but then she decided against it. She wanted to translate the Italian part of her mother's letter first. She assumed Madame Gabor could do it for her, but she wanted time to read it, process it, and then write down all her questions for the fortune teller, and she was sure there would be many.

When she entered her dorm room, it was empty, and while she would've been glad to see her roommate and friend, she was grateful for some time to herself to start the translation. She opened the browser on her laptop and searched for a translator program. After choosing the one from the top of the list, she typed in the content from the letter. The results didn't make much sense to her, though, so she decided she'd have to take it to Madame Gabor after all. She looked at her watch and saw that it was 3:30 already. She quickly left a note for Cat and then grabbed her purse with the letter inside it.

It was a half-hour drive to the fortune teller's shop, and she remembered that Madame Gabor closed at 4:30 on Fridays, so she pushed the speed limit to get there in time. She got there in time, but there was a note on the door stating that the shop was closed due to a family emergency.

She got into her car to go back to campus, but when she reached the turnpike, she went the opposite direction. She wanted to go to the large San Francisco library to do some more research—there was no way this could wait until Monday.

Thirty-seven
Cairo Egypt

When the plane landed in Cairo, it was just after the stroke of midnight, and after they disembarked, Kellan tugged on the leash to lead Ray to a quiet corner in the dark where he could change back.

"What now, Master?" Ray inquired. "Will you be feeding again? I saw a beautiful stewardess who looked quite delicious. I could fetch her for you."

Kellan looked at the dumpy man with amusement. He wasn't sure how the crony would be able to charm a woman, any woman, but he appreciated the offer—it just meant he was taking to subservience.

"Yes, why don't you go get her for me"—he patted his lackey on the back—"I'll wait right here for you."

Ray smiled and patted his hands together. "Oh yes, Master. I'll bring her back right away." He was chuckling to himself as he walked off, and it made Kellan smile—he hadn't had a friend in a very long time.

Much to Kellan's surprise, Ray returned a few minutes later with a luscious redheaded flight attendant. She looked every bit as delicious as his minion had claimed, and very sexy too, so he decided to satisfy two hungers with the young woman.

"Why are we back here?" she asked in an annoying high-pitched voice. "What do you want to show me?"

"I want to introduce you to my master," he answered and thrust her forth toward Kellan, who was waiting under a lamppost.

She stared at Kellan and gave him a seductive smile. "Oh, well it's my pleasure to meet *him*," she cooed. "You're a handsome fella."

He cringed on the inside from her piercing voice, but he forced a smile for her benefit. "You are very lovely yourself," he reciprocated before reaching out a hand for her, which she accepted with grace.

She made a soft mewing noise as he pulled her into his steely embrace and claimed her lips in a deep kiss. He tried to stoke the embers of passion inside him, but she wasn't Aria, so it was difficult. He broke the kiss off and nodded to Ray to excuse himself—he didn't need an audience. His minion understood the gesture and backed away with a devilish grin.

Kellan considered pulling the woman out of the light streaming upon them, but he wanted to see the fire in her eyes, so he kept her in place. He searched them, but they weren't deep and mysterious like Aria's, so he turned her around to avoid seeing them again. His hands cupped her breasts while his mouth traced the veins in her neck. Her mounds weren't full and soft like Aria's, though, so he let them go, and knowing that she wouldn't be able to satisfy his sexual appetite, he gave up the seduction. She groaned in obvious disappointment, but he ignored her cries and sank his fangs deep into the back of her neck.

He muffled her high-pitched scream with his large hand as he swallowed mouthfuls of her blood, which tasted bitter like oranges. He didn't relish the flavor, so he spat most of it out.

He had two choices at that point. He could let her go or finish her off. Choosing the latter, he pulled out his knife and cut her carotid. Blood soon filled her throat as she clutched it and crumpled to the pavement. The gurgling sound he heard was much more pleasant than her voice.

"Ray," he called out in the dark, "Come here." Hurried footsteps filled the night air as his minion raced back to him.

Ray was panting to catch his breath as he eyed the dead woman at Kellan's feet. "What now, Master? Did she satisfy you?" He chuckled maniacally and rubbed his stubby hands together in anticipation of Kellan's answer.

Kellan looked at the crumpled corpse and scowled. "No, not at all, but I'm not worried about it. We have more important things to focus on." He began to walk north, and Ray had to double-time his steps to keep up.

"Where are we going then, Master?"

Kellan pointed northeast and replied, "We are headed to the pyramids of Giza. We will need camels to ride, and I see some over there." He gestured to their right.

Ray squinted in the darkness and responded, "Master that is a wonderful gift of sight you must have because I can't see a thing in this blackness—Luna isn't cooperative tonight. But I will do as you say and check it out." He took off running east.

Kellan thought about what he'd say to Isis, assuming she'd accept his presence in her court. The protector of the dead wasn't always known to be the most forgiving or cooperative. He didn't want to do or say anything that would upset her and bring about her wrath.

Perhaps I should take her a gift.

The stomping of hooves permeated the air as Ray drew closer with a pair of camels. "Master, you were right about the camels. Did I do well?"

Kellan accepted the reins of one of the beasts, although he made the animal nervous, and praised his helper, "Yes, you did a good thing. Now, mount up and let's go. We have a long ride before sunup."

Ray did as he was told without question while Kellan mounted his own jittery animal. It was obvious that the camel could sense that Kellan was a predator. He petted the creature to soothe its nerves, and after a few minutes, it seemed to work.

They raced northeast toward Giza in silence. Kellan was too busy thinking about his beauty, Aria, to talk. Soon he'd have her as his, and that made him elated—something he hadn't felt in centuries. He was also thinking about what he'd have to do to get to Isis's court, and it wasn't going to be easy or pleasant.

Thirty-eight
San Francisco

Aria parked on Larkin Street and then entered through the huge heavy double doors of the San Francisco Main Library. She inhaled deeply as she walked through the main corridor, taking in the pleasant scent of the old books—it was possibly her favorite scent in the world.

Well, maybe it's not as good as the musky smell of my mysterious vampire lover.

She put her fingers to her temples and rubbed—she didn't want to go down that road. She looked around the vast foyer at all the bookcases filled with the words of great authors throughout history. She'd love to walk around for hours looking at all the books, but she was on a mission, so she went to the computer to research specific literature. As she sat down, though, she felt stumped. She typed in Gypsy curses, which brought up a few titles, and she typed in Romance languages, which brought up some titles as well. On a scrap slip of paper, she wrote down the card catalog numbers for the books using a little golf pencil the library provided. Then she went in hunt of five books to start her off. The library would only allow her to check out two books at a time, so she'd have to do her research while there.

Long fingers quickly brought up the last search results on the computer and then wrote the information down on a tiny piece of paper. The

little pencil was still warm from the woman who
had just been holding it. It smelled like her too.

Aria sat down at an empty table with her
stack of books. One by one, she cracked them
open and flipped through the pages, jotting down
anything that caught her interest on the little
scraps of paper she had grabbed from the bin.

"Aria, right?" a voice suddenly startled
her, and she looked up to see a familiar face.

"Yes, that's right. You're in my English
composition class, aren't you?" she asked the
familiar looking girl.

"Right, I'm Beth. Here"—she ripped out
a piece of notebook paper and handed it to
Aria—"take this or you're going to have a
hundred little pieces of paper to keep track of."

Aria smiled sheepishly. "Thanks, Beth, I
appreciate that."

"Sure. Well, I'll see you in class next
week," she said and walked off with a little wave
of her hand.

Aria got back to work on her hunt for
information as soon as her classmate left. She was
reading over information on curses when she felt
her phone vibrating in her pocket. She pulled it
out to see that Chris was calling. She slipped the
phone back into her pocket and continued
reading about old-world Gypsy curses, although
she had yet to find anything that matched up to
what her birth mother had written. She went on

to plan B and browsed through the first book on Romance languages.

An hour later, Aria was still going through the books and taking notes when she was once again interrupted. This time it was by one of the staff.

"Is there anything I can help you find, dear?"

Aria smiled at the matronly woman. "Not unless you can speak fluent Italian. I'm having trouble with conjugating some verbs. At least that's what I think it is," she replied with a shrug.

The woman beamed. "It so happens that I am. Can I see what it is you want to translate?"

Aria happily handed the woman the letter. Then she worried about the content of the letter, specifically the part being translated. If it was indeed a curse, it may raise some questions—certainly some eyebrows.

"Oh, dear," the woman said with a look of surprise.

Shit.

"Well, I'm able to tell you what it says, although it sounds strange to me," she said with knitted brows.

Aria picked up her pencil to write it down. "Go ahead, please."

"Okay, it says 'I am light, where the darkness dwells. I will fight those brought from hell. In the gloom of the night, I am too strong for you to fight. Romani blood sets me free. Ayres name protects me from thee. I am safe from the plight that comes from your immortal bite.' That's all it says, but it's odd, isn't it? It sounds like something from the folklore of the Old World." She looked at Aria for her reaction.

Aria tried to think of a plausible answer. "Yes, that's odd. I found the letter in an old trunk I purchased at an antique shop, and I was just curious about it"—she looked off into the corner of the library to avoid the woman's piercing gaze—"The shop owner said the trunk had come from a writer, so maybe that is from a story they were working on." She looked back at the librarian with what she hoped was a believable smile. *Are you buying any of this crap?*

The librarian set the letter back down on the table. "Huh, interesting. Well, I'm glad I could help. Did you need to check any of those out? We are going to be closing up in a few minutes."

Aria looked at the books and felt flustered. "No, that was all I was looking for, so I don't need them. I'll go put them back on the shelf."

The librarian waved a hand at her, though. "Nonsense, we'll take care of it. Have a good evening."

Aria couldn't help but feel like she was being rushed out of there. "Thank you," she said politely and gathered her notes. "You were a big help."

The woman just smiled in return and gathered the books up in her skinny arms.

As Aria made her way to the exit, she couldn't help but feel like the librarian was watching her leave.

Kellan and Ray continued to travel in silence as they reached the souk in Giza. Sunrise was another forty-five minutes away by Kellan's estimation, so the marketplace was closed. He halted his camel, though, in front of some bronze statues.

Ray pulled up beside him. "Master, is there something wrong?"

Kellan pointed to a small sculpture of Isis. "I need the statue on the end. Fetch it for me."

Ray hopped off his ride and collected the item. Just as he began to walk away, though, there was a shout from close by.

"Stop thief!" A man came out from under the tent and chased after him.

Damn! Kellan dismounted and intervened just as the man tackled Ray. He picked the merchant up by the back of his tunic and flung him several yards away. The angry man leapt to his feet and charged Kellan with his fist ready to throw a punch, but Kellan sidestepped him while reaching his leg out to trip him. Anger boiled up to the surface as he grabbed the man's arm and yanked him upright—he didn't have time for this horseplay. He grabbed the man's head and, while the merchant's arms flailed, twisted it until there was a large cracking sound piercing the still air.

The lifeless body crumpled back to the hardened soil.

While Ray picked the dead man's pockets, Kellan mounted his camel. "Let's go. We must rush now."

"As you wish, Master," the dumpy man replied and ran to his own camel.

Twenty minutes later, they were stopping in front of the Sphinx. "We must wait now, but it won't be long."

Ray's body trembled while he looked around in the pitch-black night—he could only make out very large terrifying shadows. "Can I ask what we're waiting for, Master?"

"We are waiting for the sun to rise."

"Oh, and then what are we going to do, Master?"

Kellan looked down at his lackey. "You are going to wait here for me to return."

"And where are you going, Master?"

Kellan looked toward the horizon at the first hint of pink coming up behind Mount Catherine and replied, "I'm going inside the Sphinx."

Ray's mouth gaped in confusion while Kellan continued to monitor the skyline. Soon, it was time, and he braced himself for the unbelievable pain he was about to experience. He faced the Sphinx and waited. First, he felt like he was in the ninth layer of hell as his flesh began to burn from his bones. Then he saw a light coming out of the Sphinx's eyes, beaming straight at him, and he felt himself being ripped apart into a million pieces.

It was a torturous minute later, that felt like a hundred years, when the pain subsided, and he could see again. He blinked away the moisture pooled in his sky-blue eyes and looked all around him. He had done something only the strongest of vampires could do—he had survived the *riddle of the Sphinx*. He had made it to the lair of Isis.

Forty

Kellan knelt, set the statue in front of himself, and bowed his head. Now he had to respectfully wait until he was accepted into Isis's court.

"Who comes before me?" a loud feminine voice boomed. "Stand up, announce yourself, and pay your homage."

"May I lay eyes upon you, Isis?"

"You may."

Kellan rose to his feet, with the statue held out in front of him, and drank in the sight of the god of gods. She was without a doubt the most beautiful sight he had ever taken in. She had an aura around her that glowed four times brighter than Gaia's—perhaps it was even brighter than the sun's. She had perfectly oval eyes, which were dark and mysterious, pouty lips which were a perfect blushing pink that matched her cheeks, and a long slender neck adorned by tousled black hair. She was dressed in silken ivory robes inlaid with gold-spun thread, which accentuated her perfectly sculpted bosom and taut waistline topping delicate hips. She was the image of femininity, and it was no wonder that she was the icon of fertility.

When he found his voice again, he announced, "I am Kellan Montcroix, and I have brought you this." He placed the statue on the marble floor and backed away.

She eyed the offering without expressing any enthusiasm but told him, "That will do. Now, what is the purpose of your visit?"

The judgement he could see in her eyes sapped his confidence, but he had come all that way for Aria, so he pressed on. "I have crossed paths with a mortal, who is like no other human out there past or present."

"Explain yourself," she interrupted him.

"I have bitten her three times and left her for dead, yet she walks among the living under the rays of the sun. She's either an incredibly resilient mortal, or she's the strongest vampire walking the planet."

"I see." Her eyes became shadowed as she looked away in deep thought.

"I came here because you are the mother of all, so you must know what she is."

Isis focused her piercing gaze on him and cocked her head. "Tell me, child of the night, what is the answer you desire? Do you wish her to be human or vampire? Do you wish me to stop her heart since you have not been able to do so? Tell me what you long for."

Elated that he wasn't turned away, Kellan rushed his words. "I long for her. Her blood sings a melody to me that I've never heard before, and I can't get it out of my mind. Please don't make me walk the earth for eternity with that tune stuck in my head."

She leveled her gaze on him again. "So, you would have me smite you then to end your obsession?"

He bowed his head and humbly replied, "If that is what it takes, Goddess."

She examined the statue he brought her and sucked in her full bottom lip while she mulled over his predicament.

"Have you seen the oracle?"

"Yes, but Gaia had no answers, and she suggested I come to you."

Isis set the statue down on an ivory pedestal and clasped her slender hands. "I know all of my children but have no record of such a woman. I know of no creature who survives the immortal bite. However, I faintly recall a prophecy mentioned to me once by Anubis." She looked over her shoulder and called out, "Nefartari," and a lovely young woman appeared. "Bring me the crystals to summon Anubis."

Aria lie on her bed and read the translated portion of her mother's letter for the tenth time. It was certainly a curse and a clue to her past. It mentioned Romani blood and the name Ayres.

Is that my family name—Ayres? Am I Romani?

She had to see Madame Gabor, and she didn't want to wait until Monday. She went online to the white pages to search for those with the last name Gabor in the local area, and she found a listing for Zelda Gabor. *That sounds like a fortune teller to me.* She dialed the number and counted three rings before a woman answered.

"I've been expecting your call," the woman said.

Aria almost laughed at the obvious marketing ploy, but instead, she answered, "Um, hello? Is this Madame Gabor, the fortune teller?"

"Yes, dear. We met the other day when you came to the shop, and I've been expecting to hear from you."

She must have caller ID.

"Um, how did you know I was calling you now, though?"

"That's easy, child. Madame Gabor knows all and sees all."

Aria tapped her hand on her nightstand. She didn't know how to respond to such a bold statement. "Well, great. The reason I'm calling is I have a note I'd like for you to look at with me. I think it's a clue to my family history, but I'm not sure. I'm hoping you can help with that." She bit her lip in anticipation of the Gypsy's response, which seemed to take a long time.

"Can you bring the letter to me? I live at 1232 Chestnut Hills Drive."

Aria felt her pulse race. "Yes, I can come right away."

"Good. I'll be waiting."

Aria rang the doorbell on the charming little blue clapboard house and tapped her foot nervously while she waited for Madame Gabor to answer. Finally, the door squeaked open and the white-haired woman appeared.

"Come in, my child," she said warmly and gestured toward her foyer.

"Thank you, Madame Gabor," Aria responded in kind as she stepped inside the warm house.

She looked around the quaint room and smiled. The walls were painted country blue and were decorated with photos of family members. There was a fire crackling away in a stone fireplace, and the antiquated furniture, although a little shabby, pulled everything together perfectly.

"Please call me Zelda. Now, have a seat and let's discuss what is happening in your life."

Aria sat in an armchair decorated with a bright blue afghan and nervously pulled the letter out of her pocket. She then folded and unfolded it repeatedly while staring at her hands.

"You look nervous, dear. Would you like some tea? It's chamomile."

That sounded beneficial. "Yes, that would be nice, and, please, call me Aria."

Zelda's thin lips turned up in a smile, which temporarily smoothed out the lines around her mouth. "I'll be right back then, Aria."

She disappeared around the corner, and then Aria heard the rattling of dishes from the other room. Her phone vibrated in her pocket, so she peeked at the display—it was Chris again. She hit ignore and put the phone back. He'd just have to wait.

"Here we go," Zelda said as she handed a tea cup over to Aria. "Now what is that paper you are nervously handling?"

Aria took a deep breath and began, "Do you remember that I'm adopted?" She waited for the other woman to nod. "Well this is a letter from my birth mother. My adoptive parents kept it all these years, but I just found out about it," she said softly and handed the letter to Zelda.

The Gypsy put on her reading glasses and scanned the letter. Her face grew taut, and she pursed her lips as she read. Then, when she must have reached the end, her eyes widened, and she grinned while clutching her amulet with a wrinkled hand.

"I was right the other day—you are of Gypsy ancestry, which means you have your own evil eye," she explained with zeal. "And this is a curse written by one of your ancestors, possibly your mother."

Aria interrupted, "I see that, but what about what she says about my father?"—she wrung her hands and bit her bottom lip—"'Your father came to me, under the cover of darkness, and brought the kiss of death. He would force you into the shadows as well, if I didn't hide you from him and his kind,'" she quoted from memory. "She is saying my father is a vampire. What am I supposed to do about that? What does it mean for me?"

Zelda nodded with understanding, and Aria saw something cloud the woman's features— apprehension. Her pale knuckles grew whiter from pinching her amulet, and her mouth set in a hard line, which didn't help Aria's nerves.

"What is it? What are you thinking?" she pleaded.

Zelda met her concerned stare, and her face softened. "I think you are the *coveted one*. The one my tribe has been waiting for. I believe you are the one chosen to be the savior."

Aria shook her head and put her hands up in defense. "I think you have the wrong girl. No, I *know* you have the wrong girl. I can't be anyone's savior! I'm a twenty-year-old college sophomore. I'm a girl for Christ's sake!"

Zelda laughed lightheartedly. "Joan of Arc was a girl. Cleopatra was a girl. History is full of strong women, Aria, and you are no exception even if you choose not to believe it."

Aria's arms flailed in front of her. "My sex aside, what do you mean when you say 'coveted one?'"

Zelda's cheeks grew rosy as her face lit up. She put her hands together and rubbed them, as if they were hurting, before picking the letter back up. "Aria, you are coveted because you are the first of your kind," she softly explained.

Aria blanched. "That right there. What does that mean? What 'kind' am I?"

"You are a half-breed of vampire and human, which is unheard of, but you're not any ordinary human either. Your mother was a powerful Gypsy—magic runs through your blood, dear, and you can't avoid it in your life. The sooner you accept who you are and what your purpose is, the better off you'll be."

Aria vigorously shook her head. "No, no, no, no, no. I can't be half-vampire. I can't have this in my life. I should be dealing with acne, homework, and boyfriends, not killing monsters. You need to find someone else." She pleaded with her eyes as well as her words.

Zelda shook her head back. "You don't seem to understand how monumental this is, Aria. You are the only one born to do this. There is no one else. You are the coveted one, because you are one of a kind."

Aria held one hand up in front of herself in protest. "Slow your roll, Zelda. You haven't told me what it is you think I am born to do. Start there, please."

Zelda nodded and clutched her amulet. "I will explain. There was a prophecy foretold centuries ago among the Gypsy clans that there would come a time when a coveted babe would be born. The babe would be a powerful Gypsy hybrid who was conceived during an eclipse in a rare calendar year that contained seven eclipses"—she rose from the couch and crossed the living room to open an antique chest and pull out a large book—"The full prophecy is in here, I think." She looked up from the book and asked, "Do you have time to keep talking today?"

Aria's eyes were as big as half dollars as she attempted to process everything thrown at her so far. "I will make the time."

Zelda got up again and walked out of the room while calling over her shoulder, "Great! I'm going to go put on another pot of tea, and then we will figure all of this out."

Forty-two
Giza Egypt

Nefartari returned to Isis's hall moments later with her arms full of crystals, which she laid out on the cool marble floor in a large circle. She then backed away to stand next to the wall with her hands clasped and her head bowed.

Isis opened her arms wide in a large sweeping gesture, closed her eyes, and chanted something under her breath. A cold breeze suddenly blew past Kellan while the ground vibrated from heavy footsteps, which sounded like the rumble of thunder. Then a mist swirled upward from the center of the circle while the crystals began to glow.

Anubis appeared within the circle, and the sight of him made Kellan quiver. He was an impressive vision, standing close to eight feet tall with the body of a man and the head of a fierce black canine. He glowered at Kellan but then became humble when he looked at Isis.

"How may I be of service to you, Goddess?" he asked in a voice that boomed and vibrated the walls.

Isis looked at the god of the dead with a cool gaze. "Anubis, this vampire says there is a woman who has survived three of his immortal kisses, but she can still walk under the sun. I know of no child having this gift, but I recall you speaking of a prophecy once. Tell us what you foresaw."

"It was prophesied among the Gypsy nation that a coveted hybrid babe would be conceived at the exact moment that there was a day masked by night. This would fall within a calendar year containing seven of those days. She was to be born to a powerful Gypsy and an immortal"—he looked down at Kellan—" This woman whom you speak of must be the coveted one since she walks in the sunlight."

"I see," Isis stated calmly. "What else do you know about this half-breed, and why have I not known of her existence?"

"Because she is the first magical being of her kind. Since her birth, she has lingered in limbo between mortality and immortality."

"How do I make her fully immortal?" Kellan interrupted.

"Am I to take it that you are besotted, and she's the mate you've chosen?" Anubis looked at him with a raised brow.

Kellan bobbed his head in confirmation. "Aye, that I am. She has bewitched me."

"There is a second part of the legend, Isis. When the coveted one has come of age, there will be an influx of vampires"—he switched his gaze back to Kellan—"Is the woman close to her twenty-first year?"

Kellan looked up at the god and shrugged his own massive shoulders. "I guess so. We haven't exactly had a conversation."

The god of the dead scowled at him and switched the sword he carried from one hand to the other which made Kellan more than a little nervous—the god could take his immortality away, and it wouldn't be in a painless fashion.

"Since you have found her, I'll assume she has reached it, or she's close to it. Anyway, when the vampires come, the Gypsies will be banding their clans together and will become stronger than they have ever been—especially with her on their side. Therefore, you must sway her to embrace her vampire half, and to do so, you must douse her with water from the Nile River *and* impregnate her."

Kellan moistened his lips with the tip of his tongue. "I may already have."

"Make sure to override any human birth control methods she may be using just to be sure, and don't forget about the water. If you fail and the Gypsies sway her to their side, it may be the end of vampires—*all* vampires."

"There you have it," Isis began, "you have your orders. The rest is up to you." She disappeared in a swirling light, and Anubis followed in a burst of flames.

Kellan suddenly had the sensation of being in a vacuum, and then he found himself on the outside of the Sphinx again. As soon as he felt the flames licking his skin, he changed into a crow to end the suffering.

Ray was right there where he'd left him.

Zelda flipped through the dusty antiquated book while mumbling something in Italian. Then, about two-thirds of the way through the book, her eyes brightened.

"Ah, here we go," she happily cried and tapped the pages. "Okay, it's like I told you so far. It speaks of the eclipse and half-Gypsy babe"—her finger ran down the page along with her eyes—"Oh, wait, here's something of importance. How old are you, hon?"

Aria grinned and clapped her hands together. "I'll be twenty-one one week from today, and I can't wait." Zelda looked nervous by her news, though, and that stopped her little celebration. "Is something wrong with that?"

Zelda looked at her with fear in her eyes. "Well, I'm afraid it complicates matters. As I said at your reading, you are a warrior, and according to the legend, when the coveted one reaches her twenty-first year, the Gypsy clans will band together to battle a great evil on the horizon."

Aria felt her heart pounding in her ears. "What evil? My mysterious lo—" She caught herself before she revealed her indiscretions to the woman. "The vampire?"

Zelda clutched her teacup with a shaky hand. "I don't think so. I think there's more to it than him. So, I need to get with the matriarchs of the Gypsy High Council and see what they know. That's all we can do for now"—she shut the book and took it back to the antique chest—"Leave me your phone number, Aria, so I can call you when I have more information. I'll give you mine, too, in case anything else happens in the meantime. You can call whenever you need to or come by the shop." She pulled some paper and a pencil out of a little drawer on her end table and wrote her phone number down.

"My number is 555-492-2129," Aria told her as she accepted the slip of paper. "And, of course, it goes without saying that I would like you to call as soon as you know something."

"Of course, dear. Now, you had best get going back to school before the sun is completely down. Which reminds me, in case you didn't know, there is truth in the saying that a vampire can't enter your home unless it is invited. So please be careful whom you spend time with— some vampires are powerful enough to shapeshift."

Aria blanched, and her eyes went round. "Do you mean they can look like other people?"

Zelda slowly bobbed her head as she went to the front door. She tossed over her shoulder, "I know that some are able to shift into animals, so I assume it's also possible for them to look like whatever person they want to, but I'm not sure. Just be careful."

"Oh, I will be," Aria assured her, "As much as possible."

"We'll talk soon," Zelda hollered as Aria climbed into her car, and she waved back at the Gypsy in response.

It was a long drive back to campus as she nervously watched the sun dip low in the sky and replayed their conversation. *"Battle a great evil on the horizon"*—*what is that about? And I haven't invited anyone into my house, so how did he get in?* She had a feeling it was going to be a very long night.

Close to twenty-five minutes later, she pulled into the campus parking lot. The sun had already disappeared, so she wasted no time in getting from the car to her dorm. She had made sure no one was around before running across the parking lot, though.

Cat was lying on her bed and reading from her accounting text book. She looked up with a raised brow and said, "Hi. Glad you're back, but weren't you going to stay there all weekend? Did you have a fight or something?"

Aria quickly responded, "No, I just have stuff around here that I need to do, so I thought I'd come back early and get it done. Plus, I'll see them at Thanksgiving."

"Like what? What do you need to do? Maybe I can help."

Aria looked away so her discomfort with the conversation wouldn't be as obvious. "Just some school stuff. I have a paper due that I need to do some more research for."

Cat tilted her head and wore a sly smile. "Is it on vampires?"

"No!" Aria answered too quickly and too loudly. "I mean," she continued with a shaky laugh, "why would you ask that?"

Cat's face screwed up, and she stared her friend down. "Wow, take it easy. I'm just teasing because you were reading those books. Geesh."

"Oh, yeah, that's for a different class."

"To study vampires? That's odd. What class?"

Aria had to think fast or tell her friend the truth and risk her ridicule. "Um, my lit class. I'm studying pop culture." She could see that Cat was suspicious, so she needed to change the topic—to another uncomfortable one. "I just remembered I need to call Chris back really quick," she mumbled and dug her phone out of her pocket.

Cat's eyes grew large with interest. "Oh yeah? Are you going to go out with him again?"

Aria held up a finger in response because he had answered already. "Hi, Chris, I'm sorry I missed your call earlier. I was in the library, and well, you know their policy on phones." She broke off with nervous laughter.

"It's all right," he softly replied, "I wanted to see if you wanted to go see that movie yet. There's a showing tonight in an hour. Are you up for it?"

Aria looked at the dark star-streaked sky through her window and told him, "I'm a little jet lagged from flying back from Idaho earlier, and I have a paper I'm working on now, but how about an early matinee tomorrow?"

"Yeah, sure! There's one on at 2:00. How about that one?" he asked with a lot of enthusiasm.

She couldn't get romantically involved with anyone at this chaotic, mysterious, and scary point in her life, but she figured a date would be okay—as long as the sun was up. "Yes, that sounds good."

"Great! And after it's over, we can go to dinner," he suggested.

This time of year, it would be dark out then, but she didn't want to hurt his feelings, so she replied, "Um, okay." She'd worry about how to get out of it tomorrow.

"Okay, I'll pick you up at your dorm at 1:30. I can meet you outside," he offered.

"A vampire can't come into your home unless you invite him in." Nonsense, Aria, if he was a vampire, he wouldn't be out in the daytime. Would he? She shook her head to clear her thoughts and answered, "Okay. See you then. Bye." She clicked the end button on her phone and put it back into her pocket.

"Soooo?" Cat prodded. She had been watching Aria talk on the phone the entire time. "It sounds like you have a date."

Aria rolled her eyes at her roommate. "Yes, you both win. I have a date for the movies."

"Awesome! And guess what? There's a kegger at the park again tomorrow night with a new band in town, who I hear is really good, so we can all go dancing," she exclaimed.

Aria chewed her lip while she tried to find the right words. She decided to be practical. "You know there is a killer on the loose, right? Don't you think it would behoove us to stay in at night?"

Cat looked at her sideways and then laughed. "'Behoove?' Someone's getting fancy. And, no, I'm not going to stop having fun because there is one maniac on the loose. Besides, I don't think he'll come around here anymore, and we'll be with a lot of other people, so it'll be safe." She rolled her eyes upward and jabbed her finger to accentuate her words.

Aria knew she wasn't going to win this fight—Cat was a stubborn woman. So, she mumbled, "Whatever," and left it at that. At this point, she could only hope that the vampire wouldn't attack her friends, or that she'd be the warrior Madame Gabor said she is if he does.

Ray and the Doberman climbed off the jet in San Francisco with the other passengers when they heard a scream behind them. Commotion followed, and Ray hung back long enough to ask an attendant what had happened—even though he already knew the answer.

The frazzled attendant exclaimed, "One of the passengers was murdered. Her throat was slashed."

Ray faked surprise, "Oh my lord! We were on the same jet as a murderer? I can't believe that!"

The attendant looked at the Doberman and swallowed hard. "With that dog, I'm sure you were safe."

Ray patted the quiet dog on his head. "Yes, my furry friend goes wherever I go and always makes me feel safe and sound."

Kellan stood on all fours and tugged on the leash. He didn't have time for this chatter—he needed to find Aria. He wanted to see his mate. He pictured the bottle of water taken from the Nile which was nestled in Ray's suitcase and smiled to himself. All he had to do was sprinkle some on her and then impregnate her, and she'd become fully immortal and bonded to him. Something occurred to him, though, and his smile faded. Anubis had mentioned an influx of vampires, which could lead to trouble—he may have to battle for her. Therefore, he would need to change her before the others came. They may be savage beasts, but they did respect the ritual of pairing up. Once she was bonded as his mate, no other would come after her.

When he and Ray were alone in the man's humble motel room, Kellan shifted into a crow. In his bird voice, he gave his minion a clue. "College," he said. "Going to college." Then he flew to the windowsill and waited for Ray to open it. "You go home," he ordered before flying off in the direction of the school.

He didn't need his minion any longer.

Kellan buzzed the sky all around the campus in search of his raven-haired queen. He started to feel frustrated as he planted himself in a tree across from her dorm, but then he saw a familiar face—the young man she had gone to dinner with—and his heart rate quickened. The man was walking up to her dorm just as she came out of it. His wings flapped wildly as he drank in the sight of her. There was a definite change—she was stronger looking and moved with lithe, confident strides. He could see the predator in her. *She is going to make a remarkable vampire.*

He followed them as they drove off in the man's black Mustang. It was hard to keep up with the car as it cruised down the highway, but fortunately, they didn't go too far. They had pulled into a movie Cineplex and went inside while he watched from a lamp post nearby. He decided that he would shift into a mouse and sneak inside with the patrons just to keep watch on her.

He flew over the Mustang on the way to the front door and left his droppings as he did. *I'll mark my other territory later tonight.*

Forty-five

Another surprisingly uneventful night had passed, along with a quick morning, and soon Aria was at the movies with Chris. They were enjoying *Ghostbusters* and laughing in all the same places, but she still felt unease. The fact that she had made it through a couple of nights without a visit from her mysterious lover gave her pause.

Did he set his sights on someone else? Am I free? She knew it wasn't all that simple—there was still an "evil on the horizon" to contend with.

She was brought back to the present when Chris slipped his arm around her shoulders, and while she wasn't comfortable with it, she didn't want to cause a scene either, so she left it there. After the movie, during dinner, she'd try to explain to him that she appreciated his friendship but didn't want anything more. Maybe she could convince him that it was too soon after Kyle. She certainly couldn't tell him that she was physically involved with a vampire.

Keeping this all concealed is a pain in the ass!

She started to feel claustrophobic under the weight of Chris's arm, so she excused herself to use the ladies' room. Little did she know that a mouse, sitting underneath a chair, was watching her every move from two rows behind.

It was 4:30 when the movie finished, and Chris suggested they grab dinner at a new Thai restaurant in town. She thought about begging off, but then Cat's words about not living in fear

ran through her mind, and she reconsidered. She
kept a watchful eye out as they made their way to
his car, though.

The parking lot of the Thai restaurant was
packed, so they opted for the Longhorn
Steakhouse restaurant around the corner. The
only table left was an intimate one in the shadows.

"This is nice. It's probably better than the
Thai place too," Chris claimed while he looked
over the drink menu. "Are you going to have a
cocktail with your dinner or wait until after?"

Aria looked up from her menu into his
warm brown eyes. "I'm not twenty-one yet. Not
for another week."

"One Week? So, like on September 16th?
That's awesome—we'll have to plan something
special," he said with a broad grin.

She bit her lip and looked away at the wall
décor. "Um, sure. That sounds nice."

He leaned in and lowered his voice. "You
can pass for twenty-one now if you want to have
a drink with me."

Aria examined the drink list on the menu
and decided to take him up on the offer. Maybe a
drink would give her the shot of courage she
needed to broach the topic of just being friends.

"Okay, if you think so," she said with a
smile. "I'll try a Piña Colada."

"There you go. That's the spirit"—he
grinned mischievously and examined the menu

again—"You know, I've never had one of those, so I think I'll give it a try too."

The server came back and took their drink orders while giving Aria a scrutinizing once over.

"So, are you having raw cow again?" he teased.

She couldn't stop herself from smiling at his jab. "I was going to order the chicken parmesan, but now that you mention it, beef sounds delicious."

"Huh, the chicken sounds good to me now," he replied with a chuckle. "I would suggest that we order both and share, but there's no way I'm eating rare meat"—he winked at her—"But I'll still share."

Aria slowly sipped her cocktail when it came; although her nerves made her want to chug it. Two drinks in, she was feeling buzzed, but she still didn't tell him that she only wanted to be friends. He was extra happy too, so she didn't know if he would remember it anyway.

"So, how was your trip?" he asked with a silly grin that made her laugh until she snorted.

"It was good. I saw my girlfriends and had a nice visit with my folks."

"Excellent!" he chimed just as the waitress stopped by to see if they wanted another cocktail. "I'll have another. How about you, sugar lips?"

"No, I'd like to switch to a Dr. Pepper if I may."

He waved his hand at her. "Pfft. You're a party pooper."

She feigned a hurt expression. "No, I'm not. I just think one of us should be able to drive.

In fact"—she rubbed her hands together—"I'm looking forward to driving your car."

"Can you drive a schtick?" he slurred.

She nodded. "Why, yes, I can. I grew up driving sticks. The Camry is my first automatic."

His eyebrows shot up in surprise. "Okay, but can you handle"—he raised his arm to show off his bicep—"muscle?"

She couldn't resist. "Muscles bigger than that."

"Ouch!"—he put his hand over his heart and pouted—"hat turts. Oops, I mean that hurts."

Their meals came then and soaked up most of the alcohol. He was still a little fuzzy, though, so he let her take the car keys when they finished.

When they were on their way out, Aria stopped in her tracks. She could faintly smell musk over the strong odor of sizzling meats. Her eyes scanned the room and settled on the back of someone's head, which was full of long black hair and topping massive shoulders. It got her feet moving, and she ushered Chris out the door.

"What's wrong? Did you see a spider?"

She quickly responded, "No, I just need some fresh air." *I'm not sure what I saw.*

"Would you like to go to the keg party?" he asked.

She bit her lip and looked up at the night sky. *There will be lots of people there, and this time I won't wander off to the park. I just hope I'm not leading the lambs to slaughter.* "Sure, but I don't think I'll be drinking any more alcohol."

Chris stumbled in a small pothole. "Whoa! I-I-I might not either."

They laughed in unison, and both failed to see the sultry vampire staring from a hundred feet away.

Forty-six

The crow followed the Mustang as it made its way to the local park pavilion. Kellan changed back into himself and crept behind the couple while maintaining a safe distance. He could have easily attacked and taken Aria someplace to make ravenous love to her, but he wanted to observe her for a while first. He wanted to watch the hybrid creature interact with the mortals, so he could see how much his venom had affected her.

His hand reached into his pocket and clutched the small bottle of Nile water. He was eager to start the second half of her transformation.

"Hey, sexy, are you here for the party?" a young co-ed asked while approaching him.

"Aye, I suppose I am," he replied and grinned at the scrumptious morsel. He was feeling famished, so she'd make a nice appetizer.

"Awesome! Let's get started," she said in a sultry voice while raising the short skirt she wore to reveal a flask strapped to her thigh with a garter. She grabbed the flask with one hand while raising the skirt farther with the other to expose her red lacy thong.

Kellan licked his lips as he admired the skimpy garment along with her moxy for showing it off. Aria was the one he wanted, but they weren't fully mated yet, so this wouldn't be breaking the bond.

She took a swig from the flask and offered it to him, but he waved it away.

"That's not what I like to drink," he told her with a carnal growl.

"Oh, are you like those guys"—she pointed over her shoulder—"Do you only drink beer? Is the hard stuff too much for you, sexy?"

Kellan laughed a deep throated chuckle. "No, I like something stronger."

He pressed her against a nearby SUV and kissed her passionately while his hand traced her silky thigh upward until it was under her skirt at her apex. His other hand pressed firmly against her small but perky breast. He teased her nipple, making it hard, but it wasn't as hard as he was.

She moaned into his mouth while her hands wandered. She traced the muscles of his abdomen with her right hand while her left ran over his pulsing manhood.

She broke the kiss off and groaned, "You're so hard for me."

This woman is a cock tease.

His mouth moved to her neck while he deftly yanked down the thong and began to massage her smooth mound. He liked the little bit of downy curls Aria had left on hers better.

"Oh, yes, right there," the woman sighed as his finger slid between her swollen lips to massage her firm bud until she was wet to his liking. Her juice was making the movements slippery and easy.

"Turn around," he commanded, and she immediately obeyed.

He spanked her ass once before spreading her open to receive his thick head and strong shaft. When he was deeply embedded in her slick sheath, he began to move in a rhythmic symphony with her. Every time she lifted herself up on her tip toes, he prodded deeper inside her and with more force than before.

"Oh, my god," she bellowed into the night air. "Oh, that feels god damned good. Fuck me harder!"

Kellan could feel the pulsating waves of ecstasy shaking her body all around his hardness. She clenched him with every orgasm, and they were piling upon one another. Then, when he felt his own burst of pleasure coming, he sank his teeth into her bared shoulder and sucked hard.

The girl cried out from the pain of the bite, but she was helpless to fight against it because of the spasms of rapture pulling her under a tidal wave of molten passion.

Kellan pulled himself out of her body and caught her as she went limp. She wasn't dead yet—she had just fainted. "La petite mort," he said under his breath. *The little death*. He bit into her neck this time and continued feeding until he was full. Then he shoved her lifeless form under the SUV and went in hunt of his love.

He didn't like where he found her, though. She was slow dancing with her dinner companion, and the man's arms were tightly wrapped around her sexy waist.

Forty-seven

Aria had her hands resting on Chris's shoulders while he had his arms wrapped around her waist for a slow dance. The band was playing Eric Clapton's *Wonderful Tonight,* which she normally enjoyed, but it presently made her uneasy. Dancing a slow dance with Chris meant something different for him than it did her. She was just dancing, while he was courting. He was a decent man, but she was in no position to get close to anyone right now. Even if her heart was ready, she didn't think it would be safe.

"Don't you two look cozy?" Kyle's voice rang out behind her, and it was laced with nothing short of contempt. "Chris, are you having fun with my sloppy seconds?"

Aria was about to turn around and slap him, but Chris surprised her by pulling her in tighter.

"Kyle, back off," Chris growled in a threatening tone that surprised her.

Unfortunately, Kyle wasn't about to listen. "Seriously, dude, you can have my hand-me-downs. I don't care because I've got no use for her anymore. I already did my damage."

Aria yanked herself out of Chris's embrace and turned around to slap Kyle—hard. His mouth gaped open in surprise while his hand went to his stinging cheek.

"Kyle, leave her alone. I'm bored, so let's just go," his date protested. He ignored her, though.

"You fucking bitch!" he snapped at Aria and pulled his hand back to strike her, but Chris thwarted the blow and delivered a punch strong enough to make Kyle stumble backward.

Kyle immediately tried to punch his opponent back, but Chris quickly dodged the blow and threw an uppercut to his jaw. Then, before he could recover from the strike, Chris swept his leg out from under him, which caused him to land squarely on his ass.

Aria looked at her date with surprise and admiration. She figured him to be the kind of man to verbally defend a woman's honor, but she didn't know he would be strong enough to physically do it. He seemed more of a pacifist to her. Nonetheless, she was happy to see him put Kyle in his place.

"Fuck you!" Kyle screamed as he scrambled to his feet in front of the crowd of onlookers. He spun on his heel and took off in a run back toward the dorms with his date left behind.

"Wow"—Aria looked into Chris's eyes— "thank you. I appreciate you defending my honor, kind sir," she said with a southern drawl and fanned her face with her hand.

Instead of getting angry, he laughed at her jesting and gave her a playful slap on the ass. "Is your hand okay there, slugger?" he teased.

She looked at her hand, which was stinging yet, and told him, "Yes, it's fine."

"Aria, I can't believe you laid into him like that," Cat squawked as she approached. "I'm proud of you girl! And I must say, Chris, I have a newfound respect for you, handsome." She batted her lashes playfully. "What are you two kids going to do the rest of the night?"

Aria smiled at her date. "I believe we are going to dance," she yelled over the music as an upbeat song came on.

"Yeah, we are! Woo-hoo!" Chris hollered and started to move with her.

For at least a couple of minutes, Aria could sweep her worries under the rug and enjoy herself. She had no idea, though, that if Chris hadn't stepped in, Kellan was more than ready to. In fact, he was seeking retribution while she danced carefree.

Forty-eight

Kellan stalked the asshole who dared to raise a hand to Aria while thinking about all the horrible things he could do to him, and when the punk walked in between the buildings on the college campus, Kellan decided to make his move.

The boy turned around at the sound of Kellan's footsteps behind him, probably thinking it was Aria's date coming after him for more. He immediately balled his fists up at his sides, preparing to defend himself.

"What the fuck do you want?" he snarled.

Kellan could make it quick, but he wasn't going to. He would make the douche suffer for even having thoughts about striking a woman—a vampire's woman. Sure, he had killed a woman earlier, and many before her, but that was only for survival. He looked up at the sky. The moon was full, and the sky was clear, which was perfect because he wanted to see the look on the creep's face when he realized what was happening. He also wanted his image to be burned into the boy's brain in case there is an afterlife.

"Who the fuck are you?" the boy yelled as Kellan got closer.

"The last person you'll ever see," he hissed.

The boy put his hands up in self-defense. "That's what you think, asshole."

Kellan laughed at the punk's avid display of bravery. Then he made his advance. He spread his arms wide and growled, "Take your best shot."

The boy threw a punch, and it made direct contact with Kellan's steely abdomen. "Ow," he yelped as he withdrew his throbbing hand.

Kellan laughed again at him. "Did that hurt?" he taunted. "My turn now."

He threw one punch at the boy's nose, which sent him backward on his ass. He had heard the unmistakable crack of bone, and it lit him up inside.

"Ugh!"—the boy covered his face with his hands—"You broke my fucking nose!"

Kellan stepped forward and grabbed him by his arm, yanked him to his feet, and slapped him across the face.

"So, you like raising your hand to girls, eh?"—he slapped him again but harder this time—"Does that make you a tough guy? Are you the big man on campus who hits girls?" He shoved the boy backward until he fell on his ass again. "Well, tough guy, you raised your hand to the wrong girl."

"Who are you?" the punk cried out without getting up. "I'm sorry, but I didn't hit the bitch"—he realized his mistake, and his eyes went wide with terror—"I mean her. I didn't hit her," he whined while scrambling backward. "Who is she to you anyway?"

Kellan smiled, and he could tell by the boy's expression that he saw his fangs glistening in the moonlight. "Who is she to me? She's mine." He advanced slowly to build the dread.

"I'm sorry, but I didn't know that," the boy squawked and scrambled farther backward. "I had no idea she was yours."

Kellan chuckled maniacally. "Do you want to hear something funny? She has no idea either."

The boy's eyes went wide with surprise. "What?"

However, Kellan didn't answer. Instead, he closed in the gap between them, grabbed the boy's head, and twisted it until he heard the neck bone break. He would have played the torture out longer, but he needed to get back to Aria, so he left the body there and strolled back to the park.

Forty-nine

Aria stood with Cat while Chris went to the refreshment area to get her a Pepsi. "I can't believe Kyle had to be such a dick," she exclaimed.

Cat rolled her eyes and looked over at Chris. "Tell me about it, but what the hell was that with Chris? I had no idea he was such a badass. It makes him even more attractive, don't you think?" She took another sip of her beer while looking at Aria for her reaction.

Aria shrugged and looked over her shoulder at Chris, who'd stopped to talk to some boys. "I guess so. I'm still not wanting to start anything though," she said nonchalantly.

Her friend shot her a look of exasperation. "I can't figure out why not. He really likes you, he's good looking, and he's nice. Add to that the fact that he can kick some ass when he needs to and you've got the perfect man."

Aria shook her head at her roommate. "I know, but—"

"But what? You have no excuse not to move on. You and Kyle have been over for a while now, and you haven't shown anything other than a passing interest in anybody else. Unless there's something you aren't telling me. You never did say where the hickies came from"—she gave her a hard stare—"Who was it? I think it's time you fess up."

"Um"—Aria fidgeted nervously—"I don't want to talk about him. He's no one special." She broke their eye contact and looked over Cat's shoulder. "Oh look"—she pointed toward the corner of the pavilion—"there's Marissa. I'm going to go say hi." She took a step around Cat, but her roommate quickly grabbed her arm.

"No, you don't. Every time I bring it up, you change the subject. Should I be worried? Is he someone's boyfriend? Husband? What's the big secret?"

Aria was tired of the secrets. She was tired of keeping everything that was going on locked up inside. "Okay, I'll tell you." She leaned in to tell Cat in her ear because another loud song had begun. "I don't know who he is. I was horny and drunk, and it just happened." She shrugged for effect while her friend stared at her with her mouth gaping. Thankfully, Chris had just returned, so the conversation could end—at least for now.

"What did I miss?" he asked when he saw the look on Cat's face.

"Nothing. Nothing at all," Aria told him and accepted the cup of soda.

"Okay, well, would you like to dance some more?"

She looked around the pavilion at all the people having fun and suddenly felt like she didn't belong. The music got louder, the smells of perfumes mixed with an assortment of aftershave grew stronger, and everything began to spin.

"Chris, I'm suddenly not feeling very good. I'm going to walk back to the dorm."

He waved her off. "Nonsense, I'll drive you, hon."

"Oh, you don't have to do that. Stay and have fun."

He shook his head at her, though. "I'm only having fun because I'm with you, and I'm going to take you back. I want to make sure you get there safely."

She tilted her head to look over his shoulder in the direction Cat had walked off in. "Okay, let me tell Cat I'm leaving."

She caught her friend's attention and waved good-bye. Cat pointed to her then to Chris and raised her eyebrows. Aria knew she'd hear about it later, but she nodded. *Oh, yeah. She's going to ask a ton of questions.*

"Are you feeling any better?" Chris asked once they were back at Hudson Hall.

The corners of her mouth turned up. "Yes, I think so. I think the noise was just getting to me after a while, and I'm tired. After a good night's rest, I'm sure I'll be as good as new."

He ran a hand through her dark hair. "I hope so. I had fun tonight, so thank you."

Aria felt herself blushing. "I had fun too." She reached for the doorknob, but he put his hand on hers to stop her. Then, when she looked at him, he leaned in and gave her a soft kiss. It was unexpected, but it was nice.

A growl pierced the air, and two surprised faces stared into the blackness of the night.

"What was that?" Chris wondered aloud.

Aria swallowed hard. "I'm not sure, but I'm going inside. Good night, and I'll talk to you tomorrow." She went inside, locked the door behind her, and took the stairs two at a time.

Once back in her room, she wasted no time in getting ready for bed. Then she climbed under the covers and started flipping through the most recent issue of Vogue, trying to relax herself, when the sound of a cat's mewing caught her attention. She looked out the window at the old oak tree close to it and found the source of the noise—there was a stuck kitten. She opened the window and reached for the little bundle of fur, which timidly walked across the branch to her waiting hands.

"What are you doing out there, buddy?" she cooed to the kitten. She could feel the vibration of its purring as she cuddled it close to her chest and stroked its silky soft fur. "Here"— she placed the kitten on her bed—"you stay put, and I'll be right back."

While she was in the restroom, Kellan changed back into his vampire form and waited on her bed.

"Now"—Aria began as she re-entered the bedroom area with a little bowl of water—"where did you come from?" Her question was met with silence, though. "Kitty?"

The moon shone through the window, but shadows were cast over her bed. She walked with tiny steps so as not to step on the kitten if it had hopped down to the floor. When she got closer to the bed, though, it hit her—a wave of sensuous musk.

"From your dreams," a deep husky voice replied, "I came from your dreams."

She wanted to scream. Really. Something stopped her, though, and she'd forever tell people it was fear, but in truth, it was something else—something carnal. Perhaps it was the strength in the hand stroking her cheek. Perhaps it was the sensual voice that had caressed her through the air. Perhaps it was the steely muscles now rippling under her fingertips. Perhaps it was the tingling and dampness in her nether regions that always occurred when she smelled the musk. More likely, though, it was the fact that every time they had joined their bodies, he had lit her up like a starry night.

His hand moved off her cheek to run down the length of her neck, then the dip into the collar on her pajama top, and spread out over her breast. His thumb stroked her nipple while his mouth came down on hers. His tongue lingered on her lips before prodding them open and forcing her to accept his voracious invitation. He delved deeply in her intoxicating mouth to taste her sweet nectar while his hand continued to knead her breast. Then he gave a swift tug on her top, and it was over her head before she could blink. A low growl escaped his throat as he cupped both of her breasts, which eagerly sprung forth and filled his hands.

"Mm," he murmured as he took a rosy peak into his mouth. He suckled the bud while his free hand worked the flesh of her other soft mound. Then he took it into his mouth and feasted some more.

Oh, he was driving her crazy, and her hands dug into his full head of hair urging him on. The expertise of his hot mouth was waking up an

animal inside her that she had never met until he
came along.

"Take me," she heard herself gasp.

"I fully intend to, my pet," he growled and
stood to his full height while scooping her up and
tossing her onto the bed. His hands immediately
went to the waistband of her pajama bottoms, and
he had them off her soon after. "Now it's time
for these," he murmured and removed her black
panties. "You have a beautiful body, my queen."

He made a sexy purring sound as he
planted heated kisses on her abdomen and
worked his way down to her hips and thighs. His
scorching trail continued a blazing path down her
right inner thigh and then back up the softness of
her inner left thigh.

"Shall I continue?" he asked huskily while
moving inward toward her landing strip of soft
curls.

"Oh, yes. Please don't stop," she cried
out.

His tongue obliged her by running over
the softness of her folds before splitting them
apart and teasing her ripened pearl.

Explosions of fire and stars burst behind
Aria's eyes, and she began to tremble. She
couldn't believe how good he was making her
feel. She couldn't believe how badly she wanted to
feel the length of him inside her. This stranger.
This animal. This *vampire*.

As if to answer her unspoken pleas, he
slipped a finger inside her hot, wet, and
welcoming passage. Her body shuddered as he
moved it around inside her. He was playing her
better than Beethoven played the piano, and she

could feel herself bursting all around him. Suddenly, his mouth left her body, and she shuddered from the expectation of what was coming next.

"Are you ready for me?" he growled, and she moaned in response. "I'll take that as a yes."

With a flex of his hips, he found his way to her molten hot center. She felt herself stretch gloriously around him as ripples of shuddering pleasure overcame her, and she ran her nails down the length of his massive back. He responded by plunging his tongue back into her mouth while his steely tumescence plunged into every inch of her femininity causing liquid fire to burn through her insides as she was pulled into a flaming vortex of pleasure.

"Oh my god!" she yelped as undulated ecstasy washed over her body. "Oh, that feels so good!"

He let out a fierce growl as his own rapture overtook him, and he held her tightly pressed against him while his body shuddered inside her. When his convulsions stopped, he dug into the pocket of his pants and pulled out the bottle of water from the Nile and sprinkled it on her.

This time, he didn't bite her. This time, instead, he whispered into her perfect ear, "I love you."

Fifty

Saturday evening, the vampire society, Daughters of Bathory, was called to order by Gail Woodson—wife, mother, librarian, and high priestess. She addressed the collective with an authoritative side that only they saw.

"Ladies, let's come to order," she boomed while rapping her gavel on the podium, and eight pairs of eyes turned in her direction. "I'm happy to report that the time has come for us to summon the first of our brethren—Jareth."

Excited murmurs flowed through the collective as questions were fired one after the other.

"To answer your main question, yes, *she's* here. The enchanted Gypsy is about to come of age, and she has surfaced in the area," Gail told them.

"How do you know that she's the anointed one?"

"I've met her myself, and I sensed the stirring inside her. This brings us here today. Now, join hands and let's say the chant."

More murmuring buzzed through the room as all nine women joined hands.

"Let's chant to summon Jareth."

Together, they recited, "Elizabeth Bathory, our mother of the immortal, bring us our brethren, Jareth. Grant us the passage into the arms of your child, Jareth, whom we wish to call brother. With your blessing, through his third immortal kiss, we shall be born again."

Outside, thunder rumbled, and lightning streaked the sky as a sudden storm struck up. Winds made the trees bow, and limbs were breaking off and coursing through the air.

Gail looked at the members of the secret society and told them with certainty, "It worked."

Fifty-one
Sunday

Aria had trouble falling asleep, although she feigned it when Cat got home. She didn't want to talk about her little confession at the park, and she certainly didn't want to confess what had just happened. How do you explain to someone that you willingly gave yourself to a blood-sucking vampire? Although, she'd reflected, that hadn't happened this time. For whatever reason, he didn't bite her.

Around 3:00 am, she drifted off into a sound sleep, but *he* plagued her dreams—every single one of them. They were all play-by-play erotic dreams involving him, and on a hotness scale of one to ten, they were elevens.

Now, she was dreaming that he was driving himself into her so hard that the bed was shaking, but then her eyes flew open, and she realized it was Cat shaking the bed. Her half-closed eyes glanced at her large display clock and saw that it was only 6:00 a.m.

"Wakey, wakey," Cat called out to her while her eyes tried closing again.

"What do you want?" she managed to groan.

"I want to talk. You dropped that bomb on me, and then, when I got home last night, I heard you gettin' busy in here with somebody. So, before we head to breakfast, I'd like to get the dirt from you."

"I don't want to talk about it. There's nothing to tell you," she lied in a whiny voice while pulling the covers up over her head.

Cat plopped down on her bed, though. "Come on and talk to me. Who is this guy? Does he attend here?"

"No, he's not a student here," she replied.

"Oh, so how old is he? What does he do for a living?"

Aria laughed and received a curious look from her roommate. *I don't know. He could very well be one thousand years old, but he looks damn good for his age. What does he do? He feeds on human blood.*

"Well?" Cat probed again.

Aria rolled her eyes and sighed. "Look, I don't know anything about him. We don't talk. We just—"

"Fuck?" Cat interrupted.

Aria's eyebrows shot up, but then she shrugged. "Well, yeah, we just have sex."

"Huh"—Cat looked at her sideways and bit her lip—"I'm shocked. I didn't know you had it in you to get some strange."

"Well, that just goes to show that you don't know everything about me. Now, you go on to breakfast, so I can get some sleep. I'm exhausted."

Cat rose from the bed and chuckled. "After what I heard last night, I guess you would be." She gave Aria a half-smile before grabbing her purse and leaving.

Aria heaved a big sigh of relief to have the conversation over while curling up on her side.

She closed her eyes and gave way to the haunting
erotic dreams once more.

A knock on her dorm room door woke Aria up. She tried to ignore it and go back to sleep, but the person was persistent, so she got out of bed and answered it. It was Marissa, and she was holding a package.

"Hi, Aria, I'm glad you're home. The UPS guy dropped this package off for you yesterday, but you weren't here, and I didn't want to leave it in the hall"—she looked both ways—"because you never know if there are thieves around."

Aria was touched. "Thank you, Marissa. I really appreciate you hanging on to it for me," she gushed before accepting the box. She looked at the return address on the label and saw that it was from her parents. *An early birthday gift perhaps?*

"No problem. We need to look out for each other, right?" she commented with a wink.

Aria nodded in agreement with her before spinning on her heel and stepping back into her room. She located a pair of scissors in the small desk she shared with Cat and cut the tape on both ends of the carton. Inside, there was white tissue paper, a birthday card, and a velvet jewelry box. She quickly opened the jewelry box to reveal a breathtaking pendant necklace. The pendent was a beautiful shade of blue, and it had a ruby above it and a blue gem below it. It all hung on a thin leather cord, and it appeared to be quite old. She immediately pulled it over her head and snapped a picture with her cell phone to send to her parents with a thank-you note. She ran to the bathroom and admired how it looked on her in the mirror. It hung perfectly around her slender neck, and the stones caught the light in a way that made it seem like they were glowing. She snapped a second photo and emailed it with the first one to her mother. Then she uploaded it to her various social media accounts for all her friends to envy.

She went back to the box and pulled the birthday card out of its blue envelop. It was a sentimental card for daughters, and her mother had written a message inside. She mentioned how proud they are of her and how special it is to be an adult. The she wrote about the necklace. She claimed she found it in an antique shop in the neighboring town. She said it caught her eye, and she knew it would look great on Aria.

Specifically, she wrote, "I saw it lying in a case, and it made me think of you. Like you, it is both hard (strong) and soft (delicate). The stone is your strength, Aria, and the blue color is soft like your compassion for others. I knew you'd have to have this necklace because it represents who you are—an incredible woman."

Aria read the note twice before setting the card on her night stand next to her alarm clock, where she noticed something that didn't belong there. It was a small folded piece of paper that had one thing written on it—Kellan Montcroix. She said the name to herself a couple of times.

Is that him? Is that his name?

She opened the contacts app on her phone and found Zelda Gabor. She tapped the name, and it dialed the number for her.

"Aria," the Gypsy answered, "I was just thinking about you. I need to see you, dear."

"Good, because I need to see you too. Can I come over now?"

"Yes, of course. Come to the house."

Aria looked at her watch and said, "It's 2:00 now, so I'll be there around 2:45."

"All right, dear. I'll be watching for you. We have much to discuss," Zelda told her, and then the line went dead.

Aria took a quick shower, dressed in a yellow sweater with blue jeans, and ran a brush through her wet hair before putting it in a braid. Her mother's words of wisdom about going outside with a wet head in cold weather flitted through her mind, but she was in a rush. Thirty minutes after hanging the phone up, she was in her car and heading to see Zelda.

Thankfully, traffic was light that afternoon. On the way there, she kept repeating the name in her head—Kellan. It was a strong name, she thought, and befitting for a vampire. She knew it was time to tell Zelda everything about him. It was time to confess to the Gypsy that she was lovers with her vampire stalker.

Kellan had been prowling around Aria's building all morning long. He'd even climbed the tree once to look at her through the window. Her curtain was drawn, though, so he could only see through a tiny corner. It was enough, though, to let him know that, despite the hour, she was still sleeping.

That may be a good sign. Hopefully, it means that her vampire side is strengthening. Maybe the Nile water had affected her, and maybe she's even with my child.

When he saw her leaving her room, he shifted into a crow and flew to a tree just outside the dorm entrance. He was prepared to follow her, but an uneasy feeling overcame him—he felt like he was being watched. He used his excellent eyesight to scan the area for predators, but he saw nothing of consequence. He did see another crow, though, and it was looking straight at him. It wasn't a mating attempt, he knew, because the other bird was also a male. It didn't feel territorial, either, and as far as he knew, there weren't any female crows around. He noticed that Aria had caught the other bird's attention, and then he noticed something disturbing. He saw that the eyes on the gargoyles by the dorm entrance had started moving—they were looking for evil. They, too, sensed that another malevolent being was nearby. They, too, recognized the other crow as a vampire.

When Aria reached Zelda's house, she saw the woman tending to what was left of her flower garden.

"Hi, Zelda," she greeted her new friend and confidant.

"Hello," Zelda called back to her, "I'm glad you could drop by. Come inside with me, and we'll catch up."

When Aria followed her inside, she noticed that a serving tray with two teacups was already set out on the coffee table alongside the large book Zelda had brought out last time. The fortune teller sat on the small sofa, and Aria chose the armchair again.

Zelda looked at her with a smile, but then her expression changed. Her eyes widened, her smile turned into a thin line, and her pale wrinkled hand flew to the talisman she wore while she stared.

"That necklace—where did you get it?"

Aria touched the large blue stone and explained, "I got it from my parents for my birthday. It was given to me just today in fact." She saw something odd in Zelda's expression, so she continued, "Why? Do you like it?"

"Yes, dear, it's quite lovely, but I'm asking because I've seen it before."

She went to an antique oak desk, opened a drawer, and pulled out another old book that looked similar to a scrapbook. She sat back down and began to quickly flip through its pages, while Aria studied her face.

How could she have seen it before?

Zelda's mouth turned up into a sly smile as recognition shone in her eyes.

"Here, look at this." She motioned for Aria to sit on the sofa next to her. "I have a fascinating story for you."

Aria sat next to her and looked down at the book she was holding on her lap. Her eyebrows shot up in surprise, and her hand shook as she pointed at the photograph she was entranced by.

"Is-is-is th-that what I think it is?"

"It is. It's your necklace in this book from the Salem Historical Society," she answered with excitement oozing from her voice.

Aria's pulse raced as she frantically tried to put the pieces of the puzzle together. "I don't understand, though. How?"

Zelda shot her a calming look. "Well, it says here that this necklace belonged to the Ayres family, and they were one of the most powerful Gypsy clans. It says—"

Aria interrupted her, "Wait! You said Ayres? Let me see that"—she looked in the book where the name was mentioned—"that is the name mentioned in the curse." Now her voice rang with excitement too. "Ayres name protects me from thee," she recited from memory.

"You're correct. You're from the Ayres family line, which means this necklace has always belonged to you, and it has found its way home," she replied with a big smile.

Aria fingered the gem, and she blinked away tears. "But how?"

"It found its way to you because it's a part of who you are. It belongs to you, and you belong to it. How did your parents acquire it?"

Aria stared blankly at the ivory wall in front of her. In a soft voice, she slowly answered, "Mom found it in an antique shop"—she met Zelda's curious gaze—"In my card, she wrote that she knew I had to have it."

Zelda's eyes twinkled, and her kind smile brightened. "Do you see how powerful Gypsy magic is? You're a part of it, dear. This necklace represents your family's evil eye. Let me explain the stones to you. First"—she pointed to the large blue stone—"this is lapis lazuli. According to Gypsy legend, it provides access to the mystical realms and esoteric knowledge. It is known as the stone of total awareness."

"I'm sorry, but what does esoteric mean?" Aria interrupted.

"It means you are part of the select few. You are part of the unexplained."

"Yeah, I'm beginning to see that," Aria replied while raising her eyebrows to it all.

"The ruby"—Zelda tapped her fingertip on the red stone—"shields the wearer against psychic attacks and will also help to reduce your fears. It is a leadership stone, which is perfect for you."

Aria's jaw dropped. "Leadership? I'm not a leader, I'm a follower."

Zelda chuckled softly and patted Aria's hand. "Don't worry about that. You'll have the skills and courage you'll need when the time comes."

Aria's face went blank. "When the time comes for what?"

"We'll get to that in a minute, dear," Zelda said before taking a sip of her tea. "Now, the bottom stone is labradorite, and it signifies the moon and the unconscious state of mind. It also represents the sun, permitting the unconscious thoughts to be brought forth and applied in the physical domain so that you can achieve your purpose in life."

"I'm sorry to interrupt again, but what do you mean when you say the physical domain?"

"The physical domain is where all matter and all physical energy interact. It is where the mystical meets the practical. Do you understand now?"

Aria wasn't sure that she did, but she answered, "I think so."

"Your amulet, your evil eye, is a great source of power for you—you just have to learn to tap into it, and I'll help you learn how to do that."

Aria slowly shook her head. "I'm not sure I understand what an evil eye is."

Zelda opened her hands up in front of her. "Okay, we'll start with that then. The evil eye is two things. It is an intense stare that Gypsies can give to someone they wish to curse, and it is the amulet you wear, which will protect you from the evil eye of others. It will help protect you from harm. An invisible shield will surround you when danger is present, but I must warn you that it cannot protect against all malevolent forces, so you still need to be careful."

"Um, does it protect against vampires?"

"Vampires have different powers, so I'm not sure if it will protect you from all of them. Also, since you are half-vampire, as we have learned, that may affect it somehow. Perhaps the High Council will know the right answer."

"The High Council?"

"Yes, the Gypsy High Council is a group of twelve matriarchs and patriarchs who establish and maintain the rules of our culture. They are also the knowledge keepers."

"Hmph, Google for Gypsies," Aria muttered.

"I'm sorry?"

Aria blushed. "Oh, nothing. I was being a smart-ass. Oops"—she put her hand to her mouth—"smart-aleck."

Zelda just smiled at her faux pas, though.

"So, you said you needed to speak to me, too. What did you learn?"

Zelda looked down at her hands, which she was nervously wringing. "Before I go into that, please tell me what else brought you here today."

"I need to talk to you about the vampire," Aria began softly. She swallowed hard before continuing. "Something has happened that you should know about. Actually"—she looked up from her lap—"a couple of things have happened."

"All right, dear, go ahead. Tell me," Zelda encouraged her.

Aria picked at her cuticles, and her eyes darted all around the room. "This is hard to talk about—especially considering who you say I am."

"It's okay, Aria. Just take a deep breath and tell me." Zelda gave her a warm smile to loosen her tongue.

Aria did as she suggested and took a couple of deep breaths. "I need to talk to you woman to woman, instead of Gypsy to Gypsy."

"I'm confused," Zelda interrupted her.

"Um, what I did came from the humanity in me, not the magic." She looked up into Zelda's bewildered face to see if she was following so far. "I let him-we um"—she felt completely tongue tied—"I don't know if I can say this aloud."

"Aria, did he seduce you?"

How did she know? Aria looked down at her hands in her lap and meekly replied, "Yes, and I let him do it more than once."

Zelda reached over and clasped her hand. "It's all right, dear. Vampires are known to be very seductive—it's how they lure victims in. This is how you came to be."

"Huh. Like mother like daughter then," Aria mused.

Zelda just gave her a soft smile. "You said you had a couple of things to talk about, so what else?"

Aria dug in her pants pocket for the tiny slip of paper with the name on it. "There's this. I'm pretty sure he left it for me," she said while handing it over.

"Kellan Montcroix," Zelda read aloud. "How many times has he bitten you?" She looked up from the paper and studied Aria's face.

"Um, three. Why?"

"Well, it's possible you survived because you are half-vampire, but it's possible that he is wanting to turn you into his mate. Actually, the latter is the more likely scenario because you would be a very powerful vampire, Aria. Your combined traits make you a formidable force of nature. Both sides want you and need you."

Aria sighed and clutched her amulet to see if it would strengthen her, and surprisingly, it did give her some comfort. *Maybe there is something to this Gypsy magic.* "So, what now?"

Zelda's mouth set in a hard line while she thought. Then she looked back at Aria and told her, "Now we find out who Kellan Montcroix is or at least *was.*" She got up and went into another room, and when she came back, she was holding a laptop, which she handed to Aria. "My grandkids got me this contraption, but I'm not that familiar with it, so I'll leave it to you."

"Sure, no problem," Aria chirped as she opened the lid. "You do have internet access, don't you?"

"Yes, they bought me an internet package too."

Aria beamed at her. "Nice grandkids." She opened the browser up and ran a Google search for *Kellan Montcroix.*

Fifty-five

The crows were in a stand-off while Aria drove away. Kellan wasn't about to let the other vampire out of his sight, so when the bird left its perch, he immediately acted. He waged war in the sky as he shifted mid-air into a hawk and swooped down on the smaller crow. He reached out his talons as he got close enough to the other bird to do damage and dove. His claws made contact as the smaller bird tried to fly away, and he managed to dig them into the crow's back. Then he bobbed his head forward and used his hooked beak to do damage to the crow's head while flapping his wings to pull his talons upward. Feathers fell to the ground where a large crowd of students had gathered on the lawn to watch the fight, and cheering erupted as Kellan made his first attack.

Kellan had flesh from the other bird's back in his hooks, and he was ready to get more. As he dove again, though, a rock buzzed by his head temporarily distracting him and giving the crow time to escape.

No matter. At least I know he's hurt.

Kellan flew back to his hideaway in the cavern to recuperate his energy. He stopped the vampire from following Aria, but he knew it was a temporary fix. The other would come back for her after he also recuperated his strength, and Kellan would be ready for him.

As he closed his eyes to rest until nightfall, he wondered how the other had found Aria to begin with, what he wanted with her, and just who he was. Vampires are territorial, so by that law, the other had no right to be anywhere near there. *Someone sent him, and I will find out who.* He would do whatever it took to protect his queen— his love—even if it meant the end of his immortal existence.

Fifty-six

Aria's eyes widened when she struck gold in her search for information on Kellan Montcroix, and butterflies filled her stomach while she read. According to the French Heritage Society, his family was part of Paris's aristocratic culture in the sixteenth and seventeenth centuries. His father, Gerard Montcroix, was a big wig in the textile manufacturing industry. She read that Kellan was his only son and the sole heir to the foundation when he suddenly disappeared without a trace in 1616. It stated the last person he was seen with was a woman named Gabriella, who disappeared at the same time. Rumor had it that they ran off to the colonies in America together.

Zelda had been reading along with her and commented, "I wonder if that is when he was turned. If so, the girl mentioned may have been one of his kills."

Aria nodded slowly in agreement as she scrolled down the page, and then her heart got caught in her throat. There was a photo of the family, and Kellan was standing tall and proud next to his father. Her mouth dropped open.

"Oh. My. God," she breathed softly.

Zelda let out a low whistle. "Wow! He's a looker, isn't he?"

A "looker"? Hmm, I need to change my panties now, so yeah, he certainly is. "What? Oh, yeah, he's not bad."

Zelda chuckled softly. "Honey, you're flushing and panting like a rabid dog. He's more than 'not bad,' " she teased. "Now, the question is, is he your vampire?"

"Yes, he's the one. I just hadn't gotten a good look at him before now because, of course, it was always dark out."

Zelda studied the photo too. "Well, it's easy to see how you were"—a pink color crept up her cheeks—"seduced. He looks very strong and masculine."

Aria flashed back to the lovemaking from the previous night and felt her cheeks blushing this time. "He is," she said wistfully.

"Look here"—Zelda pointed to the photograph of a stunning woman lower on the page—"this is the woman who also disappeared."

Aria looked at the photo of Kellan for a couple more seconds before shifting her gaze to the gorgeous blonde. It was totally plausible that the two attractive people would've run off together.

"Based on this information," Zelda interrupted her thoughts, "he was twenty-five when he disappeared."

"That's just a little older than me," Aria heard herself say. Then after an awkward moment of silence, while she gawked at the photograph of her lover, she looked over at Zelda and asked, "So, that is what brought me here, but what did you want to talk about?"

Zelda picked up her cup of tea before she answered, "Well, do you recall when we discussed the battle with a great evil that would occur when the coveted one—well, you—came of age?"

"Yes, how could I forget?"

Zelda sipped her tea and then explained, "The High Council thinks there is someone or some group setting out to destroy the Gypsies, and they believe the person or group is summoning a great force of evil to carry out this task."

Aria's expression tightened up, and she was finally able to pull her eyes away from the photograph. "I remember you telling me last time that a great evil was on the horizon, but what does it have to do with my twenty-first birthday?"

Zelda hesitated while she searched for the right words. "Do you recall when I told you at your reading that you are a strong warrior and will be able to handle the events moving about in your life right now?"

"Yesss," she answered with a sinking feeling in her stomach.

"Well, it turns out that you are the one who will lead the collective of Gypsy clans when they go to battle"—she noticed the panic on Aria's face—"Don't be afraid, dear, as I told you at your fortune telling, I see the strength in you. You were born for this—you were destined to be a warrior for good."

Aria took long deep breaths and chewed her lower lip while she processed the news. She knew the only way to handle the situation was with a calm and clear head—no matter how terrified she felt.

She chose her words carefully and spoke slowly. "I don't think I have the confidence or ability to take on such a task. They really should look for someone else."

Zelda surprised her when she laughed in response. "I understand your fear, hon, but this is your birthright. You have always had the power and confidence within you, even if you don't see it right now"—she got up and walked around the small room—"Imagine that your powers are being camouflaged by your current faith and system of beliefs. Until now, you didn't know magic existed, and you didn't know you have always been a part of it. Now that you know it's there inside you, you can tap into it and use it. It's a resource for you, Aria, to handle whatever comes your way."

Aria felt tears pooling in her eyes. It was from the combination of feeling honored, afraid for her life, and afraid for the lives of the other Gypsies she is allegedly destined to protect.

"But how?" she softly cried, "And how can I be a force of good when I'm half-vampire?"

"Who you are is your choice, dear"—Zelda sat back down on the couch next to her—"but the vampire side of you is a source of strength for you to draw upon just as the Gypsy side is. You're a mystical creature—the first of your kind—so it isn't exactly known how this will work, but I believe it will work out just fine. To answer your question about how, well, I have volunteered to work with you as your mentor to train you to use your gift. That is if you agree."

"Yes! I wouldn't want to work with anyone else," Aria squealed.

Zelda looked pleased. "Great, your first lesson is to learn to focus on your amulet—your evil eye." She got back up and went to the oak desk again. This time she pulled out a small book.

"Here is a book on amulets and their meanings. You'll find your stones in here and the properties they provide. The main thing for you to remember is that they will provide you with strength, courage, protection, and the path to your destiny. Think of it as an extension of you, and never take it off. You must learn to trust in its power. Here, let me demonstrate." She closed her eyes and touched her own amulet with one finger. The purple stone began to glow, and Aria jerked backward with a gasp.

"When I put my necklace on earlier, I thought the light was catching it to make it glow."

Zelda opened her eyes with a bigger smile than the one she already wore. "It was showing you that it was exactly where it belonged. Try it now. Try to connect to your power."

"Okay, but how?" Aria asked as she fingered the necklace.

"Just relax and imagine seeing it as an extension of yourself, such as another limb. Just like you can tell your toes to wiggle, you can connect to the necklace to tell it to do your bidding. Imagine making it move for you."

Aria closed her eyes and concentrated on her erratic breathing first. Once she had that under control, she did as Zelda had suggested— she pictured the necklace as one of her limbs, and she pictured moving it. Nothing happened, though, so she started over. She pictured it as one of her muscles this time, and again, she envisioned moving it. She opened her eyes in time to see a little flicker of light.

"I did it! Or at least I think I did. Did I?"

Zelda nodded and grinned at her. "Yes, you connected with it. I'm proud of you."

Aria's eyes went back to the stone, which no longer glowed and sighed. "It's gone," she pouted.

Zelda chuckled warmly. "That's all right, dear. It takes practice and patience. However, the sooner you learn to use its power, the better. Therefore, I want you to go home and practice making your connection. The important thing to remember is to relax and have faith. The power was born inside you, Aria. You are a natural—you just have to let yourself see it."

"Okay, I'll practice," Aria promised while closing the laptop lid and putting it on the coffee table but not until after looking at Kellan's photo again.

Zelda noticed what she was doing and told her, "I fully understand the power of a vampire's seduction, Aria, but you must not allow him to pull you in. If he does, you'll be fighting for the wrong side when the battle ensues, and with you on their side, they will win and destroy the Gypsies. He knows this, I'm sure, and he'll do whatever is within his power to influence you— including seduction."

Aria's memory took her back to the previous night, and it landed on something that was buried in her subconscious—he'd said, "I love you."

Her mouth twitched as she looked into Zelda's expectant face. "But what if—" She didn't know how to finish the sentence without being ridiculed, so she didn't. It was crazy, anyway, to think that love could play a role. As she moved toward the front door, she settled on, "I understand."

Zelda didn't look convinced, but she just nodded. "Let me know how it goes with your evil eye, and then we can get together for the next lesson. Remember, time is of the essence since you'll be twenty-one soon. I just hope that things haven't already been put into motion."

Aria tried to sound confident when she replied, while walking to her car, "I will, and I'll be in touch soon."

As she drove back to the campus, it wasn't the road she was seeing—it was the haunting image of her lover.

Fifty-seven

Aria stopped at the main library on the way back to campus. She wanted to check out books on Gypsy magic and how to harness it. She knew she had to learn her gifts quickly, and the best way to learn anything is to research it and then practice or apply it. She was going to throw herself into the craft until she had it mastered. She wanted to make Zelda and the Gypsy High Council proud.

When she walked in the front door, she saw the same librarian who had assisted her the last time. She gave the woman a polite smile and walked to the computers to do her search through the digital card catalog.

She found a few books about Gypsy folklore and magic, so she jotted the reference numbers down on one of the small slips of paper and stood up to go hunt them down. Just as she turned to go, though, she stopped herself and sat back down. She ran another search—this time it was on Kellan Montcroix. She was somewhat surprised to see that there was a book on the shelves with his family mentioned in it. It was a book published by the French Heritage Society— the same reference she had found online. She quickly wrote the book number down and headed for its shelf.

The book was well-worn, and dust filled her nostrils when she pulled it off the shelf. She opened the cover to see how many times it had been checked out before and saw that only three dates were stamped on the due-by insert, and the last time was in 2014.

Well, that explains the dust.

She tucked the book under her arm while she quickly hunted the other three down. Soon, she was sitting at a table and flipping through the book titled *Industrial France*. She found Montcroix in the index and turned to page 272 to read about the family. There was more information in the book about Kellan's father, Gerard Montcroix, than what she'd read online at Zelda's house. He was a pioneer in the textile industry, it seemed, and had been the head of several foundations. She skimmed through the paragraphs looking for anything and everything she could find on Kellan. She told herself the research was to prepare for the battle, but in truth, she was obsessed. No mortal man could do to her body what this vampire did, and no mortal man on the planet could compare to him in the looks department.

Not even if George Clooney and Brad Pitt had a baby together.

She found a photograph of him by himself and traced over his face with her fingers. Every nerve inside her turned electrical when she recalled the sensations his perfect lips had provoked. Lethal or not, he knew his way around her body. Dangerous or not, she found herself craving more. She took the book to the copier, deposited a dime into the slot, and made a color copy of the photograph.

Bells suddenly rang loudly overhead, and people ran past her toward the exit. She grabbed the printed copy of the photograph and rushed behind the other patrons to pile out the double doors to the parking lot. She had left the book on the copier, but she held the other three in her arms along with the photo of Kellan.

"I don't see any smoke," she heard someone say.

Aria looked through the windows from where she stood and didn't see any flames or smoke either. Then the librarian who had assisted her came out of the building and announced, "False alarm. You can come back in."

She filed back into the building with the others and went straight to the checkout counter to take out the three books on Gypsy folklore and magic. She didn't need the *Industrial France* book, and the library had a three-book maximum policy.

"You were here the other day needing help deciphering some Italian, weren't you?" the librarian asked.

Aria noticed the woman's nametag this time. Her name was Gail. "Yes, that was me. Good memory."

"Well you are hard to forget with those blue eyes," Gail told her with a smile. "I've never seen such pale blue eyes before, and they are the perfect complement to your dark hair and fair skin."

Aria felt herself blush and shyly looked away. She never did figure the thing out with her eyes—she'd bring it up to Zelda the next time they spoke.

"Do you have your library card with you?" Gail asked.

"No, I need to get one for this branch," Aria told her and felt foolish for not having mentioned it beforehand.

"Sure, it's no problem. Just fill out this short application, and I'll make one up for you." The librarian handed her a half-sheet of paper with only a few boxes on it to collect basic information. She had to fill in her name and address and then give Gail her license or Student ID to photocopy, and that was it.

"So, do you have practice fire drills often?" she teased while she filled the form out.

The woman chuckled and told her, "That was crazy. I think one of the kids pulled it, but there's no way to be certain. I'm just glad it was a false alarm."

"Yeah, me too," Aria agreed. "I left a book on the copier during the chaos. Sorry about that."

"Oh, that's fine, hon. I'll put it away when I copy your ID." She took Aria's Student ID and walked off in a hurry to make the copy. When she came back, she said, "I think you know my son, Chris Woodson. I've heard him mention your name once or twice."

"Yes, he's a friend of mine," Aria said surprised. "Well, he's a new friend of mine. We just met recently."

Gail winked at her. "If I remember correctly, he spoke very highly of you." She handed Aria her new library card. "Our laminator isn't working today, but the next time you come in, I can laminate this for you."

"Oh, no need. I'll take care of it. Is that it then?"

Gail looked up from a note she was jotting down. "Oh, yes, you're all checked out and ready to go." She gave her a smile that looked a little plastic this time, though.

Aria backed away from the counter with her three books. "Okay. Thanks for your help."

She quickly turned toward the exit and made her way back to her car. Something about Chris's mom was creepy—especially the way she had stared and that last smile.

The sun was hanging low in the sky, and the first shadows of the evening fell upon her as she drove back to school. Something was different this evening, though. Instead of feeling afraid, like she had before and she should now, she felt something else—anticipation. That left one problem, though. What would she do about Cat? She didn't want her friend to get hurt, or worse, but she wanted her lover to come to her again too.

Fifty-eight

Before the sun had disappeared for the day, Kellan had flown back to the school to look for Aria. He wanted to be there as soon as night fell so he could protect her from any attacks by the other vampire. He didn't know what he was going to be up against, but his adrenaline was pumped and made him ready for it—even if there was more than one adversary.

He climbed the tree outside her window but stopped three-quarters of the way up because he found her looking out of it. She was staring out into the coming darkness as if she was looking for something.

Is she searching for me? Have I influenced her enough to make her willing to come with me?

The questions fired off in his mind as he stared at her captivating beauty, which was being illuminated by the orange and pink rays of the setting sun. Then he heard her talking to someone—her roommate he guessed—so he listened in with piqued interest.

"Where have you been all day?" the other female asked her.

"Nowhere special. I just had errands to run is all," he heard Aria say as she crossed the room to her tiny bed.

"Oh, are you seeing Chris tonight?" the girl asked.

So, that's his name then. Chris. After I take care of the vampire, I may have to take care of him too.

"No, I hadn't planned on it," Aria was quick to respond.

"Oh. I ask because...I guess you haven't heard yet, and I thought he'd be the one to break the news then."

"Break the news about what? What are you rambling on about?" he heard Aria question the girl.

"Something happened last night, Aria. It's Kyle. I have news about Kyle."

"What about Kyle? That he's a colossal douche? I already knew that," Aria huffed.

"No, Aria, he's gone," the other girl said so softly that Kellan almost didn't hear her.

"Did he drop out of school? That doesn't surprise me, but I'm glad nonetheless."

"I wish that was all," the girl answered in tears this time. "He's dead, Aria. He was found with a broken neck this morning."

Kellan didn't hear any response from his mate, but he watched through the break in the curtains as she rose from her bed and walked around the room a couple of times.

"I'm going for a walk," he finally heard her say, and his heart raced. He could hold her soon.

Or be battling to save her.

He scurried down the tree and around the building to check for his enemy. He went to see if the gargoyles were talking.

Fifty-nine

Gail tapped the gavel on the wooden podium to get everyone to settle down. "Tonight, ladies, is a special night. Tonight, we get to take action."

She ran her hand over the photo of Kellan. Pulling the fire alarm had been genius. It had given her time to see what the enchanted girl had been copying, and she had recognized the photo—it was of the vampire who had been killing within San Francisco. She knew this because she had been at the downtown library branch the night of the murder. She had watched as the vampire killed the patron on the way to her car at closing time.

Yes, she knew of his presence. Yes, she knew that the women killed lately had been the work of a vampire. She knew this for certain because she was friends with the medical examiner. The medical examiner, Alicia Freeman, was a member of the collective, and while she was keeping the actual cause of death a secret from the police, she had told Gail and the other cult members everything. The problem was, though, they didn't know who the vampire was. He wasn't someone they had summoned, so his identity was a mystery—until now.

Gail flipped on the overhead projector and shone the photo of Kellan on the pull-down screen. Gasps radiated through the room, and

Rose Duncan, who swore she didn't need glasses to see, put the ones she kept in her purse on.

Over the oohs and ahs, Gail addressed her friends. "Ladies, this is the vampire we have been wondering about. He is the night stalker in San Francisco."

"Oh, he can bite me any time he wants to," Jenna Knight exclaimed, and murmurs of agreement rang out.

"How do you know for certain it is him?" Betty Colbert asked in a haughty voice.

Gail jabbed a finger at the photo while she answered, "I know it's him because I saw him that night. I got a good enough look at him to make the comparison."

"Can we summon him to make the change?" Alicia inquired.

Gail shook her head and said, "No, not yet at least. Unfortunately, he is moving around in the life circle of the enchanted one. She copied this photo today, so she must know of his identity, and I think he is intending to sway her to her vampire half."

More murmurs burst out within the group, and Gail had to loudly clear her throat to settle them down.

"How will he do that?" Rose asked.

Gail scanned her eyes over the entire group when she responded, "Through seduction of course. The seduction of a vampire is the most influential force out there."

"You never said who the girl is," Alicia pointed out and then looked at the other members to get their backing.

"Her name is Aria Sandoval." Gail laughed lightly, which received startled looks from the collective. "The funny thing is, she is my son's latest crush."

"Oh, we can use that," Alicia mentioned over the other giggles.

"Yes, we can use that to get information," Betty chimed in.

"Of course, but I think Jareth can get us more. Now, let's get to the business of calling him forth." Gail snapped the projector off and retrieved the spell from her book. "Let's try the spell on page 183 this time."

Together, they chanted, "Elizabeth Bathory, mother to the shadow dwellers, we summon thee to send us your son, Jareth. We wish for him to take us into his arms and help us fulfill our immortal destinies. So mote it be."

The lights in the room flickered before going out completely, and the women squealed with delight laced with fear.

"Who summons me from my hunt," a male voice boomed just as the lights came back on. Standing at well over six feet was an exquisite blonde-haired man. He had a piercing gaze, and it went from face to face before settling on Gail's.

"We are the Daughters of Bathory," she announced. "We summoned you here because we need your help, brethren."

His mysteriously blue eyes narrowed while his mouth turned up with amusement. "What do you want my help with, and why should I give it to you?"

"You should help us because we are on the same side, and we know about the coming battle between the Gypsies and the immortals. We also know who the enchanted one is, and we have access to her," she answered confidently.

His eyes opened with surprise, and he laughed snobbishly. "And you think you can help the immortals? How do you wish to accomplish that?"

"We will summon more of your kind and then bring Countess Bathory forth."

His face grew taut. "You don't have that kind of power."

"We will have it once we have the girl," she answered with a Cheshire grin.

He put one finger to his chin in thought. "You haven't told me what you expect from me in return."

"We want only one thing from you—immortality."

Sixty

Aria stepped outside into the chilly night air and began to rub her temples.

Kyle is dead? I can't believe it. What the fuck?

She kicked a rock, sending it skidding into the parking lot, and then turned to walk to the grassy knoll in the center of campus. The dried lawn crunched beneath her feet as she wandered aimlessly lost in her thoughts. She tried to make a list of enemies Kyle had while she plopped down on the grass. He was a jerk to a lot of people, but she couldn't imagine anyone getting violent enough to kill him.

Then again, look how mad Chris got.

Nausea overcame her as her mind went to a dark thought. So far, she only knew he was killed sometime between last night and this morning when they found his body. Chris had been incredibly angry.

But could he? No, he surely wouldn't be that vicious. Would he?

She clutched her stomach as the bile rose and took several deep breaths. She noticed something familiar on the last breath—the smell of sinfully delicious musk. Her eyes scanned the darkness, which was partially illuminated by the full moon, and found a large shape coming closer to her. Common sense would have had her on her feet and running in the opposite direction, but she found that she was currently lacking any. Instead of thinking about a method of escape, she found herself wondering if her breath was bad and if her panties were clean.

Kellan approached his beautiful obsession with confidence. If she'd wanted to escape, she would've tried by now. Instead, she stared at him while he got closer and wet her lips with the tip of her soft tongue. He could smell her pheromones, and they were calling to him to quench their thirst.

Aria stared at him when he came into full view. He was even more gorgeous in person than in the photo she'd been coveting for hours, and the discomfort between her thighs grew more intense.

She intended to say hello, but instead, "I want you," came out.

She felt herself blush when he chuckled, but she liked how deep and masculine it sounded. She'd never paid attention to things like that before with him because she was always terrified. Now, even though she was mesmerized by his features, she could really notice him because she wasn't afraid. Something besides his breathtaking face caught her eye, though. Her necklace began to feel increasingly warm against her skin, and it even began to glow underneath her sweater. It was just a soft flicker at first, like before, but this time it grew into a warm light flooding the blackness around them.

Kellan saw the amulet glowing through her sweater. He knew it was meant to protect her from evil like him, but since he had no intentions of doing her harm, he had no idea how the amulet would behave. He was glad to see her wearing an evil eye, though, because of the other vampire in the area. Before coming to her now, he'd checked the gargoyles, and they were silent except for the stare they always gave him.

"I want you too, my pet," he growled as he kneeled on the grass next to her. "I want this more than you know."

Kellan put his hands on her face and leaned in to give her the most passionate kiss he'd ever given anyone before. His tongue probed her perfect lips and slipped inside to tangle with hers while his hands slowly glided over her shoulders. He gave them a gentle squeeze before moving his right hand over her left breast. It felt perfectly molded against him while he slowly kneaded it before giving a light pinch to her nipple.

"Mm," she moaned softly while they kissed, and then her hand found the one playing with her breast. She gave it a squeeze and pushed it harder against her, and he responded to the silent request by pinching her peak again.

"Oh my god," she cried out as passion brought her blood to a rolling boil. She'd never wanted anything as much as she wanted to feel him inside her right then and there. "Please," she groaned.

His kisses trailed down her neck while his hand trailed down as well. He nestled it between her thighs, and he could feel the heat through the leggings she wore.

"Please what?" he taunted while his mouth trailed down to the V-neck portion of her sweater. He pushed his right hand up underneath it and unhooked her bra, which he moved out of the way for his mouth. He took her taut peak between his lips and suckled gently at first and then harder as she urged him on with her moans. His left hand continued to rub over her mound, which was still concealed by her clothing.

"Please take me somewhere," she pleaded.

Kellan let go of her, stood to his full height, took her by the hand, and pulled her to her feet. Then he scooped her up into his strong arms and held her protectively against his massive steely chest.

While Kellan carried her to a dark area on the campus, Aria inhaled his masculine scent until she found herself brushing his hair away from his neck, so she could kiss it. His skin was smooth, and his neck was thick and strong. She darted her tongue out for a lick, and he tasted like nothing she'd sampled before. She could taste the virile testosterone coursing through him, and it overpowered her senses like a drug.

Kellan found a private area and laid her down on the grass while moving over her to capture her lips once again. He nibbled on her bottom lip, but he was careful to avoid contact with his fangs. Then he drew her tongue into his mouth with a sucking motion, and he felt the vibrations from her throat as she moaned with delight. Swiftly, he pulled her sweater up over her head and then tugged her bra off. His mouth went back to work on her nipple while his other hand caressed the softness of her other mound. He drew the hardened bud into his mouth and flicked it with his tongue while her hands were pulling through his long hair. Her amulet continued to glow, which put a soft light around her features.

"Kellan, I want you. Take me," she begged.

He looked up into her face and smiled. "You saw the note," he observed. "Good, I was hoping you'd find it, and I fully intend to take you, my love. I'm going to take you to the highest peaks of pleasure."

He moved his kisses from her breast to her abdomen while he removed the last barrier of her clothing. As soon as her flesh was exposed to him, he put his mouth to work on it. He flicked his tongue against her ripened center of sensation, and then he kissed, sucked, and nibbled his way down to her core and thrust his tongue inside her. She was hot, wet, and ready for him, and he could deny himself no longer. He rose above her, unfastened his black pants, and let himself spring free. He put his thick head at her opening and gently probed. It was greeted with another trickle of nectar, which urged him to plunge further. His hardness found her inferno, and he moved in and out of it in slow measured strokes.

Aria licked his chest, which was bared to her now. She once again got drunk on his masculine essence as she lapped at his flesh. Her hands moved down his muscular torso in slow circles until they rested on his hard hips. She dug her nails into his flesh while he brought her to the peak of ecstasy multiple times.

"You smell so good," she breathed against his chest.

"You taste so good," he growled and plunged a little harder.

"Oh my god," she howled again and then bit into him until she tasted blood. The salty flavor did something to her insides to make her feel exhilarated.

She began to buck her hips wildly until he was buried to the hilt. Her claws dug into his back now, but she reached one hand around to feel him as he moved in and out of her slickness with fluid motion.

"Bite me," she cried out into the heated air around them.

Without question, Kellan leaned in and gently bit into her neck. Her sweet vanilla and honey flavored blood filled his mouth while the thick aroma of orchids filled his nostrils.

Suddenly, he pulled himself out of her and put his hands on her waist to lift her and flip her over. Then he wrapped his arm around her and pulled her to her knees. While he kissed her back, his staff found her entrance and dove in as deep as it could.

Aria cried out from the feeling of him touching every inch of her insides. It was pain wrapped up in pleasure, and it blanketed her senses until she was almost numb. She bowed her head and clawed at the ground while he repeatedly took her to the point of no return. She didn't ever want to come back to reality after being shown the joys of womanhood by this man—this vampire.

Kellan was overcome with joy at her receptiveness, her passion. He felt her pleasure surround him as he was buried deep inside her molten core. Then his own pinnacle of gratification was upon him, and he released his hot seed into her with rapturous content.

They both cried out in completion, and he rolled to the ground with her falling on top of him. Her head was nestled to his chest, and their hearts were beating in unison. He gently stroked her bare skin with his fingertips as her breathing slowed.

"That was perfect," she purred against his chest.

"You are perfect," he replied, "and I'll do anything for you, my love. I'll protect you until my last breath."

Aria lifted her head and searched his face. She couldn't see his sky-blue eyes, but she could recall them from that first night with perfect clarity.

"We aren't supposed to be together," she stated softly.

"It's your choice to make, Aria."

She cocked her head slightly. She loved the sound of her name coming from his lips.

"I know," she sighed while laying her head back down on his broad chest. "But I don't know what to do."

"You are half-vampire, but that doesn't make you evil. You are a creation from the gods, a one-of-a-kind creature with a divine purpose. The path is yours to choose"—he planted a kiss on the top of her head—"but I believe you are my soul mate, and I'm going to find a way to prove it to you. I will find a way for us to make a path together."

She looked up at him and inched closer to his mouth. "You're off to a good start, at least in the bedroom department," she whispered huskily and leaned in for a perfect kiss.

Sixty-one
Monday

Aria was reliving the magic of the night before in a lucid dream when her alarm clock blared. She reached out and sent it flying across the room where it landed in the closet.

Cat popped her head out of the bathroom with her toothbrush in hand. "Did someone wake up on the wrong side of the bed, or was it just a lonely bed?" she teased. When Aria didn't budge, she nagged her, "You know you can't keep missing classes if you expect to pass them."

"Who are you, my mother?" Aria growled as she tried to muster the energy to climb out of bed.

Cat scoffed, "Don't bite my head off. I'm just looking out for you."

Aria screamed her defense in her mind. *Why do I have to go to school when I'm a powerful Gypsy warrior responsible for saving innocent people from blood-thirsty vampires?*

"Oh my gosh, listen to this," Cat exclaimed and turned the volume up on her radio.

"What?" Aria grumbled, but she tuned in.

A news reporter was talking about grisly murders that occurred last night. Authorities reported that the bodies of two more women in the San Francisco city limits had been discovered, and the cause of death was exsanguination.

"That's horrifying," Cat exclaimed. "I can't believe the crazy shit going on lately."

"You don't know the half of it," Aria replied as she bolted past her confused roommate. As soon as she reached the porcelain bowl, she retched up all her stomach contents.

"Damn, girl. Are you okay? Are you sure you're not preggers?" Cat leaned in and held her hair back.

Aria sat up and tore off some tissue to wipe her mouth. "I'm not pregnant," she groaned as she stood up and walked back to her bed. "I'm just—" She didn't finish the sentence because she fell back asleep.

"Okay, you rest then," Cat whispered while she pulled Aria's blanket over her. Then she grabbed her bags and quietly left the room with the door locked behind her.

Aria tossed and turned in her sleep. She was dreaming that she was back in the park and in the fog. She was walking around aimlessly when she heard her name called. She turned to the voice behind her, and there he was.

"Good evening, beautiful," he purred.

"How could you? How could you kill those women?" she yelled at him.

He moved closer and reached for her. She tried to turn away in time to run, but his hand caught her arm, and he pulled her into his vice-like grip.

"Darling, you know I have to eat. You are well aware of what I am, and you seemed accepting of it last night when we made love under the moon and the stars."

Aria struggled to get away, but he just held her tighter. "I wasn't thinking," she rebuttled, "I was under some kind of spell."

Kellan laughed haughtily. "Aye, you were under the spell of love, my sweet. Do not deny your feelings for me."

"You're a monster! I could not possibly ever love you," she spat at him.

He planted kisses on her neck while she struggled to get free, and then he spun her around and claimed her mouth as his bounty.

"But you do love me, admit it. And now you're pregnant with my babe."

Aria's eyes flew open. Her heart was pounding in her ears, and it took her several deep breaths to calm it down. She bolted upright and grabbed her datebook. She looked at June, July, and August, and then she flipped to September. There it was, or rather, there it was not—her period. She was officially four days late. She ran to the bathroom and dry heaved.

This can't be happening. I can't be pregnant because, if I am, either the father is dead, or he's a vampire, which is still technically dead. Oh Lord!

She dry heaved some more and then passed out on the bathroom floor.

Sixty-two

"Aria, wake up. Aria, are you okay? I'm going to call for an ambulance." She heard her name being called, but she couldn't respond. Stinging to her cheeks finally brought her back, though.

"Oh, thank God," Cat exclaimed. "I was about to dial 9-1-1. What happened?"

Aria looked around the bathroom and rubbed the sore area on her head. "I don't know, I'm not sure. I felt sick to my stomach again."

"Well, we're going to the hospital now. I'm taking you to the E.R." Cat helped her off the floor and outside to her Jeep.

It took only ten minutes for them to get to the hospital, and Aria was quickly checked in. Cat paced the small hospital room while Aria changed into a gown.

"Would you quit pacing? I'm going to be fine. I'm sure I'm okay," Aria said for her own benefit more than Cat's.

A nurse came in three minutes later and checked her vitals. "What are the symptoms that brought you in today?"

Aria didn't want to say them aloud because she knew the assumption that would be made. "I've been vomiting, I'm extra tired, and I fainted earlier," she replied meekly.

"Oh, I see. And when was your last menstrual cycle?"

Aria picked at the bracelet the triage nurse had put on her. "Um, about 32 days ago. I'm four days late."

The nurse nodded like the diagnosis had been made. "Okay, well the doctor will want a urine specimen then"—she reached for a plastic container in the cabinet—"The bathroom is just around the corner, and you can leave the sample in there." She gave Aria the container and left the room through a door that said *employees only*.

"Four days?" Cat asked and then let out a low whistle while she averted her eyes.

Aria jabbed a finger at her while trying to close the back of her gown before she stepped out into the hallway. "Don't you say it. Don't you even think it."

While they waited for the doctor to come in with the test results, Aria tried to keep the conversation light—anything but babies.

"How is your vampire paper coming?" Cat inquired.

Aria choked on the sip of water she was taking, and Cat rushed over to pat her on the back while she tried to catch her breath.

Red in the face, Aria finally managed to squeak out on a hoarse voice, "It's fine."

"Can you imagine what the world would be like if they really existed?"

Aria blanched. "Um, no. I mean that would be something. Is it hot in here?"

Cat looked at her with a squint. "No, I'm cold to tell you the truth"—she looked up at the wall clock—"I wish they'd hurry up."

There was a knock on the door, and a woman wearing a stethoscope entered the room. "Hi, Aria, I'm Dr. Freeman. I've read your chart, and I've got the results of your urine test here. It came back negative on the pregnancy test, so the next step is to run some bloodwork. I'll send the nurse back in to take a sample, and I'll see you as soon as the results come back on it."

Alicia Freeman exited the room and walked to the nurse's station to issue the orders for the blood work. The medical examiner picked up occasional shifts in the ER when they were shorthanded. She smiled to herself, happy that they were short on doctors today. It gave her a chance to examine the alleged coveted one. It gave her a chance to see what was so special about the girl that made the gorgeous immortal want her.

Sixty-three

Kellan scoured the school campus and the area surrounding it in search of the other vampire. He was, specifically, looking at every creature he came across. Every bird, every squirrel, even every mouse was scrutinized. While in beast form, it was often difficult to tell if the creature wasn't all that it seemed to be—he had to carefully study its behavior. Animals that are predators in nature are the most difficult to discern. In vampire form, it was easier. Vampires have special pheromones that can be smelled. Of course, he could rely on gargoyles to announce the proximity of another vampire, but the ornaments weren't that popular in the area. In fact, the only ones in a fifty-mile radius, he discovered, were those on Aria's dorm building and an old apartment building downtown.

He soared over the walkway between the buildings where he'd dispatched the loud-mouth punk. There was a lot of activity going on there. Students, mostly female, were paying their respects by leaving flowers where the body had been discovered. He recalled hearing Aria's roommate mention the name Kyle yesterday.

Too bad, Kyle. You messed with the wrong woman.

Thinking about antagonizing Aria made him think about her amulet. He wondered how long it would take her to harness its full power, and what her powers would grow into. It's quite possible that she would've been able to handle the jerk on her own had the other male not stepped in.

What is his name again? Chris?

He hadn't decided what to do about the man yet. While he was glad that the man had stood up for Aria, he still didn't want him eating out of his food bowl. Of course, Aria had seemed to make her choice—the right choice—last night when she'd given herself to him, so maybe she would give Chris the brush off. If not, then Kellan would just have to do it himself, with or without her blessing.

Just as he was about to leave his perch across the walkway from Aria's building, he saw her get out of a Jeep. Her roommate was with her, and she walked around the vehicle to put her arm around Aria. Kellan soared around to the back of the building and perched in the tree outside her window. Something about her looked off.

Sixty-four

"I'm glad it's just an infection, not that I'm glad you're sick, but you know…"

Aria gave her roommate a weak smile. "I know what you mean," she breathed on yet another sigh of relief. "I don't know what I would've done if I was pregnant with"—she looked away toward the window—"Kyle's baby." *Or my vampire's.*

"Especially now," Cat exclaimed and shook her head. "Gee, I wonder if there are any leads in his murder."

Aria shrugged and walked to the window. "Turn on the news," she suggested while peering through the glass. She thought she saw something moving around outside it, but now she didn't see anything.

I'm losing my mind, starting with my behavior last night.

She was still staring out the window when Cat announced, "There are no suspects yet."

Aria's mind went back to Chris. "Hey, you don't think that Chr—" She stopped and sighed. *I shouldn't project my unfound suspicions on her.*

"Now they're talking about the two women who were found. They still can't figure out how they bled out."

Anger boiled up inside Aria. She was angrier at herself than she was with Kellan, though, because she'd allowed him to get close to her. She'd willingly let her guard down with him—she'd craved him. Zelda had warned her, but she didn't listen. Her amulet had cautioned her too. She looked down and pulled the necklace out from under her sweater.

"That's pretty," Cat called out from the bathroom, "Where did you get it?"

Aria fingered the lapis lazuli. "My mom found it in an antique shop and sent it for my birthday," she answered wistfully.

"Well, it's lovely, and speaking of your birthday, what do you want to do? We have to celebrate it right"—her eyes grew large, and she fanned her hands—"I know what we can do! We can go to Boxers for the all-male review."

"Hmm," Aria sighed. "I don't know, maybe." She didn't know if she would make it to her twenty-first birthday with the evil threat looming, or if she did, if it would be the last birthday she'd get to celebrate. *What I would give to have a normal life.*

"Well, try not to get all worked up about it," Cat replied in a voice dripping with sarcasm. "Hey, if you aren't going to class, let's go eat because I'm famished."

Aria looked over her shoulder at her friend. "I'm not feeling up to it, but I'll eat a sandwich if you bring me one back."

"Do you want pickles on it?" Cat teased, and Aria tossed a pillow at her. It hit the door, instead, and landed on the floor.

After Cat left, Aria curled up on her bed with her back against the wall and opened her library books on Gypsy magic and legends. She searched the index of each of the three books for information on amulets and talismans, and in the third book, there was a plethora of material. So far, everything she read about her stones matched up to what Zelda had said. The lapis connected her to the mystical realm, the ruby was for leadership, shielding against psychic attacks and helping to reduce her fears, and the labradorite would help her discover her destiny.

Where was that one last night? Surely a vampire lover isn't meant to be part of my destiny, even if it was part of my mother's.

She flipped through the sections on the stones and tried to find information on connecting to them, but there wasn't anything particularly useful. Zelda told her to relax and imagine it as part of her body, so she put the book down and took several deep breaths with her eyes closed. She pictured the stones in her mind's eye and then imagined them as part of her body—like another freckle.

She began to feel the stones warming against her skin, and she could even see them glowing through her closed eyelids. She concentrated on their individual attributes—she imagined them protecting her with an invisible shield. Just as it seemed to be working, though, her phone rang and ruined her concentration.

"Someone has perfect timing," she exclaimed in frustration. Then she saw it was Chris, and her aggravation intensified. "Hi Chris," she answered in a monotone voice.

"Hi, Aria," he practically whispered into the phone. "Can we get together to talk?"

Aria rolled her ice-blue eyes and glanced at her watch. "When? Right now?"

"Yes, please. I'll come there if it's okay. You are home, right?"

"Yeah, I'm home. Come on over."

As soon as they hung up, Aria piled all her library books up and hid them in the closet. She didn't need him seeing the subjects she was reading up on and asking questions—Cat was bad enough.

Chris must've been close by because he knocked on her door three minutes later. Her heart pounded as she grasped the knob to open it, and she looked down at the amulet, which wasn't glowing.

Will it recognize a killer if the killer is a human?

Sixty-five

As soon as Chris entered the room, he wrapped his arms tightly around Aria.

"Are you handling everything okay?" Wrinkles lined his forehead, and his mouth turned down while he searched her face.

She looked away from him so that he couldn't see any signs of suspicion on her face. "I'm okay," she softly replied before turning her back to him. She glanced down, but the necklace still wasn't lit up.

"I highly doubt that. I know from the little time that we've spent together that you're a strong woman, but this had to hit you hard. It had to be quite a shock."

She spun around and narrowed her eyes at him. "What do you know about it? Do you know what happened?"

Chris put both hands into his pockets. "I don't know anything more than what they've said in the news and around campus," he told her with a shrug. "To my knowledge, he died from a broken neck."

"Hmm, that would require a lot of rage—a lot of hatred—don't you think?" she fished while staring into his eyes to see if they would dilate—a common occurrence when telling a lie.

He shifted his weight uneasily and looked away from her gaze. "Um, yeah, I mean I guess so."

Aria walked slowly around the room trying to think like a homicide detective, so she would ask the right questions.

"Well, who would hate him that much? If it had just been a mugging, they wouldn't have broken his neck—it seems too personal. It feels to me like someone had a grudge with him—a score to settle—so I've been trying to think of people who might fit that description."

Chris cocked his head to the left and hooded his eyes. "Did you put me on that list because of our scuffle at the park?"

Aria pursed her lips and bowed her head. "Let me ask you this. Should you be on that list?"

His face turned red, and his fist balled. "No! It was an argument over you. I'd think you'd be grateful to have me stand up for you. Kyle was my friend, just not at that exact moment, and I came here to console you because he was your friend too once. I didn't come here to be interrogated like a suspect"—he walked toward the door—"I get that you are studying this shit but Jesus, Aria." He shook his head while he walked out the door, which he slammed behind him.

Aria grabbed a notebook out of her bookbag and sat on her bed with a pencil in hand. She jotted down some notes about Kyle, and then she jotted down notes about the other murders in the area lately. There was no common denominator, that she could see, between his death and the others. So why did it feel like they were related?

Kellan overheard everything that had transpired, and he was concerned about the infection she supposedly had. He hoped it was just a human illness, but he was worried that it may be related to the supernatural—he was worried it may be his fault. Sometimes, humans couldn't handle the conversion. There had been instances when the vampire's venom had been too toxic for the human's immune system, and they died from infection. In the vampire community, it was known as *the virus*. Kellan had been hoping that Aria was strong enough to fight it, especially since she's not an ordinary human being, but now he was worried, and there's nothing he can do but wait and see if she gets better or…

Another concern was related to the young man he'd killed. She was looking into the death of her friend, Kyle, and he didn't know if she would link him to it. It was another scenario he could only watch play out, and that didn't sit well with him. He was never one to sit on the sidelines. He had been a man of action when he was human, and that still rang true in his afterlife, such as it was.

Sixty-six

The Daughters of Bathory came together at 7:00 p.m. for their meeting, and when Gail approached the podium, a hush fell over the group.

"Good evening, sisters, we have much to do tonight, so let's get started. Alicia, I believe you have something to report," Gail said.

The M.E. stood and scanned the group before speaking. "Today I worked in the ER, and the girl, Aria, came in as a patient. At first, it appeared as if she was pregnant, but I'm able to say with confidence that she's not. She has an infection, though, and I was unable to identify the odd-looking strand. I'm going to do more lab work on the victims from the other night, to see if there are similarities."

"What if they also have the infection?" Betty asked.

Alicia's lip turned up in a slight grin. "Then the investigation begins. We find out if the vampire caused the infection or if they already had it, and that is how he chooses his victims."

"Why don't we just ask Jareth about it?" Rose questioned.

Alicia shot her a look of contempt—she wanted to be the one with the good ideas. "I want to see what the labs say first. I feel we have a limited number of favors from Jareth, so I don't want to use them up on something frivolous. The girl may just be sick."

"Maybe it has something to do with her Gypsy half," Gail suggested, and the others nodded in agreement.

Alicia made a tsking sound and suggested, "If we need to find that out, we can just have Jareth bring us a Gypsy"—her mouth turned up into a wicked smile—"We'll take a blood sample before he does."

The others chuckled at the innuendo.

"Shall we call Jareth forth to see what he's learned?" Betty asked.

"No," Gail answered, "tonight we're going to do some research on Kellan. There might be something we can use against him, and I want to find out what that is." She turned the projector on again which displayed his photo along with information she'd copied from the book. "Let's find out who this Gabriella is since she was the last to be seen with him."

She opened her laptop and brought up the browser in which she typed *Gabriella and Kellan Montcroix*. There wasn't much to go on, but there was a blurb that caught her interest. It spoke of the handsome couple being seen together at an elegant party two nights before their disappearance. It mentioned that he'd been a playboy before the mysterious beauty came into his life. Then it stated that Gabriella's last two loves had been found murdered, earning her the nickname, black widow.

Gail tapped the computer screen that was hooked up to the projector. "This has to be something. She must be the one who changed him."

"Then we should summon her tomorrow night," Alicia proposed, "Recent events may be of interest   to   her."

Sixty-seven

Aria sat on her bed and completed the assignments from her afternoon classes. Then she tried to organize her notes from the lectures, but she'd had a difficult time paying attention, and it showed on the papers in front of her.

She'd ducked Chris a couple of times, while on the way to class, and she could still recall the hurt expression he wore. She hated being in a position to suspect him of murder—if she still did. She had it narrowed down to him and Kellan.

But if it was Kellan, why didn't he bite him?

In any case, she intended to avoid both of them.

"Are you studying?" Cat asked from her bed where she had several text books laid out.

"I'm trying to," Aria admitted before putting her notes away and grabbing the library books out of the closet.

Cat looked confused. "Why do you have books in the closet?"

Aria looked down at the books she held while she thought up a lie. "I was tidying up earlier and just wanted them out of my way."

Cat cocked her head and furrowed her brows. "But your side is a mess."

Ugh, let it go already. "Chris stopped by to check up on me just as I was getting started."

"Oh, how did that go? Do you have another date planned?" Her lips turned up in a smirk, and she winked playfully.

"No, and I really wish you'd drop it. I'm not into him," Aria snapped.

Cat held her hands up in front of her in self-defense. "Sorry I asked. Why are you so touchy about it though?"

Aria gazed out the window and mentally counted to three before meeting her friend's stare. "Let me ask you this—how well do you know him?"

Cat closed the book she'd been studying from and shrugged her slender shoulders while biting her lower lip. "Um, I've known him for at least a year, but I can't say that I know him all that well. He's just always around when I'm talking to Todd and the others"—she looked down at her hands—"He's a nice guy though."

Aria considered her roommate's words carefully. "Have you ever seen him get aggressive like he did at the party?"

"Lord, no. He's always been calm and quiet up to that point," she answered with wide eyes. "I think that was just his gut reaction because he really likes you."

Aria looked away from her and fingered her amulet. "Hmm, I don't know."

"Is that why you don't want to go out with him again?" she pressed, "Because I think it's sweet."

Aria shook her head. "No, it's—" she stopped herself and looked out the window again. "complicated," she finished with a heavy sigh. "I'm going to go take a shower and then go to bed."

Twenty minutes later, Aria was tucked in under the covers with the door and window securely locked. She hoped she didn't have a visit from Kellan because she wasn't sure how to handle him if she did.

Kellan watched Aria get into bed, and then he circled the building to make sure the other vampire wasn't nearby. When he got to the front, though, the gargoyles were restless.

His heart pounded while he used his bird's-eye view to quickly scan the area. His eyes finally settled on a dark shape in the alley where he'd killed Kyle. He zeroed in on the vampire and saw him sniffing around.

He's picked up my scent, so I should go introduce myself.

He flew to the ground and shifted before slowly walking toward the alley where he locked eyes with the other vampire. The other was slightly smaller in stature, but he looked just as fierce—it was going to be a violent battle.

He approached in a slight crouch and growled, "Why are you here? Who are you?"

The vampire laughed in a deep throaty menacing way and snarled, "I think you know why I'm here, and not that it matters, my name is Jareth. I'll be the last person you see, and don't worry because I'll take good care of her."

Kellan lunged with his hands out to grab Jareth, but he was deflected and fell to the ground instead. Jareth sprang at him as he was getting back up, and they rolled around thrashing, snarling, and growling like a couple of starving wolves. Jareth bit Kellan in between his shoulder and neck causing blood to spill into the night. Kellan growled and yelped in pain before bucking Jareth off. He was on top now, and he delivered a crushing blow to Jareth's chin with his right hand while his left twisted the arm grabbing at his injured throat. Jareth bellowed in pain from the dislocated arm and injured jaw while delivering a forceful blow to Kellan's abdomen with his knee. There was a loud cracking sound, and Kellan wondered if he had broken ribs. He jumped to his left, dodging yet another punch.

The two vampires stood face to face and then ran full-force at each other. They lunged at the same time, and their bodies crashed into one another with a colossal strength that sounded like a clap of thunder and sent them both flying backward. They lunged again, and this time, Kellan's fangs sank into Jareth's shoulder. He ripped into the flesh with all his might, causing a rush of blood to splatter all over the grass while his hand pushed hard against Jareth's head. He heard the neck bones break and knew the battle was over. The body crumbled to the ground in nothing more than a pile of calcium dust.

Kellan ripped his shirt off and pressed it against his wound while walking toward Aria's dwelling. He sighed in relief. *She's safe—at least for tonight.* He still didn't know who had sent Jareth.

Sixty-eight
Tuesday

Aria woke up with chills and a pounding migraine. When she stood up to go to the bathroom, the room spun in circles around her.

"Whoa," she moaned and put her arms out to steady herself.

"How do you feel, or do I need to ask because you look like death warmed over?" Cat crossed the room and put her hand to Aria's forehead. "You are burning up, young lady. Let me go get the thermometer." She trotted to the bathroom and soon returned with the ear thermometer they shared. "Yep, just as I thought, it's 101.3," she announced. "I know you've missed a lot of classes lately, but you aren't going anywhere with this fever. I don't have a class this morning, so I'll go talk to your professors and get your assignments for you."

Tears sprang to Aria's eyes. "You'd do that for me? You're so sweet," she gushed.

"Well, I'm sure you'd do the same thing for me." A blush crept up the girl's cheeks.

Aria pretended to ponder the possibility, and she teased, "I will *now*."

Cat didn't miss a beat. "You bet your ass you will." After the giggling stopped, she turned back toward the bathroom and then returned with some pills and a small cup of water. "Here, take this Motrin. It should help bring your fever down, and don't forget to take your antibiotic. I'm going to get cleaned up, so write down your class schedule."

Aria was impressed by how together Cat was in a stressful situation. She was showing a nurturing instinct Aria hadn't witnessed before.

She did as she was told and wrote down her schedule for the day. Thankfully, she had picked up her other assignments yesterday, so she could get started on that this morning and not fall too far behind. Of course, the room needed to stop spinning first. She shuffled to the bathroom, did her business, and shuffled back to bed.

When Cat returned from her shower, she put a cold washcloth on Aria's forehead and fluffed her pillows.

"Are you sure you shouldn't be going into the nursing profession?" Aria quipped.

"I'll keep the option open as plan B," Cat smirked. "Is there anything else you need before I go, and do you want anything for breakfast? You must be hungry after yesterday."

"I'm not hungry, but I am thirsty if you want to bring me back a Sprite or 7-Up."

"Sure, I'll go get that now." She popped up off Aria's bed, grabbed some money out of her purse, and left for the vending machine in the lobby downstairs.

Aria's phone rang as soon as the door closed behind Cat. It was Chris calling. At first, she thought about ignoring it, but she didn't want him calling all day long, so she thought she'd get it over with.

"Hello?"

"Aria, I hope I didn't wake you, but I wanted to see if you would have breakfast with me. I don't like how we left things yesterday, and I want to fix it."

Aria rolled her eyes—she didn't want to deal with this right now. "I'm still sick this morning, so I'm not going anywhere. I need to get some rest."

"I'm sorry to hear that, hon. Let me bring you something then. I can get some toast or whatever you'd like." His voice had turned somewhat whiney at this point, and it was grating on her nerves. It wasn't pleasant like Kellan's deep masculine voice.

"I'll be all right, and I think Cat is bringing something back for me anyway," she explained just as her roommate got back.

Cat pointed to the phone and mouthed, "Chris?" Aria nodded in response, and then her roommate surprised her by grabbing the phone and speaking firmly to him, "Chris, she's sick and needs her rest. She'll call you when she's up to it. Bye." She handed the phone back along with a can of soda and winked. "And that's how you handle him."

Aria stared with her mouth gaping. "Wow. Look at you taking charge this morning. Thanks."

"Don't mention it. I'm off to see your instructors now"—she grabbed the list Aria had made—"I'll be back soon." She started to leave but then stopped herself and checked Aria's forehead first. With a smile, she claimed, "Better."

Aria looked down at the homework in her lap and then set it aside. She cracked open the library books on Gypsy magic instead and searched for healing spells. She found something on dandelion tea with elderberry.

"Okay great. Where do I find this stuff?" she said aloud. She doubted she'd find it on the shelves at the local Wal-Mart. She'd have to call Zelda, at a more reasonable hour, to find out where to find herbs and such for spells. She was also going to ask if there was a crystal or amulet to ward off illnesses because she hadn't seen any mentioned in the book.

She yawned and stretched her aching muscles out. Everything was hurting today, and she was extra tired. She decided to nap before she did anything else.

She started to dream right away. She was back home in Idaho in her bedroom, and the nightlight glowing softly from the corner was casting shadows across the floor. She looked around the room feeling confused about how she got there, and then she gasped when the rocker in the corner began to move. A shadowy shape started to advance toward her, and she clambered backward on her bed to get farther away from it.

"Hello again, my pet," a deep seductive voice called out to her. "I've missed you, and I've come here so we can be together."

"But how did you find me?" she squawked.

He laughed softly. "I'll always find you, Aria. You can't hide from me, not that I believe you want to."

"I do want to. You're a monster," she cried out.

He was right at the bed now, and before she could protest further, he was climbing into it.

He ran his hand up her leg as he braced himself over her. Then he leaned in and whispered against her ear, "You know you want me."

Aria cried out, "No," against his lips as they overpowered hers, but she felt the strength of her resolve weakening. She let him deepen the kiss, and she even responded to it by gently sucking on his firm, probing tongue.

Soon it was more than his tongue exploring her body—his hands were busy too. They ran up her waist and cupped her breasts while his thumbs rolled over her hardened points. Then he pulled her nightgown up over her head and had her completely naked for his greedy gaze.

"Your body is so beautiful, and it belongs to me," he growled sensuously, "And the things I intend to do to you, well…I'll let you be surprised." He grinned broadly, showing off his fangs.

Aria thrashed under his expert touch. His hands were working her into a heated frenzy as they moved over her satin flesh and made her crave the gratification she knew he could provide. Her thighs made the welcoming motion of slightly opening and then closing together, communicating her desire to have him slipping back and forth within the moisture and tightness there. He obliged her by running his hand over her treasured womanhood and probing her intimate furnace until she begged to have more of him inside her. He unfastened his pants, pulled her ankle up onto his shoulder and put the head of himself inside her.

"More," she pleaded, "I need more. I need all of you."

He chuckled lightly but gave her what she desired by sliding in every inch he had. She responded by bucking her hips wildly and digging her nails into his granite ass. She turned her head to expose her neck to him, but he went for her breast instead. As he bit into her warm flesh, though, she bit into him too—she sank her teeth into his shoulder and lapped up his salty blood.

Aria's eyes flew open and fluttered. She looked around her dorm room while her heart pounded, and her ragged breaths shook her frame. She glanced at the window and sighed in relief to see that the sun was still up.

Thank God it was just a dream, and he wasn't really here.

So why did the ache between her thighs make her wish that he was?

Sixty-nine

Kellan had been watching Aria through the window. He had seen her tossing and turning and heard the delicious moaning sounds she'd made. He wanted to be the cause of those sounds. He wanted to feel her thrashing beneath him. Last night, he didn't have time to go to her after his battle with Jareth because sunup was too close by. Tonight, though, wild bulls wouldn't be able to keep him away from her luscious charms.

He watched her while she read from her schoolbooks and took notes. He loved it when the tip of her tongue poked out and her forehead creased while she was deep in thought. He pulled his gaze away from her long enough to see her books on Gypsy magic lying on her nightstand, and it stung. He didn't want her delving into the craft because it would mean she was choosing that half of herself—the half he needed her to deny—and he'd thought their recent lovemaking had made a difference for her. He would have to woo her, but things had changed in the last four hundred years since he'd last courted someone, and he felt she was too special for traditional human methods of romance anyway. He didn't want to be compared to some ordinary boy she'd been with or who was trying to capture her interest now.

An idea came to him—he knew just what to do. He had something back in the cavern that he'd kept with him over the past four hundred years, and it was still in pristine condition. He had a rare blue diamond ring, the color of the ocean, that he would give to her as a token of his love— it was the ring he'd purchased for Gabriella.

Seventy

Aria nibbled on the toast that Cat had been sweet enough to bring her for dinner and sipped some hot tea to wash it down. Her fever had spiked to 102.0 now, so she took a second dose of Motrin and rewet the cold cloth for her forehead. She tried to concentrate on her homework assignments, but the words were blurry. She thought about taking another nap, but she was afraid she'd dream about Kellan again, so she turned the television on and was flipping through the channels when her phone rang. She thought it was Cat checking up on her, but it was Zelda.

"Hi, Zelda. How are you?" she croaked out in a weak voice.

"Hi, Aria. I'm just fine; however, I'm worried about you."

"Worried about me?" Aria sat up in alarm and used her finger to raise the volume on the phone. "Why would you be worried about me?"

"Let me explain," Zelda began calmly, "I'm worried because I had a dream about you, and it was very unsettling."

Aria's eyes opened in surprise. "Oh, I had one of those myself," she answered while a blush heated up her cheeks.

"Well, I want to discuss this with you but not over the phone. Can you come by, dear?"

Aria sighed. "I wish I could, but I'm sick. I have an infection and a fever that's getting worse, so I can't go anywhere."

"Oh, no of course you can't, so I'll come to you because it's important that we speak. I know you are at UCSF, but what building are you in?"

Aria drummed her fingers on her notebook. She didn't want to be talking to a ninety-two-year-old Gypsy and have her roommate walk in on it, but she couldn't think of a private place for them to talk. Her brain was too muddled.

"I'll meet you in the parking lot outside of your building, and we can talk in my car." It seemed as if Zelda had read her mind.

"That will work," she replied. "I'm in the second building as you pull into the campus. It's called Hudson Hall. Will you be coming now?"

"Yes, I'm headed out the door now, so I'll be there momentarily. You've seen my car, so just watch for me."

"Okay, I'll see you soon. Bye." Aria stared out the window after she hung up with Zelda. The sun was dipped low in the sky, so she knew that time was of the essence. It would have to be a quick talk, so that she could be back in her room with the door locked once it got dark. She didn't want to chance seeing Kellan again.

She quickly changed her clothes and combed the tangles out of her long dark waves before descending the stairs to the lobby and then the parking lot where she waited for the white Lincoln Town car. Fortunately, she didn't have to wait long.

Once Zelda got parked, Aria climbed in on the passenger side. She heard the doors lock, and it took her back to the night at the park when she'd tried to lock Kellan out of her car, but it didn't work. She didn't expect it to work now either, but she didn't say anything about it. Instead, she stared out the glass, scanning the area for anything out of place. The sun had inched farther away, and the first shades of darkness were blanketing the area. Chills ran up and down her spine as her mind played out the different ways this could go. Zelda must have noticed her unease because she reached out and placed a comforting hand on Aria's forearm.

"It's okay, dear. He's not going to hurt me, but if he tries, I can protect myself," Zelda assured her.

But who's going to protect me? Aria clasped her amulet with her free hand.

Zelda read her mind again. "Have you learned to use its power? Can you tap into it yet?"

Aria met her gaze and replied in a raspy voice, "I think I did a little bit—it started to glow again."

The Gypsy smiled warmly at the news. "That's good. It's a very special bond you have with it, and once you can see it clearly, you'll be able to tap into it full force. You just need to relax."

That's difficult to do after the other night. "Um, I have a question about the necklace," Aria began with some hesitation, "Isn't it supposed to be protecting me from"—she looked away and whispered—"him?"

Zelda looked away this time and wrung her bony hands. When her eyes found Aria's again, she informed her, "Our evil eyes are meant to protect us from evil, and you'll learn to control that power once you learn to control the amulet. Did he come to you again?"

Aria looked down at her lap and mumbled, "Yes, he came to me the other night." *He came. He saw. He conquered.*

Zelda pursed her lips into a thin pink line. "I see. Did he overpower you?"

Aria felt her neck and face grow hot from shame. "If you mean, did he seduce me, then the answer is yes. I let him have his way with me. That's why I ask about the amulet protecting me"—she looked down at the pretty stone— "Not only did I not stop him or try to get away, I wanted him. I wanted him to do the things he did, and that includes biting me. I asked him to bite me—why would I do that?" She looked over at the wise woman with tears in her eyes.

Zelda responded with a sympathetic smile and a soft expression. "It's not your fault, child. The power of seduction by a vampire isn't the same as by a mortal man—it's so much stronger. I don't know of any cases where the woman, or man for that matter, was able to resist the strength of it. And if the vampire falls in love, well then they become even more captivating to the object of their affection."

Aria narrowed her eyes at Zelda. "So, basically you're saying I'm screwed"—she looked away and lowered her voice—"literally and figuratively."

Zelda surprised her with laughter, and it made her jump. "Well, I suppose you could put it that way. Going back to your question about the amulet, your evil eye will protect you from harm, and since it didn't stop him the other night, I believe he doesn't mean you any—I think he's taken with you."

"Hmm, do you think he knows about my unique situation?"

"It's possible that he knows you are exceptional, but I'm not sure since it is a Gypsy legend. If he doesn't know now, though, he will learn of it when the time comes."

"To do battle you mean, right? He'll know about it when the time comes for us to battle." Aria felt butterflies in her stomach, and it wasn't the pleasant kind. It was more like when you have a surprise test thrown at you, and you haven't been studying.

Zelda put her hand on Aria's. "I know that worries you, but you'll be prepared."

"I believe you, but I'm still scared. I don't know how I can be a leader when this is all brand-new to me?" *And I don't know how I can face my lover when we are on opposite sides.*

"I understand," Zelda said with a nod. "But it's inside of you, and it will be there when you need it the most. Now, I came here because I had a dream about you. I dreamed that you were bound with rope and surrounded by a ring of fire."

Aria's eyes went wide, and her mouth fell open. "That sounds horrible. What does it mean?"

"You know, I wasn't quite sure, so that's why I wanted to speak to you, to see what has been happening. Now, based on what you've told me, I think I know what it means. The rope represents a struggle you are going through, while the fire may represent a fear of no escape. Elements are tricky, though, when they appear in dreams. They can often mean more than one thing, so I'm not positive about that part. The struggle, however, is clearly the relationship between you and the vampire. I believe you are fighting with your feelings."

Aria fidgeted in her seat. "Then what am I supposed to do? If there are feelings, how do I stop them?"

Zelda tilted her head and sighed while offering a slight smile. "You are half-Gypsy and half-vampire, but you are a woman too. Sometimes we cannot control our feelings—the heart wants what the heart wants."

"So, what if in the end, my heart wants him? What do I do about that? How do I stop it?"

Zelda opened her arms with a gentle shrug. "Magic or no, love always finds a way. Love is, after all, the most powerful magic there is."

The night had come, and with those wise words, Aria slinked back to her room and locked the door. Maybe logic and reason were forgotten when love was involved. Maybe it was a force she couldn't fight and win, but she vowed to herself to try. She vowed to use the knowledge from her ancestors combined with the power inside her to deny her heart.

Seventy-one

Kellan had been ready to go to the cavern to wait until nightfall, so that he could bring Aria the ring, when he saw her get into an old woman's car, and his plans changed. Instead, the cat crept outside the car to listen in on the conversation, and the information gathered was priceless.

He'd seen the evil eye on the woman, so he knew she was a Gypsy, and as he got closer, he could sense that she was a powerful one too. He could feel the force of her talisman trying to push him away even without the woman knowing he was there.

She must be Aria's mentor then, and where there is one, there will be others. I must make my move before they surround her and put an end to her emotional conflict.

He'd overheard Aria talk about stopping her feelings from developing, but he'd also overheard the older Gypsy telling her that love always finds a way, so he was confused.

Is she encouraging Aria to be with me?

He certainly hoped that was the case. If her mentor was reassuring her to follow her heart, then he only needed to make sure that her heart leads her to him. He needed to prove himself to her, so with that in mind, he flew to the cavern to fetch the ring after Aria went back inside the building. He would take it to her tonight and then spend the entire night with her in his arms. He would make his intentions and feelings clear and, hopefully, coax her to choose him over her heritage.

Seventy-two

The Daughters of Bathory came together earlier than usual that evening, and as soon as everyone sat down, Gail hushed their chatter.

"Shh," she scolded, "my son, Chris, is home from school while they fix a burst pipe in his dorm. He just thinks we're playing pinochle, so we'll have to conduct ourselves in a quiet manner." The ladies looked around at each other and then nodded in understanding. "Good. Now, Alicia, please tell us your news."

All eyes fell on the M.E. while she shuffled some papers around in front of her.

"I was able to compare Aria's blood to that of the victims in the morgue. They had been mostly drained, mind you, but there was enough blood to test, and the test results came back similar. They, too, had the strand of infection that Aria has."

The ladies began to all talk at once, causing Gail to shush them again.

Betty raised her hand and then proceeded to ask, "So, we can assume that the girl's infection came from the vampire, but what does that mean? Is that how humans are turned? Will we also be infected and get sick when Jareth bites us?"

"Remember that it can also be how the vampires choose their victims. Maybe they already had an infection," Rose mentioned. "Furthermore, was it Jareth who bit them or Kellan?"

Gail held one hand up before they all started talking at once again. "The only way to find out is if we ask Jareth, as we previously discussed, so let's bring him forth and get our answers."

The women got their spells out and began the chant. Then they looked around the room and at each other while they waited for some sign of his presence. Nothing happened, though, so they tried the chant once more. Again, nothing happened.

"What's going on?" Alicia asked aloud.

"I think something must've happened to him," Gail responded. "Let's try the spell without his name and see what happens."

They performed the original invoking spell, and this time there was a swirl of mist and smoke.

"Who summons me?" a deep masculine voice growled.

Gail announced on their behalf, "We are the Daughters of Bathory, and we are seeking our brethren. Might we ask your name, brother?"

The well-sculpted vampire, with eyes that threw daggers, sized them up one by one before telling them, "My name is Mikel, and you have some nerve calling yourselves my sisters, but I like it. I like your moxy. Now tell me why you are seeking your brothers."

Gail quietly explained everything about Kellan, Aria, and even Jareth.

Mikel looked amused when she finished her explanation. "So, you think this girl is the chosen one, the half-breed, but what proof do you have?"

Gail raised her chin haughtily and explained, "I've met her on two occasions, and I can sense it within her. Additionally, she has been doing research on Gypsy magic, and according to the library records, vampires. She is especially interested in one vampire—Kellan Montcroix." She could see a look of recognition cross Mikel's face at the mention of the name, so she stopped.

"Kellan has surfaced here? Hmm, that is indeed of interest to me," he said with a big grin that showed off his fangs. "I've been hoping to cross paths with him again one day"—he stared hard at Gail—"So do you want the girl then? Shall I bring the coveted one to you?"

Gail smiled just as evilly as he had. "Yes, bring her to us. We can sacrifice her to Elizabeth Bathory."

Mikel rubbed his chin, which was square and had a dimple in the center. "Hmm, I'm not sure I want you to do that. I want her to be fully turned as much as I'm sure my friend Kellan does—but for a different reason," he stated cryptically.

"So, you won't bring her forth then?" Betty worked up the nerve to ask.

"I'm not making any promises, except that I'll deal with her"—he paced the room slowly—"I may want to play with her first. Now, I'm hungry, so either I'm going to dine on one of you, or I must bid you adieu for now." He bowed to them in a grand gesture before disappearing into the night.

The ladies got up from the table and said their farewells too. What none of them knew was that Chris had been listening through the vent upstairs long enough to realize two things: they were in some kind of cult, and they planned to hurt Aria.

Seventy-three

With the ring in his pocket, Kellan stood outside of Aria's building and looked up at her window. He knew she was in her room because he'd flown past it first while carrying the ring in his talons. He saw her lying on her bed with her nose in some books again. He wondered if she was studying her craft. He also wondered how he was going to get her outside. While it hadn't worked the first time he'd tried it, he decided to use a summoning spell again. Maybe the bond he'd been forming with her, through his bites, would make the necessary difference.

He chanted, "Vin la mine şi să îmbrăţişeze destinul tău nou." *Come to me and embrace your new destiny.* Then, with hope in his heart, he waited.

Aria wasn't sure what drew her to the window, but she found herself putting her books down to look out it. There he was staring up at her—Kellan. She felt the corner of her mouth turn up slightly when he blew her a kiss. She turned her head to try to look away, but she was drawn back in by his seductive smile. While she stared at him, completely hypnotized, she felt a yearning in her abdomen. She felt herself craving his touch—his lips, his hands, his tongue, and his pulsing length. She felt an absolute need that she knew he could fill if she'd let him. She turned away from the window, ran her fingers through her hair to fluff it up, wet her lips, and went downstairs. She would still deny her heart, but she wouldn't deny her womanly desires.

Kellan walked around to the front of the building when Aria had disappeared from the window. His heart pounded with anticipation, and he could feel the blood rushing to his groin as he thought about the feel of her warm flesh pressed against him. He still had to impregnate her to complete her conversion, and it was best if it could be done with her love and trust.

Aria opened the front door and found Kellan standing at the foot of the steps. At first, she just stared, but then she felt a magnetic pull toward him—it was like watching herself in a dream. He was a puppeteer, and she was on the strings he controlled. She found herself rushing down the steps to stand before him, and she suddenly felt shy—she was small and meek next to his sizeable frame. Out of the corner of her eye, she noticed her amulet glowing, but it didn't scare her. She didn't feel it doing anything to ward him off, and she realized that she didn't want it to. She wanted to experience the mind-blowing pleasure again.

"Good evening," he greeted her, "I'm glad you came to me." He leaned in to kiss her, but she backed away.

"Wait"—she held her hand up in front of her—"I shouldn't be doing this. This isn't right. This isn't natural."

Kellan chuckled softly before grabbing her firmly by the forearm and yanking her into his hard body. He snaked his other arm around her waist and squeezed, while she squirmed to get away.

"Giving in to your body's desires is perfectly natural, and you know it's what you want," he whispered against her creamy neck before planting a couple of kisses where he could feel her heart beating rapidly.

Aria pushed against his brawny chest. "That doesn't make it right."

He stopped kissing her long enough to gaze into her eyes. "Is your evil eye warding me off? Is it protecting you from me? Does it tell you that I'm here to hurt you?"

She stopped struggling and looked down at her shoes. "How do you know about all of that?"

He chuckled again. "I've been undead for four hundred years now—I know a lot of things." Then he lowered his voice, so it was even more seductive. "I know when a woman wants me."

Aria felt a mixture of emotions at that moment. One of them was fear that someone would see them standing outside together. Cat had called and said that she probably wouldn't be back tonight—she was out with Todd—so Aria felt it was safe to take him upstairs, and against her better judgement, she did.

As soon as the door closed behind him, he advanced toward her with a lustful gaze, but then he suddenly stopped and stared with a questioning look. "Are you okay, Aria? You look peaked."

"I've been a little ill," she admitted.

"Aye, I know, but aren't you getting better with your medicine?"

She looked at him with wide eyes and backed up. "What do you mean you know? How do you know?"

Kellan wanted to tell her everything, and this was a good opening. *Here goes…* "I maintain a watchful eye on you, and I overheard your conversation with your roommate"—he saw the fear register on her face—"I keep watch so I can protect you."

Aria swallowed hard, and she was fairly certain he could hear the gulp. "From what?" she asked softly.

He saw her trembling, and it made him feel bad. He didn't want to frighten her, but he needed to keep her safe. "Not from what but rather whom—"

"You killed Kyle," she interrupted with her accusation.

Kellan waved it off like it was no big deal, though. "I'm not talking about that punk. I'm talking about something ominous and malevolent. I'm talking about the incursion of vampires."

Aria wet her lips and clenched her shaking hands into fists. Her legs began to wobble on her, and the room started to spin again. "You know about the battle? You know who I am, what I am?"

"Aye, I know, and I'm going to do everything I can to protect you."

She looked at him quizzically with a hard stare. "What can you possibly do to protect me, and why would you want to? What is your part in all of this?" She clenched her necklace to use its strength.

"There was another here, and he was after you, but I took care of him the other evening when I didn't come to you."

Her mouth dropped open, and she felt the moisture gathering in her ice-blue eyes. He stepped closer to her, pulled a handkerchief from his breast pocket, and gently dabbed the tears away for her.

"What else?" she asked when she could find her voice.

Now was the time, he decided. He reached into his pocket and pulled out the beautiful blue diamond ring while kneeling before her. "I make you mine for all eternity," he said as he held up the ring, "No other can come near you, or it would break the code." He waited expectantly while she gaped at the sparkling diamond. Multiple expressions crossed her face.

Aria's arms flew up in the air. "Are you insane? Are you drunk on the blood of a crazy person? I can't marry a vampire!" She began to pace the room with her arms still flailing and her hands balled into fists.

"It's not the same thing as marriage. It's a stronger connection than what marriage provides. It's a commitment to being life mates. It's an eternal and unbreakable bond of love," he explained while following her around the room.

"Love? Who said that I love you? How can I love a vampire?" she yelled and waved her fist at him. "It was sex. We had sex. You kill people for their blood. I can never love something that does that."

Kellan shook his head. He was beginning to taste defeat, and it unsettled his stomach. "You are half-vampire. The call for blood is in you too—your body has always just suppressed it. As for me, you knew what I was when you pleaded for me to pleasure you, and I know it wasn't just sex. I know you feel something even if you mean to deny your heart. I know that you are conflicted, and I'm trying to help you with that."

He could tell she wasn't convinced yet by the way she was looking at him. "Also, after I tasted you the other night, I was sustained—I didn't need to kill. I think I can live on the strength of your blood because you're a magical being. I'm certainly willing to try."

She shook her head. "God, you're giving me a migraine," she grumbled while she rubbed her temples. "I simply can't deal with this"—she opened her eyes and looked into his worried ones—"I can't handle what you're telling me. Just because my father was a vampire, it doesn't mean I intend to become one, no matter how I feel. I refuse to confuse lust with love. Now, I need my rest because, as I said, I'm sick. Please leave."

Kellan closed his eyes and bowed his head. "I will go, but just know that I'm not giving up on you." He put the ring back in his pocket and walked to the window. Before he opened it and shifted into a crow to fly away in pain, though, he turned to her. "I love you, Aria. It burns bright like the sun, and it will cover you like the stars."

She shook her head again. "I believe in the sun, and I believe in the stars, but I don't believe in humans marrying vampires."

Kellan nodded and turned back to the window. He flipped the lock and thrust the window up with a force that made the glass rattle.

"Wait!" she called out to him, and he turned to her with hope in his sky-blue eyes. She almost didn't want to dash it—she didn't want to put the light out, but she told herself to be practical. She held her wrist out to him. "I don't want you to kill anyone tonight, if you haven't already, so go ahead. Bite me."

Kellan took her slender arm into his while staring into her heavenly face. Her request made him love her even more, while it also made him sad to be what he was. He pressed her fair wrist to his lips and, as gently as possible, he bit into it. The flavor of vanilla and honey flooded his senses as the warm liquid filled his mouth. He drank only a little before lapping at the wound to stop the blood flow.

"Thank you," he whispered huskily.

Aria simply nodded once with her tear-filled eyes shut. The drops ran down her cheeks in little rivulets, and she sniffled. Part of it was from the pain, but it was mostly from the restlessness within her heart. Then she felt cold metal being pressed into her palm, so she opened her eyes up—it was the gorgeous ring he'd offered her. She looked up at him with both confusion and aggravation.

"I said no," she whispered on a shaky breath.

"I know, but I want you to hold onto this, though, for when you'll say yes because, in my heart, you already have." He pulled her wrist back up to his mouth for a soft kiss. Then, before her bewildered eyes, he shifted and flew out the window.

Aria stared, unable to believe what she had just witnessed. The power he had was amazing. She looked down at the breathtaking

ring in her hand and closed her eyes tightly. The
power he had over her was…inconceivable.

Seventy-four
Wednesday

Aria woke up early on Wednesday with a ringing in her ears and a lurching stomach that had her beelining for the bathroom. She had to shove past Cat, who was brushing her hair, to make it to the toilet in time to retch up what little bit of undigested food remained in her stomach.

"Ugh," Cat groaned, "I'll leave you two alone." The color drained from her face and was replaced with a look of disgust as she dashed from the room. She came back in, though, when Aria was rinsing her mouth and said, "I can't believe you aren't feeling any better yet. You know"—she winked—"since there isn't a bun in the oven." She laughed but stopped and threw her hands up in self-defense when Aria shot her a threatening glare. "Too fresh?"

"Yes, but I know what you mean. I'm going back to see the doctor today. She said she wanted to do more blood tests anyway," she groaned with a wince. She didn't relish the idea of another needle prick.

But last night I volunteered for a bite? The irony was almost laughable.

Aria felt dreadful as she looked in the mirror at her sallow face. Her cheeks were hollowed out, and dark circles were formed under her sunken eyes.

Cat caught her staring at her reflection and claimed in a sultry movie star voice, "Darling, you look beautiful."

Aria tried to scowl but ended up laughing at her silly friend instead. Playing along, she told her, "Thank you, darling," and blew her a dramatic kiss.

Cat leaned against the door frame and put the back of her hand against her forehead. "Excuse me, but I must go to my people," she drawled and giggled. Then, in her regular voice, she explained, "I have to go to class. You get your rest, and I'll get your assignments when I have free time later. Text me what the doctor says."

Aria gave her friend a weak smile. "I will. Thanks again, sweetie."

"You bet." Cat grabbed her purse and slung her bookbag over her right shoulder, causing her thick blonde hair to whip around from the left side. She brushed it back with her fingers then waved good-bye.

Aria brushed her teeth with as much strength as she could muster, then climbed back into bed. She quickly drifted off and found herself dreaming about being in the park again.

It was still foggy as she spun around in circles, straining to see her surroundings while the mist clung to her like a shroud. Her legs felt like weights as she tried to walk forth in the muddled darkness. Then there was a hushed noise and the furtive movement of black against the white.

Mixed emotions swirled inside her, much like the fog was around her, as she watched Kellan approach. Part of her, much larger than she would've liked, wanted to run to him, yank his clothes off along with her own, and let him ravish her. Her small inner voice was telling her to run like wildfire, but her mounting passion was doing its best to mute it. She could already feel her damp panties clinging to her soft flesh.

The shape emerged, and all the desire inside her was sucked out and replaced by fear—it wasn't Kellan, but he had fangs that were just as sharp. She turned to run, but the fog coiled around her legs while the night whispered secret terrors. She felt a wisp of her hair move over her shoulder, and since there was no breeze, she could only assume he'd moved it. Then she felt his icy fingertips as they glided down her neck, no longer hidden by the hair, and a cold terror gripped her in its frozen grasp.

She opened her mouth to scream, but only a guttural sound emerged, and she felt herself choked off from breath as he snaked his bony arms around her torso. Despair gripped her heart and squeezed it so hard that she thought it might burst.

"You know what's about to happen, don't you?" he taunted in a hiss.

Aria couldn't even nod—she was completely paralyzed by the terror enveloping her in its clutches.

"And he thought he could save you," the malicious voice whispered against her neck. He was getting closer. She could feel the saliva dripping from his fangs as they drew near. She could almost feel the sting...

Aria's eyes flew open, and she drew in jagged breaths while her hands clutched the damp bedding. Her heart was pounding so loudly that she thought her eardrums might burst. Of the nightmares she'd had before, this one was certainly the most nightmarish, and she knew it was because it could come true. Kellan said he'd killed the vampire he caught coming after her, but she knew it wasn't the only one. The battle hadn't even begun yet.

With the battle on her mind now, she forced herself out of bed to grab her books on Gypsy magic—she had a lot of studying to do. She reached toward the nightstand to grab her pencil for taking notes and heard a slight clinking sound. She looked down at the floor to see what she'd knocked off and saw the blue diamond ring Kellan had offered to her. She picked it up and turned it over in her hands. It was exquisite and unlike any kind of ring she'd seen advertised before. The perfect blue diamond was pear shaped and nestled between two smaller marquise-cut white diamonds, and it had an intricate gold filigree band. It was so delicate, yet it seemed to fill the room with its brilliance. There was something special about holding it, so she slipped it on her left ring finger. Her fingers were long and slender, so it came as a surprise when the ring wasn't too big, as they usually were. Instead, it was a perfect fit—like it had been made just for her.

She walked to the window and held her hand up so the sunlight could catch the stones, and little dots of light were reflected throughout the room. The brilliant flashes of color playing before her eyes took her breath away.

She reached with her other hand to take it off, so she could put it in her jewelry box until a night when she could give it back to him, but when her fingers grazed it, she stopped and stared at it some more. She rolled her finger side to side, bedazzled by the sparkles, and decided she couldn't take it off—it was tugging too hard at her heartstrings.

She went into the bathroom and used the ear thermometer, which read 100.3 on the display—her fever was going down despite how poorly she'd felt when she first woke up. She realized, too, that her stomach wasn't as upset.

Good, maybe the antibiotic is finally kicking in, and I won't need that second blood test. She decided to wait until tomorrow to see if she still needed to go to the doctor.

She also decided to go see Zelda since she was feeling better.

Seventy-five

Kellan smiled on the inside as he watched Aria admiring the ring on her finger. He sat, as a squirrel this time, on the tree branch outside her window and fell in love all over again. The ring was perfect for her in every way imaginable.

When she'd slipped it on, a rosy pink flush had illuminated her cheeks, and her soft smile brightened the room, almost causing him to fall out of the tree from excitement.

Is she accepting my proposal?

He looked up at the sun and wished he had the power to pull it down—he couldn't wait to hold his mate in his arms.

He watched her as she brushed her lush dark hair with slow, deliberate strokes before gently tousling it with her hands, making it spill forth over her shoulders in cascading waves. Then he watched as she put on some makeup, and he wondered why she thought she even needed it. After putting on her lipstick, she looked down at her hand and smiled, and Kellan thought his heart might burst from love.

He saw her get her purse and head out, so he shifted into a crow and flew around to the front of the building to watch her. In his happy-go-lucky state, though, he failed to notice the eyes on the gargoyles moving side to side.

Seventy-six

While on the way to see Zelda, Aria kept looking at the ring she wore on her left hand. She considered taking it off, so Zelda wouldn't see it, but then she decided that keeping secrets from the Gypsy was probably not a good idea—especially a secret this large. It would, after all, affect the clans too if she married, or became a life mate of, a vampire.

She was still thinking about the situation when her phone rang and startled her. She saw on the display that it was Chris again, and that reminded her that she hadn't returned his last two calls, so she answered the phone now.

"Hi, Chris. I'm sorry I didn't call you back yesterday, but I fell asleep, and then I was studying," she explained before he got a word in.

"Hi, beautiful, I was worried about you. How are you feeling now?"

"I'm feeling better today and thanks for asking. I'm driving now, though, so I shouldn't be on the phone," she said trying to excuse herself out of talking to him.

Disappointment filled his voice. "Okay, well, I'd like to talk to you later. It's kind of important."

"Oh, um, I'll call you back when I'm done with my errands," she offered, "Unless you want to tell me now."

"No, it can wait, I think, but please be careful."

She laughed at his warning—he had no idea of what she had to worry about. She quickly flashed back to her dream, and shivers ran down her spine.

"I'll be careful," she assured him, "bye."

She hung up just as she pulled into Zelda's driveway, and the woman must've seen her because she was opening the front door as Aria exited her car.

She waved as she called out, "Come inside, Aria. It's nice of you to drop by."

"Hi, Zelda. I was hoping we could do some training today," she replied while walking into the house. "I'm feeling better, and I want to get a jump on things before something gets a jump on me."

Zelda's eyes narrowed a bit, and she cocked her head. "I'm going to need you to explain that last part, please. Would you like some tea?"

Aria's lip turned down, and she raised her brows. "We might need something stronger than tea today."

Zelda appeared amused at first, but when she saw that Aria's expression wasn't changing, hers did. She grew grave with concern and motioned for Aria to sit on the beige sofa, forgetting about the refreshments.

"What troubles you today, Aria?" Zelda assessed her from head to toe and then back up again until her eyes settled on Aria's new ring. She reached out and gently touched it with her fingertips, and a knowing expression crossed her aged features. "Is this from him? Did he give you this as a token of his love?"

The other woman's intuition surprised Aria. "Yes, but how did you know?" She watched Zelda's eyes while she stared at the ring—there was a twinkle of wisdom in them, and something about it made Aria feel happy. It looked a little like approval from the Gypsy.

She tapped her finger to her temple and smiled back at Aria. "Madame Gabor sees all and knows all." After the laughter stopped, she confessed, "I knew he was falling in love with you, and that exquisite ring looks like it came from another time and place. I've never seen anything like it in all my years, and you know that's a long time."

Aria giggled at her friend's reference to her age and looked down at her exquisite jewelry. "I wonder when he got it then, since you think it's old, and why he still has it"—she looked up at Zelda—"I mean, he's been a vampire since the sixteen hundreds, so why does he want me? Why hasn't he already married—or as he calls it, mated—off? I wonder whatever happened to Gabriella."

Zelda opened her hands and shrugged. "You'll have to ask him those questions. I can only imagine that he's been waiting for the ever-elusive true love that most seek to find. Something about you, my guess is your coveted status, drew him in, and I'm willing to bet he's not going to give up on you."

Aria sighed heavily and looked upward toward the ceiling. "That's what I'm afraid of, and that brings me to my problem. What do I do? Please guide me."

Zelda's soft smile wavered, and worry clouded her wrinkled features. She reached out and touched the back of Aria's hand. "I'm afraid that only your heart can guide you. I could say that you shouldn't be with him because of what he is, but you are half-vampire, so that may not be the right answer. Maybe this is your destiny. Maybe he is your future."

Aria rubbed her temples and groaned. "This is too big of a decision. I don't want the responsibility of it."

Zelda wrapped an arm around her and squeezed. "If you recall your reading, I told you that you are a warrior and would be able to handle everything that is going on in your life. Well, my dear, that still rings true. You can handle this also. It's all a part of your destiny—you were born for this. Both of your parents were strong, even though they were on opposite sides of the good versus evil spectrum, and that makes you innately strong too." She still saw doubt on the girl's face. "Aria, I believe in you, and I believe you will find a way to accomplish what you desire, both with your mind and your heart."

Aria perked up a little. "Do you really think I can have it both ways? I mean, I don't see how that would work, but do you?"

Zelda nodded slowly. "I think that if there is a way, it will reveal itself to you and your vampire in time."

Aria got up from the sofa and slowly paced the room. She didn't know if she could trust her heart to make the decision that her mind should be making. She looked up at the ceiling, ran a hand through her long hair, and decided that she needed to get her mind off it by throwing herself into her magic. Nature would have to take its course in the matter of Kellan.

"Changing the subject, what comes next in my training?" she asked with enthusiasm. "I think I should focus my energy on that right now."

"Well, young lady, I think it's a good time to find out what your powers are."

Aria picked up her pace as she continued to move around the room, and her excitement about the possibility of possessing a magical ability bubbled over. "Are you saying that there is more than the evil eye? I thought I'd just be learning more about how to use it."

Zelda chuckled at her naivety and opened a drawer on her end table. "I found this old book of mine that I'd forgotten about, and I discovered something in there that might help us. We need to go to the shop, though, because we'll need some things that are there." She stood and grabbed her handbag while Aria walked to the door and held it open for her.

"I can't wait to see what comes next," she exclaimed exuberantly. "I'm anxious to prepare myself because, according to Kellan, there was another vampire, and he thought it was coming after me."

Zelda turned paler than she usually was, and her hand flew to her amulet. "Oh, no," she gasped, "it can't be starting already"—her worry-filled eyes met Aria's—"Time is of the essence now, so we mustn't delay. After we figure your powers out, we must go before the council and reveal all to them."

Aria's excitement over learning more magic was replaced with dread as she thought about the battle to come and the distinct possibility that she'd have to fight Kellan—the one she may have been born to love.

Seventy-seven

While on the way to Zelda's shop, a news broadcast interrupted their conversation. The reporter explained that there had been another ghastly murder in the San Francisco area involving exsanguination, and authorities were imposing a curfew for the local high school and college students. All students, who aren't working, are expected to be in their homes by 8:00 p.m., and all athletic events were canceled until further notice.

"8:00 isn't early enough," Aria mumbled under her breath, "It's dark before then."

Zelda heaved a sigh. "I know, but what can we do? We certainly can't tell the authorities what is really going on. We can't tell them what we know."

Aria quickly glanced at her before looking back at the road. "I failed to mention earlier that Kellan claims he killed the vampire that was coming after me. He also said that if he drinks my blood, he isn't hungry anymore and, therefore, doesn't kill. If that's true, there must be another one that has come because Kellan drank from me last night. I told him to bite me, so he wouldn't kill."

Zelda nodded her head and spoke in a respectful tone. "That's interesting that your blood sustains him, and that's admirable of you to offer it up. As for the possibility of another vampire in the area, that doesn't surprise me—

there will be more coming. They, too, are going to be preparing for the battle."

Aria parked on the street in front of Zelda's shop, and they bustled to get inside. Zelda locked the door behind Aria and ushered her to the back of the room before closing the black curtain.

"So, what did the book say to do exactly?" Aria inquired as Zelda set her crystal ball and a lit candle on the table. "How do we find out what I'm capable of?"

Zelda smiled secretively and winked. "Anxious?" she teased.

"Ugh, you know I am," Aria cried out and rubbed her hands together.

"Well, all right then. Let's get to it, shall we? Remove your amulet and swing it west to east over the crystal ball." Zelda removed her own amulet as well and began to swing it north to south over Aria's.

"What are we doing exactly?" Aria asked.

Zelda closed her eyes to concentrate but answered, "We are calling the four corners, which is typically used in witchcraft but can also be used in Gypsy magic. Just continue to sway the amulet, and allow it to connect with mine."

Aria did as she was instructed, and before long, there was a whoosh of air that made the candle flicker.

"We are connected. I can feel it, can you?" Zelda asked as her eyes flew open.

Aria did feel something—she felt a strange surge of energy flowing through her. "Yes, I can feel it. I feel invigorated."

"Close your eyes while you continue to swing the amulet. Search your mind's eye and see the sun rising and falling. Do this over and over to reveal your true self. See the sun and then the moon. See the cycle that allows for life"—she watched Aria's face as she did what she was told, and she looked into her crystal ball—"I see something. It's becoming clearer to me, so keep concentrating."

Aria pictured the sun rising and opening the flowers, and then she saw the moon rising and moving the tides. She pictured this repeatedly while her arm grew tired from the swaying of her amulet—she hoped she could stop soon.

In an excited whisper, Zelda informed her, "I see lightning with gusty winds, and I can see blazes of fire licking the sky. Aria, you can open your eyes and stop the pendulum. I believe I know what your power is, so let's test my theory."

Aria cocked her head and stared at the Gypsy, filled with expectation. "What do you think it is?"

Zelda smiled in her secretive way again. "Before I say for certain, I want you to put your amulet back on, clasp it, and try to picture the storm I saw. Imagine the lightning and winds and envision what the thunder sounds like. Put yourself there in the middle of it."

Aria clasped the cold stone and closed her eyes. She pictured the last thunderstorm she'd seen, and she could vividly remember the wind making the trees bow and lightning streaking the gray sky. She could even recall the rumble of thunder shaking the windows—she could hear it perfectly.

"Aria, open your eyes," she heard Zelda whisper softly yet sternly. "Now look out the window."

Aria looked outside, still recalling the sound of thunder, and she couldn't believe her eyes. The sky had been only slightly overcast when they'd arrived at the shop, but now it was black, and rain was pelting the window and running down it in streaks. Thunder rattled the walls with its fierce boom and made Aria jump with a nervous excitement. She looked at Zelda and studied her joyful face.

"Did I do that?" she managed to squawk out while she flapped her hands in excitement. "Did I cause the storm?"

Zelda smiled peacefully. "I think you know the answer already."

Aria paced the room but kept her eyes on the window and the tumultuous storm outside. Then she turned back to Zelda full of muddled thoughts.

"I don't want to look a gift horse in the mouth, but what good will it do me? I'm sure farmers will be glad I can make it rain, but how will it help me in battle?"

Zelda tilted her head and thoughtfully nodded. "I understand your confusion—you are failing to see the bigger picture here. Try something else for me. I want you to focus, like before, but this time look at the candle and imagine the flame growing bigger and bolder. Imagine the fire burning bright enough to light up the room."

Aria stared at the wisp of a flicker and tried to imagine it being ten times its size. At first, nothing happened, but then something amazing took place—it grew. It became strong and steady as she held her stare on it, and the shadows in the corners of the room were lit up, taking away their mystery.

Aria made a gasping noise that echoed off the walls, while Zelda clasped her hands in glee and twirled around, making a whooping sound of joy as she did so.

"This is so exciting!" she cried out and looked at Aria with wild eyes. "Do you know what this means?—she reached out and took her by both wrists—"It means you have the power to control the elements."

Aria nervously bit her lip, pulled away from Zelda's grasp, and paced the room again. "As I said, I don't want to seem ungrateful, and it is a neat power to have I suppose, but what good will it do me in battle? How is this supposed to help any of us?"

Zelda stopped her from pacing by placing a firm hand on her arm. "I understand your skepticism, but I don't think you would have been given the gift unless it was meant to serve you. I'm not sure in what way that will be, but I know it will come to you when you need it. That is the way of Gypsy magic, Aria—it's there to protect us."

Aria wrung her hands and looked out the window again—she saw that the storm had let up.

"The rain is ending, so does that mean my power is limited? Is there an expiration time on it?"

Zelda chuckled at her choice of words. "I think, my dear, that it's because you moved your focus away from it. I wouldn't worry about the strength of your powers—you are the coveted one after all. Now, I think it's best I get home. My son is bringing my grandchildren over tonight, so I need to do some baking." Her face lit up at the mention of her family members, and it made Aria miss her folks.

"I think maybe I should go back home for a couple of days before the battle," she thought aloud as they exited the shop, and fear knotted inside her. "Would that be okay?"

Zelda ran her tongue over her dry lips and averted Aria's gaze. Her own fear and anxiety mingled hot in her throat.

"I'm not sure what to tell you, Aria. You have a lot of training to do, you need to meet the council, and we have no idea when the battle will begin or what kind of evil will be surfacing in the meantime. I hate to say it, but I think it is the wrong time to travel."

Aria's voice was thick with regret as she claimed, "I wish I hadn't left a day early when I went home recently. I wish I'd told them what amazing parents they are."

"I'm sure they know, darling, and I'm sure they feel the same way about you."

They drove back to Zelda's house and talked about her powers and the High Council. Neither of them had foreseen the evil lying in wait at her dorm.

Seventy-eight

The sky had cleared up, since the unexpected thunderstorm, and was a beautiful shade of orange and pink when Aria got back to the campus. She found herself strolling across the wet, beaten down grass and staring up at the heavens with a pleasant smile on her face when she suddenly heard her name called out—it was Chris, and he was running toward her. He'd phoned twice, while she was on her way back to school, but she'd ignored both calls. There was no ignoring him now, though.

Chris leaned over with his hands on his knees to catch his breath. "Aria, I've been trying to get in touch with you," he puffed. "I was worried about you when you didn't answer the phone or call me back." He shot her a questioning glance filled with hurt.

Aria felt a blush creeping up her neck, and she avoided his stare. "I'm sorry, but I was busy, and then I forgot to call you back," she lied. "I just now got back to campus."

He forced a slight smile and patted her upper arm. "Well, I'm glad to see that you're all right, but can we go somewhere private to talk?" he asked while looking around for eavesdroppers.

Aria pointed to a spot over his shoulder and told him, "Let's go over there to that bench."

Once they sat down, he nervously cleared his throat and looked down at his folded hands in his lap. "Aria," he hesitated, "I don't know how to begin or exactly what I should say."

She quickly held up a hand and said, "Chris, I think I know what you want to talk about"—she subconsciously touched her ring with her right hand—"I think that you want us to be more than friends, and we can't be." She looked up into his blank stare and brushed her hair back from her cheek. "I'm already involved with someone." She paused for his reaction.

"Well, that's good to know, but it isn't what I wanted to talk about. But since you brought it up, I must ask something. Were you involved with someone when you went on dates with me?"

Aria saw pain cross his face while he struggled to get the question out, and it made her feel terrible. She'd never intended for him to get hurt. Of course, she'd never intended to fall in love with a vampire either.

"No, I wasn't involved with him then. He was pursuing me at the time, but I kept him at arm's length. I—"

"What changed then? Why him and not me?" he interrupted her.

Aria broke her eye contact with him. His tone had become gruff, and it grated her nerves. "Chris, it's complicated, and I don't feel like I should have to explain myself. Now, you said this isn't what you wanted to talk about, so what is it? What warrants three phone calls?"

He looked taken aback by her tone as well, and when he spoke again, he talked in a softer voice. "Firstly, I wanted to see if you were feeling better, and I can clearly see that you are.

You even have some pink in your cheeks. Secondly, I wanted to tell you to be careful"—he looked away from her bewildered stare—"and that is where this gets complicated, so let me try to break it down."

Aria couldn't imagine him telling her anything more shocking than what she'd been learning about her past, present, and future, so she encouraged him to be blunt.

"Whatever it is, just tell me," she prodded. "I can handle it."

Chris slowly turned himself to face her again and eased into it. "I overheard some people talking about you, and it was weird, but they were talking like they wanted to do you harm."

Aria's eyes widened to the size of half-dollars, and she leaned in closer. "I'm sorry, but just to make sure I heard you correctly, you're telling me someone wants to hurt me?"

His face screwed up, and his lip twitched. "In a nutshell, yes," he whispered hoarsely.

She jumped up from the bench and paced in front of him, and as she did so, the gentle breeze that had been blowing picked up momentum. She took in a deep breath of it while her hand went to her amulet, which was concealed by her sweater, and she pictured the wind gathering its strength and becoming something fierce. Soon, students were chasing papers, trying to hold their skirts down, or their hair in place as they crossed the campus and ran for shelter.

"Aria?" Chris shouted over the whoosh of air.

She turned on him and held her arms out to her sides. "Who?" she bellowed at him. "I want to know who."

Chris couldn't hide the shame that crept up his neck and settled on his face. He leaned forward and pretended to tie his shoe while she waited for an answer. Then he swallowed the lump in his throat that was almost choking off his air supply and told her, "It was more than one person. There is a group of—" he hollered but stopped when she suddenly bolted. Then just as quickly as it had begun, the wind died down to a gentle breeze once more.

Listening in from the hollow of a tree, an owl overheard the conversation. *So, the young lad wants to warn her? We'll see about that...* Mikel had only another hour to wait before he could make a move.

Seventy-nine

Aria ran to the dorm and up to her room. Cat was sitting on her bed and watching TV when she walked in, and she didn't bother to peel her eyes away from the show that was on. Instead, she held up one hand in a weak wave.

"Hey," she mumbled, "how are you feeling, girlie?"

"I'm feeling a lot better," Aria replied.

"That's good to hear. By the way, Chris called me looking for you—twice."

Aria put her fingers to her temples and rubbed. "I know," she groaned, "I talked to him."

And, according to him, I'm in danger. No shit, but what does he know, and how does he know it?

Cat finally looked up from the TV, and her eyes caught the glint from Aria's ring. "Whoa, whoa, whoa. Look who has a new bling! Where or who did that come from?"

Aria touched the ring and lied, "It's a birthday present from my mom and dad."

Cat got up from the bed and approached her for a better look. She took Aria's hand and touched the individual stones in the ring. "This is just gorgeous!"

Aria smiled sheepishly. "I know. My mom has great taste."

"I'll say. So, what did Chris want besides your body?" She made a kissing face and winked dramatically.

"That's about it," Aria said with a giggle.

"Aw, that poor pup is in love," Cat crooned. She went back to her bed and began flipping the television channels. "Hey, your birthday is two days away. Did you decide if you want to go to Boxers for the all-male review? I think it'd be a blast"—she looked at Aria and grinned like a possum—"Maybe Chris can go and get a job there," she said huskily.

Aria spit out the sip of soda she'd just taken and snorted at the image of Chris up on stage. She had the feeling he was far too shy for that line of work, and he certainly didn't have the right build for it. Kellan on the other hand...She fanned her face at that image.

"Someone is turning awfully red. You're picturing him dancing, aren't you?"

"I am not!" Aria scoffed and waved a hand at her friend.

Her eyes moved to the window and saw the dark shadows of the early evening peeking through, and it made her stomach flutter. He'd come to her soon—she was certain of it. So, the question was what should she do about Cat? It occurred to her that she didn't know where he slept. She imagined him having a coffin in a crypt somewhere, and shivers ran down her spine. She wouldn't ever be going back to his place if that was true.

She looked down at the glamorous ring and wondered if she should remove it before he showed up tonight. She hadn't committed herself to the idea of being his mate, so she didn't want him thinking she had. If he saw her wearing the ring, and she ended up giving it back to him, the hurt feelings caused could lead to her demise. She didn't know what kind of temper he had, and she didn't want to test it either.

At least not until battle—then I'm afraid I'll have no choice.

"How's your lover?" Cat suddenly asked and made her jump.

Aria's eyes darted around the room to avoid looking at her roommate. "Oh, he's okay."

"Just okay? Did you stop putting out already?" she teased while running her hands through her long blonde hair. She gathered it all up and put it on top of her head in a knot. "What do you think? Can I pull off a bun?"

Aria squinted and shook her head. "Um, that would be a firm no, and I haven't seen him lately."

It was Cat's turn to squint now. "You're lying," she accused.

"What?" Aria tried to look as innocent as she wanted to feel.

"Your tell—you wring your hands when you're nervous. It's your tell."

Shit.

"So, what's his name?"

Aria felt tongue-tied as she quickly came up with a name. Somehow, she didn't think Kellan would go over smoothly. "Eric. His name is Eric."

Cat narrowed her eyes suspiciously. "Eric what?"

Aria was losing her patience with the interrogation. "Just Eric. That's all you need to know for now."

"All right, be stingy then. Now, let's go do something. I'm bored, and Jason doesn't want to get together," she said with a pout.

Aria looked at her watch. It was only 6:00 p.m., but it was already black outside. "You did hear about the curfew being imposed, didn't you?"

Cat's face fell. "You had to bring that up, didn't you? Well, it's not like they are going to be running around to check our rooms, and what if they do? What's the worst that can happen?"

You have no idea.

Aria shrugged and scowled while she tried to think of a convincing answer for her friend. "I don't know, but better safe than sorry, right? I mean, the curfew is for a reason—women are dying."

Her reasoning fell on deaf ears, though. Cat looked down at her chipped nail polish and casually claimed, "Well, I think that's just living in the city. People are killed here every day."

Aria looked at her with disgust and shook her head slowly. "That's a healthy outlook for you," she exclaimed sarcastically. She was dismissed with the wave of a hand, though, as Cat climbed out of her bed and reached for her sneakers.

"Whatever," she groaned, "I'm going to go get a snack or find something to do. I bet something's going on somewhere, but it's not in this room." Before Aria could continue to protest, she was gone.

As soon as the door closed, Aria dashed to the window and peered into the blackness below. She couldn't see him anywhere, though, and that made her worry that he was out hunting.

Eighty

The bobcat had found the crow sitting outside a window, and it pounced just before the bird realized it was there. It swiped its claws and caught the bird's wing as it tried to fly off. The squawking creature fell to the ground after receiving the crippling blow, and the predator followed close behind just as the sun descended out of sight.

Kellan used every ounce of strength left in him to get up and hobble away just as he heard the thud of paws hitting the ground. He could feel hot breath on his neck as he looked up to the sky and found the power to shift into his vampire body. Just as the change took place, he once again felt the white-hot pain of claws contacting his flesh—this time, it was his leg that suffered, and he yelped into the darkness. He spun to face his attacker and was surprised when he found himself staring into familiar vampire eyes.

"Mikel," he snarled, "you were foolish to come here."

"So glad to cross paths again, Kellan," Mikel growled just as menacingly. He was crouched with his arms wide open, and his eyes narrowed with hatred.

Kellan was in a similar pose, and they side-stepped each other in a circular fashion. He knew this battle wouldn't be as easy as the one he'd fought a couple of days ago—Mikel was of equal strength, agility, and expertise in the art of war. Kellan knew this because they'd battled two hundred years ago when Mikel had trespassed on his hunting grounds. It was a close fight then, and this one would be even closer due to his wounds. It helped, though, that his heart was blackened with vengeance, and the hatred gnawed at him as he thought about protecting Aria.

Since he was injured, he waited for his opponent to lunge. Mikel sensed the hesitation and made his move, leaping at his enemy. He struck Kellan in his injured arm while tackling him to the ground. Kellan bellowed in pain while he bucked his hips and pushed with his hands to get the vampire off him. Mikel was sent flying backward against the back of the building, but he quickly recovered from the blow, and he circled his opponent like a shark in bloody waters. This time they both leapt, and Kellan landed a lucky blow to Mikel's cheek with his right hand. The crunching of bone was music to his ears and urged him on, so he hit hard and strong with his other hand into Mikel's stomach, all the while ignoring the searing hot pain from his clawed flesh. Mikel was knocked off balance, and Kellan was ready to rain down a flurry of blows when he heard a gasp coming from the left.

Both vampires looked to see Aria frozen in place. The cold light of fear shone in her eyes as she stared with her mouth gaping like a fish out of water. Kellan turned to his opponent when he heard the shuffling of feet, but Mikel wasn't trying to strike him. Instead, he was running away. Kellan took one step after him, but Aria's shout made him stop in his tracks.

"No!" she cried, "Please don't go."

Kellan rushed to her side and took her by the shoulders to look down into her exotic eyes. "I must go after him while he's injured, my love. It's better that way."

Tears streamed down her porcelain cheeks as she melted against his powerful frame. She'd seen his injuries, and it made her heart thud.

"You're hurt too, though," she softly wept against his chest. "Stay with me."

Kellan sighed and kissed the top of her head. He was putty in her delicate hands—the hands that displayed his ring, his love. As he looked at it gracing her long slender finger, he noticed something else. Her amulet, which normally glowed a soft blue light, was now glowing a bright amber. He wondered if that meant her heart had opened to him—it certainly felt like it had.

Eighty-one

The meeting had been called to order, and the minutes had been read. Now everyone was waiting to hear what Gail had to say.

She cleared her throat and began, "Let's get down to business. I'm tired of pussyfooting around with this girl. Mikel hasn't done his job, and I'd like to know why, so let's summon him."

The summoning spell was chanted, and the vampire came forth in a swirl of smoke. His face was bruised on the left side, and his cheek appeared to be caved in.

Before Gail could question him, he growled, "You bitches can't summon me every time you have the notion to do so." He stared each of them down and then grinned, as much as he could with a broken face, and added, "Unless one of you wants to be supper."

"While that is part of our request, it's not what we want just yet. We'd like to know why the girl isn't dead yet, but we can see from the looks of you that you must've come across Kellan. Is that right?"

His eyes narrowed to slits, and he snarled, "Aye."

"Did you kill him or at least hurt him too?" Betty asked.

Mikel tried to smile again but winced from the pain. "Aye, he's hurt. I could've finished the job, too, but his wench showed up, and she was wearing her amulet. I don't think I could've killed both."

Alicia scowled and claimed, "She must be feeling better and growing closer to him."

He nodded in affirmation. "As I made my exit, I saw her go into his arms."

Gail bowed her head in disgust while the others all began talking at once. They would have to execute the next part of their plan.

Just as she held up her hand to quiet the group, Mikel surprised them all by seizing Jenna and pulling her out of her chair. He brandished a knife, which he'd pulled from his pocket, and held it to her throat.

"You said you wanted to be immortal," he hissed, "Well, I can't bite you, for obvious reasons, so I'm going to have to go about this another way."

While the audience gaped, he made a small incision in Jenna's wrist, missing the main veins, to draw blood. After drinking from her, he went around the table and did the same to the others. Gail had fetched bandages, so they fixed each other up when he was finished.

"You've had your fill, so you may leave us now. How long, though, before the transformation takes place for us?" Gail asked.

Mikel chuckled as much as his broken cheek would allow. "It takes three bites before the change takes place, so I'll be back." He turned to the others and bowed in a grand gesture. "Ladies, I bid you adieu." Then he disappeared into the night.

Gail touched the bandage on her sore wrist and told her followers, "Now that he is taken care of, we can get down to business. We will summon Gabriella, so she can separate Kellan and the girl and bring her to us for sacrificing." They all agreed and eagerly chanted the summoning spell.

After two tries, a swirl of mist appeared, and a floral fragrance filled the air. Gabriella's long wavy blonde hair tumbled over her perfectly rounded shoulders while piercing emerald eyes scrutinized the women before her.

"What is the meaning of this?" she demanded in a light feminine voice that was still full of authority.

Gail gathered her wits before answering the exotically beautiful vampire. "Gabriella, we have summoned you because we want to help you defeat the Gypsies." She saw the smirk on Gabriella's face, so she added, "We have access to the prophesied Gypsy half-breed."

The vampire didn't seem impressed by that information either. She waved Gail off with one sculpted hand and laughed.

"I don't need *you* to help me gain access to the charmed Gypsy, but you have piqued my interest. Tell me about her," she encouraged while pacing the room.

"She lives here and dates my son," Gail continued, "but someone else is infatuated with her, and he's someone you know."

The vampire didn't hide her confusion. Her brows knitted together, and her mouth turned down. "Someone I know? How would you know whom I associate with?"

Alicia spoke up, "While we don't know much about you, we do know of a romance you had in 1616."

Gabriella's eyes rolled upward, and she pursed her lips while she dug deep in her memory. "Tell me more," she commanded.

Gail said his name in a hushed whisper like it was a big secret from the others in the room. "Does Kellan Montcroix ring any bells?"

Gabriella mouthed his name with no sound while her eyes widened from surprise. "Kellan is here, and you say he is in love with the lass?"

"Yes, that's correct," Alicia responded.

The vampire's fangs glistened while her eyes became slits. "I'll have to put an end to that—I want him back."

Eighty-two

Aria snuck Kellan up to her room and locked the door. While he sat on her bed and watched with a curious gaze, she rushed to the bathroom to fetch the first-aid kit. When she returned to him, he tried to pull her in for a kiss, but her mind was set to bandaging his wounds, so she pushed him away with more strength than he knew she was capable of. She looked at the gashes on his arm and leg and began to feel hopelessness. The wounds were too deep for just a bandage, and there was a lot of blood seeping out of them.

"You're losing too much blood," she pointed out. "I want you to bite me. You need to replenish." She held her wrist out to him while grabbing one of the Gypsy magic books from her nightstand with her free hand. She quickly flipped through it to a section she'd seen on potions while she felt the piercing sting of his fangs on her wrist.

Kellan drank in her honey and vanilla nectar, and a warm glow spread throughout him. It wasn't just from the blood supply, it was also from the supply of love he was receiving from her. He'd finally gotten through to her heart, and that made all the difference. He stopped before taking too much blood and planted kisses over the bite while studying her silhouette. He loved how serious she looked while she flipped through the book.

"Is that the Kama Sutra you're reading by chance?" he teased.

She shot him a look of disapproval but then broke out in a grin. "No, silly, I'm finding a magical solution to your ailments"—she gave him a lust-filled gaze this time—"I don't want scars on that gorgeous body."

His smile was larger than life, and his eyes studied her hand. "Speaking of gorgeous bodies, the ring looks perfect on you." His voice was soft and loving, and it drew her in. "I can't tell you how happy I was when I saw you wearing it today."

"Today?" Her brows shot up in surprise. "Are you around during the day and how?"

He reached out to lightly touch her arm while she still flipped through the book's pages. "I am always around you, but I have to shapeshift during the day."

Aria looked away from the book to stare into his mesmerizing eyes. *His eyes look close in color to mine…*

"Do you mean like you did the other night when you suddenly changed into a bird?"

Kellan simply nodded with a sexy grin.

"Shouldn't you be sleeping in a crypt during the day? Don't you have a coffin somewhere?" she asked with her head tilted to the side.

His face contorted into a look of amusement, and his booming laughter filled the tiny room. "You watch too many movies, my love. It's true that we need a dark place to hide from the sun, while in our vampire forms, but I've never known a vampire that slept in a coffin.

I, myself, have a cavern I sleep in, but I'd much rather spend my days watching you."

"Stalker," she mumbled with a giggle. Then she turned serious and pointed to a page in the book. "Here's one I can do." She quickly moved around the room gathering items as she went.

Luckily, Cat was big on seasoning her food, so she had some of the ingredients on top of the dresser they shared. In a bowl, Aria mixed some baby powder, cinnamon, ginger, and water to make a paste, which she then carefully applied to his open wounds. She saw pain cross his face while she dabbed, and it tugged at her heart. She'd panicked when she'd seen him fighting the other vampire and caught sight of the gashes, and that's when she knew how much she truly cared—that's when she knew she loved him. After the paste was applied, she clutched her amulet and closed her eyes. In her mind, she tried to envision his wounds closing, much like she'd been able to picture the thunderstorm.

She opened her eyes and checked one of the gashes with hope in her heart, and much to her surprise, it was closed. It was red and swollen but closed. She touched it lightly with her fingertips before wiping the rest of the paste away—the gashes were barely scratches now. She squealed with delight and hopped up and down.

"It worked! I can't believe it, but it worked," she sang.

Kellan admired her work and touched the scratches. They were still a little tender, but it wasn't anything he couldn't handle. He locked eyes with her and smiled, but it quickly changed into a look of concern when there was a key in the lock, and the door opened.

"Oh!" Cat chirped when she saw him lying on the bed. "I'm sorry." She quickly bobbed back into the hallway, followed by Aria.

Cat was wide-eyed, and her mouth hung open. "Who is the hunk? Is that him—Eric?" She gestured to the door.

Aria shifted her weight nervously from one foot to the other and picked at her cuticles. She wasn't prepared for this, and she was sure her roommate could sense her unease.

"Um, yes, except his name is really Kellan. Now, can you leave for a few hours, so I can spend some time with him?" she rushed her words.

Cat looked toward the door and back at Aria with a mischievous gleam in her eyes. In a slow sultry voice, she said, "Sure, I can leave you two lovebirds alone."

"Thank you," Aria replied over her friend's giggles.

"Oh, and let me just say, damn, he's hot!"

Aria looked toward the door this time and then back to her friend with a sly grin. "Yes, he is, and he has a silver-tipped tongue too," she replied with a wink before spinning on her heel to go back inside.

"Uh! Not fair," Cat cried as she walked away.

Aria was still snickering as she stepped inside the room, and she found Kellan with a silly grin on his perfectly sculpted face.

"You know," he drawled, "I could hear everything you said."

Aria felt her cheeks flame. "Oh, no, I didn't know that."

He was still grinning, and he laughed at her embarrassment. "So, you want a few hours with me, eh? What am I, a stud horse to you?" he teased, and her cheeks turned even rosier.

"Um, I um—" she began, but he held up his hand to stop her.

"It's okay"—he winked, still smiling—"I don't mind. In fact, I think I should put my 'silver-tipped tongue' to good use. Shall we?"

Aria slowly stepped toward him and lazily ran her hand up his chiseled abdomen. "We certainly shall," she purred. "If you're feeling up to it. You were hurt pretty badly."

He looked down at his burgeoning erection bulging through his black pants and smiled. "I am definitely *up* for it."

Aria shook her head while the corners of her mouth turned up. "I can see that," she whispered and ran her fingertips over the bulge.

Kellan's shuddering breath came in tiny pants as her fingers continued to play over his tumescence. He, in turn, let his hand roam up her thigh to her apex and played over her clothing too. He could feel her swelling for him, and he ached to be inside her with his mouth and tongue, followed by his distended virility, so he unbuttoned her pants and tugged.

"Let's get you naked for me," he growled. "I need to taste you."

"Uh-uh," she said and wagged a finger at him. "This time, I want to taste you." She gave him a wink as she unfastened his pants and set his rock-hard masculinity free.

Kellan's quick intake of breath was music to her ears as she began at the base of him and ran her tongue up his silky length. She slid it over his tip and then down the other side before taking the head of him into the lush sweetness of her mouth. He gasped and groaned as she went down as far as she could accommodate him while swirling her tongue side to side. She continued the bobbing motion while taking hold of it with her left hand, slowly stroking up and down.

The sweet suction of her mouth became too much to bear. "You have to stop," he groaned through gritted teeth. "You have to stop, or I'm going to release, and I want to feel you on me yet."

Aria ran her mouth back up him and kissed the head. "So, you want me on top this time?"

His lust-hazed eyes widened, and he made a growling noise. "My god, woman, you know how to work me up. Right now, though, I just want you on top of my face."

Aria, who had stripped down, climbed onto the bed next to him and helped him remove the rest of his clothing. She slid up his naked body, with her satin flesh meeting his rock-hard muscles, and plunged her tongue into his hot mouth. The moaning sounds he was making sent tickling vibrations into her throat as they plundered one another. Their hands explored each other while they kissed, but when his found her moistness, she broke the kiss off to gasp from pleasure.

He put his arm tightly around her and rolled her onto her back with him on top. He then blazed a trail of steamy kisses down her neck and to her pretty pink peaks. He cupped each breast while his tongue flicked the nipple before taking it into his wet mouth to suckle.

Aria squirmed under the weight of him, her body begging to have him inside her flesh. She desperately wanted to feel him prodding, thrusting, pounding...

Kellan sensed her urgency and chuckled softly. "Not yet, my love. First, I want to feast on your swollen lips."

He moved down her abdomen, placing more kisses while his hand roamed her inner thigh. He let his fingertips graze across her silken lips as his mouth got closer to her mound. He wanted to know what secrets hid inside that soft, yielding flesh. He used his tongue to slowly separate them, which caused a cry of pleasure to escape her. Then he took the left side into his mouth and gently suckled before giving it a little nibble. While she writhed in ecstasy, he dragged his tongue over to the right side and did the same.

"Oh my god!" she hollered. "Oh, that feels good!"

Kellan chuckled again. "You did say something about 'silver tipped' I believe."

Then he moved his tongue up her slit again, but this time his destination was her swollen pink pearl. He used the tip of his tongue to stroke her there, sending her into shivers of ecstasy. He worked the slippery, throbbing nub into slow circles while she clawed at the bed and cried out her passion. He was drowning in her taste, and the lash of his tongue kept her prisoner to desire while he tantalized and teased her.

"Please, you're killing me. Please fuck me!" she begged.

"Oh, but it is a sweet death, is it not?" he teased while working his strong finger inside her, igniting her desires further.

Aria writhed and wriggled against his hand, lost to the pleasures bestowed upon her. His caressing tongue and fingers made her ache for him more than ever before, and she grew embarrassingly damp. She was wet and ready, begging for it.

"Please, fuck me now," she cried out once more.

Kellan slowly withdrew his probing finger, slid it up her slit to tease her, and then raised himself over her body. His mouth found hers again while his thick, throbbing head found her wet heat. The vampire moved slowly and sensually as he stoked her furnace to a scorching inferno.

Aria's whole body was on fire with pleasure as he moved in and out of her. He prodded her womanhood with deliberate expertise, and she was awash with overlapping waves of rapture. Her toes curled, and her back arched as she reached shattering climax after climax.

Kellan felt the pleasure ripple through her as she clenched his thick head. He was quickly drawn to his own rapturous ending, but he didn't want it to be over, so he stopped flexing his hips to roll over onto his back with her on top. He never left her body.

Aria felt him go deeper into her as she was flipped on top, and she used the pleasurable sensation to her advantage by grinding her hips back and forth. Her bouncing breasts caught the attention of his large hands while she continued her journey to orgasm.

"That's it, baby, take your pleasure. Make yourself come for me," he commanded in a husky voice. "I want to feel you all over me."

Aria's tempo picked up as she got closer to the stars, and suddenly, they were bursting behind her eyes. "Oh, God!" she screamed as the tidal wave of pleasure pulled her under.

Kellan had been fighting his own release, struggling to hold on just a little longer. The need to explode built inside him, a rising crescendo, until he could fight it no more. He clasped her hips, pulling her hard into his final thrust, and spilled his seed deep inside her.

He rolled her to his side and was still semi-hard as he lay panting next to her with her legs entangled over his. She'd placed her head on his chest, and his arm was protectively wrapped around her slim torso.

Her half-lidded eyes slid closed as she breathed his name. Her body was spent and deliciously sore as she settled into his embrace and melted against his powerful frame. She'd never felt as safe as she did at that moment. She could feel his love vibrating through her as her breathing slowed to match his. Tangled emotions overcame her as her hand slid over his torso to snuggle him closer.

"I love you," she whispered.

"And you know I love you," he purred back before reaching to turn off the lamp. Then, by the amber glow radiating from her amulet, they fell asleep in each other's tender embrace.

Eighty-three

Gabriella sniffed the night air in hopes of catching Kellan's masculine scent. She wasn't from the area, so it was a chore to locate the college campus. It hadn't surprised her when none of the women who'd summoned her offered to take her there—they were afraid for their lives. Little did they know that she only fed on males. She craved the testosterone in blood, and she could recall that Kellan had had a lot of it.

She finally stumbled onto the college campus and sniffed out some prey—she didn't want to keep walking around on an empty stomach. She moved across the grass, hidden within the shadows from the buildings, and stalked the boy. The midnight thirst was upon her, and her throat grew parched at the sight of his pulsing neck. She stepped out of the darkness to reveal herself to him.

"Hi, where did you come from?" Chris asked on a shaky breath.

He was on his way to see Aria to tell her more about what he'd overheard at his mother's house when the gorgeous woman suddenly appeared. His eyes wanted to go down to her overflowing bustline, but he couldn't tear them from her perfect porcelain face and intense green eyes.

Gabriella sized the young man up. He wasn't very large, but he'd satiate her thirst. Her tongue instinctively played over her razor-sharp canines while the blood-hunger made her body quiver with anticipation. The dark juices from his sinewy throat would soon be hers.

"I'm new in town, and I went for a walk and got lost," she cooed while batting her lashes playfully. "Can you help me back to town?"

Chris stared at the beautiful creature. He'd help her all right because he felt the compelling urge to. He was drawn into the woman.

"Yes, ma'am, I'll help you. Where are you trying to go?"

Gabriella stepped forth and reached out for his hand. She gently pulled him into the shadows between two buildings before facing him and saying on a sultry whisper, "Right here."

She leaned in and kissed his full lips, pricking his bottom lip with one of her fangs. His blood was hot and salty upon her tongue, and she wanted more of it—she wanted to have it flowing freely into her greedy mouth. Seducing this young man wasn't in her plans, so she got down to it. Her fangs tore crimson holes in his neck, while his hands tried to roam her body. When the salty blood ran in thin rivulets into her ruby-lipped mouth, she began to feel revitalized. She took long pulls until her hunger was satiated, and his heart beat no more. Then she discarded him like garbage onto the dried grass and went back to her hunt for Kellan. This time, she found him.

Gabriella peered at the sleeping couple through the window. Kellan was as perfect in form as he had been four hundred years ago, and she couldn't wait to wrap her legs around him. Of course, she'd have to pry him from the little half-breed wench.

Shouldn't be too hard. He loved me once before.

She watched them until it was time to seek her shelter from the sun. She changed into a dove and flew over the city until she found a cavern to hide in, and by all the luck, his scent filled the hollow opening.

Eighty-four
Thursday

Aria woke up feeling wonderful. She was still nestled up against Kellan, and he was softly snoring. She drank in the sight of his sleeping form and what his face looked like when it wasn't full of lust—it was perfectly chiseled, like the rest of his body, and aristocratic. He didn't look like he came from this time or this country. She recalled reading that he'd lived in Paris, and that made her wonder how he got to the United States as well as when and why he came here. She'd ask him when he woke up, she thought as she looked out at the dawn. Then she panicked—the sun was up, and he wasn't someplace dark. She climbed out of bed and raced to the window where she draped Cat's blanket to drown out every shred of light.

Kellan woke up from Aria's stirring and quietly watched her work to protect him. It made him love her even more, if that was possible. He eyed her nude body from head to toe as she reached up to hang the blanket, and when she turned around, he was already fully hard.

Aria caught him staring, and her hands flew to cover her breasts and mound. He laughed at her modesty, and it was a warm and inviting sound.

"You can't tell me you're suddenly shy, my love," he purred sensuously.

Aria shrugged and softly replied, "I'm a little shy."

"Well, you certainly weren't shy last night," he reminded her with a sexy grin.

She noticed his erection and licked her lips at the memory of last night. "No, I suppose I wasn't, was I?" she asked huskily while she climbed into bed with him. She clasped his hardness while leaning in for a kiss and whispered, "And now I remember why."

"You're a beautiful vixen and impossible to say no to," he murmured while laying her on her back and rising above her.

He wasted no time in easing his hardness into her softest spot, and with slow strokes, he brought them both insurmountable pleasure once again. He thrust harder every time he felt her reaching climax and rode her waves of delight with her until his own eruption spewed forth. Then he collapsed beside her and pulled her into his body.

"Aren't you worried about the sun being up?"

He looked at the darkened window and grinned. "No, I think you took care of that for me."

She looked at his fangs glistening in the light from her amulet and suddenly craved them. "Will you bite me? I want you to," she pleaded.

"Well, if you want me to, I will certainly oblige." He leaned in to her neck, but she pushed his head down.

"No, on my breast like you did the first time."

"Yes, my love, anything you wish." Kellan carefully nipped at her full mound until her honey and vanilla sweetness spilled forth into his wanting mouth. He wasn't sure why, but she tasted better this time than any other before it.

When he was done feeding, he nuzzled up against her soft body once more and began planting kisses on her neck and collar bone.

"Oh, no you don't," she told him sternly, "I have to start getting back to classes today before I fail them." She saw his face fall, so she added, "But I would love to make love again if I didn't have to go to class."

"I understand, my darling. You have your human obligations to tend to yet. But I will come to you tonight and make sure you make good on that promise," he said with a sly smirk.

She smiled back at him and squeezed her breasts for his benefit before donning her bra. "I hope you do," she said seductively.

They both dressed, and she gave him a long drugging kiss.

"How will you get out of here safely? Are you going to change into something?"

Kellan looked down at his clothing and laughed. "Well, I can't very well leave like this— I'm disheveled."

Aria lightly pushed against his massive shoulder and laughed at his silliness. "You know what I mean."

He pulled her against him and squeezed tightly. "Of course, my pet. Now, when you see the black crow or cat watching you, you'll know it's me," he purred against the top of her head.

She looked up into his sky-blue eyes and smiled brightly. "Stalker," she teased.

He kissed her passionately with his hands running through her silky hair and then held her tightly once more.

"I'll miss you, my love."

Aria beamed. "I'll miss you too, gorgeous," she returned.

"I'll leave you now, so you can prepare yourself for your day," he told her. "If you'll just get the window for me after I change, I'd appreciate it."

Kellan shifted into the crow before she pulled the make-shift curtain back and opened the window for him. As soon as it opened, his heart began to thud. A familiar wave of roses mixed with ambrosia floated in—Gabriella had been there. He was sure of it.

Eighty-five

After Kellan left, Aria made her way to the showers and hummed the entire time. She couldn't remember a time in her life when she'd felt this happy. It all ended when she got back to her room, though, because Cat was on her bed crying her eyes out.

"Oh my god, what's wrong?" Aria asked while plopping down beside her.

Cat looked up with tears streaming down her puffy face. Through shuddered breaths, she managed to squeak out, "I found out, on my way back, that Chris-Chris—" She broke off into fresh sobs.

Aria panicked. "Chris what?" she asked but was afraid to hear the answer.

Cat shivered before finally choking out, "Chris is dead."

Aria jumped to her feet and paced the room full of rage. *How could he? How could he kill my friend and then make love to me?*

Her fists clenched so tightly it made her knuckles hurt. First, there was Kyle, and now Chris is dead too? She shook her head in disbelief.

Men and their fucking jealousy!

"Aria, are you okay?" Cat suddenly interrupted her thoughts. "You aren't saying anything."

Aria looked at her friend and then the window. Sure enough, there was a crow on the branch outside staring in at her. She returned the ogling, and it was level, direct, and bored right into the bird. The crow shrank back from her gawking and flapped its wings while cawing.

Aria looked away from the window just in time to see Cat slinking out of the room with her shower products, so she got up from the bed and threw the window open. The bird didn't fly in, but it did get closer.

"How could you? How could you kill him? He was my friend!" she accused.

Kellan's head drew back from the fire behind her words. She was accusing him of killing someone, but he hadn't done any such thing. Luckily for him, crows could speak.

"No, no kill. No, no kill," he squawked at her, and she jumped back in surprise with her hand flying to her mouth.

"You can talk like that?" she asked in disbelief.

"Yes, some. No, no kill," he repeated.

Aria cocked her head and eyed him down. Then she reached over, grabbed Cat's blanket, and put it up over the window. She moved it aside enough for him to fly in, and he wasted no time in doing so. As soon as the make-shift curtain was back in place and the room was completely blackened, he changed.

"My love, why are you so angry with me? Why do you accuse me of killing? I told you that your blood sustains me," he explained.

"Chris is dead," she cried out and pummeled his chest. "Did you kill him out of jealousy? Did you kill him like you killed Kyle?"

Kellan grabbed both her wrists to stop her hitting, but he did so gently. "No, I didn't. I've not killed anyone lately, male or female. The first boy got what he deserved after trying to hurt you. Maybe you feel my methods were wrong, but you need to remember the time I come from and who I am. As for your friend, Chris, I've not done anything. You need to remember that there is another vampire out there, and you live in a city full of crime."

She looked up at him with her tear-filled eyes and mumbled, "You didn't? Do you think it was the other vampire, the one you were fighting with?"

Kellan bit his bottom lip while in thought. It was more likely Gabriella who did it—she'd probably fed on the lad. He didn't want Aria to worry about her, though, until he had time to explain everything, and he would do that tonight.

So, he simply told her, "Aye, it's possible, but don't worry because he can't harm you during the day, and I'll be with you every minute of the night."

I'll have to be to guard you from Gabriella.

Kellan began circling the campus as soon as he left Aria's room—he would get to the bottom of her friend's death. He owed it to his love.

He could pick up the scent of roses and ambrosia—her signature fragrance—at its strongest in an alley. He could even smell it over the bouquets of flowers tossed there in remembrance of the dead boy. Students were milling around the area, leaving the flowers, candles, and even a few stuffed bears. After he circled the area for the third time, trying to find her trail, he saw Aria headed that way. He perched on a ledge to watch his love as she added a stuffed toy to the pile already there. With his keen sight, he could see the stream of tears trickling down her cheek, and it made his heart ache that he couldn't hold and comfort her until tonight.

When she walked off to her class, he went back to following Gabriella's trail. It led from the alley to Aria's building and then it disappeared.

She must've shifted here to seek shelter from the coming dawn.

Fresh anger washed over him as he pictured her sitting outside Aria's window watching them. He could only hope that she'd witnessed the lovemaking—that, at least, would give him some satisfaction.

He took to the sky again and flew to the building that he'd seen Aria go into. He located her through a window and perched on the ledge to watch her as she listened to the lecture. She was chewing on her pen, and it took him back to the moment when he was in her mouth, making him aroused all over again. He wondered if she felt the exact same pleasure when he had her in his mouth.

She turned toward the window, and she must've seen him because she smiled. He flapped his wings in response to the simple gesture and waited for her class to finish.

The rest of the morning was the same— he followed her to each class and would find the window he could see her through. He kept a careful eye out for any predators in the area, but without the gargoyles to announce their presence, it was difficult if not impossible. He didn't see any out of the ordinary creatures or odd behaviors either. He hoped that Mikel had learned his lesson and would stay away and that Gabriella was resting someplace.

I could hunt her down and prey on her, but where would she be? There are too many caverns in the vast area to check them all.

He shuddered on the inside. Confronting his first love after four hundred years would not be easy. He had been ready to propose to her, with the blue diamond ring, when she suddenly vanished without a trace. It had hurt him deeply and almost tore him apart because he'd loved her so profoundly.

But I love Aria even more—it's no contest. I will find Mikel and deal with him, and I will find her and deal with her too. I swear to the gods that I will protect my love, and it will not be a wasted effort.

Then it dawned on him that Gabriella must be there for the battle. It must be on the horizon then.

Eighty-seven

Aria went back to the dorm when she had a break between classes, and she didn't have to look up into the sky to see if Kellan was following her because she knew he was. He'd been with her all morning, just as he'd promised.

Cat was in the room flipping through the television channels, but she turned the TV off as Aria closed the door.

"Okay," she said, "we need to talk."

Aria nodded slowly and sucked in her bottom lip. "You want to talk about Chris. Okay," she answered and sat down on her bed facing her friend.

Cat looked down at her hands and shook her head, though. "No, I want to talk about the stud I found in your bed last night. What did you say his name is?"

Aria felt her cheeks redden. "Oh. His name is Kellan."

"Kel-lan," Cat enunciated slowly. "That's a sexy name"—she looked up in thought—"and it's befitting for him. So, where's he from?"

Shit.

Aria's mouth twitched while she thought of an appropriate answer. She wondered if she should tell her that he's from France, but then it occurred to her that he didn't have a French accent, so that wouldn't work in case they ever conversed.

She decided on a partial truth. "He was born in France but raised in the US."

"Ooh la la, viva la France," Cat teased. "What does he do for a living?"

"His family is in the textile industry," she answered and looked down at her watch. "Well, I need to go to the library before my next class, so I'll catch you later." The truth was she couldn't handle any more questions.

"Okay, bye."

Aria ran into Marissa in the hallway, and the other girl was all smiles at her.

"Who is that luscious piece of man I saw you sneaking into your room last night?"

Aria had no idea she'd been seen, so her mouth fell open in surprise. "Um, he's my boyfriend," she answered shyly. She couldn't bring herself to say fiancé—it would raise too many questions.

"Well, he is hot! Where did you find a hunk like that?" Her eyes were sparkling with delight while she gathered the juicy gossip.

"We met at the park," Aria answered truthfully.

"Damn, I need to go play on the swings. Catch you later," she said with a wink before disappearing into her room.

Aria walked back to the alley where Chris had been found because she felt she owed it to him to find out what had happened. As she walked around, she could smell roses and something she couldn't place. She assumed, of course, it was just from all the flowers strewn around.

Sobbing caught her attention, and she spun around to face his mother, the librarian. "Mrs. Woodson," she said in surprise, "you startled me"—she followed the grieving woman's gaze to a photograph someone had left—"I'm so sorry for your loss. He was a good friend."

Gail looked at the girl with hatred burning behind her eyes. If it weren't for Aria, Kellan wouldn't be there, and they wouldn't have needed to summon Gabriella, and her son would still be alive. It was all her fault.

"I had no idea you cared so much," she sniveled.

"Well, I—" Aria was cut off by her ringing phone. She looked at the display and saw that it was Zelda. "Excuse me"—she said while holding up a finger—"I need to take this." She walked away for some privacy and answered the phone call.

"Hi Aria," Zelda cheerfully returned her greeting. "I wanted to let you know that the clans are ready to go when the day comes, and we have reason to believe it will be coming soon. We will be ready to fight under your command, so be prepared to lead us to victory."

Aria had spent a good portion of the morning daydreaming in class about the same subject, and she'd made an important decision that she wanted to share with her mentor.

"I'll be ready under one condition—that Kellan fights by my side. I realize not everyone will be accepting of that, but it's what I require" she said with as much authority as she could muster.

Zelda surprised her with a burst of laughter. "I figured that is how things would turn out, and I've already discussed it with them. No harm will be brought to your love. You do love him, don't you?"

Aria smiled to herself and felt warm inside. "Yes, I do love him. I'm not going to fight it any longer." She then went on to explain what had happened between him and the other vampire and how she'd proudly healed him with Gypsy magic.

"I've never heard of Gypsy magic working on a vampire—it must be kismet," Zelda approved.

Aria touched her amulet and sighed. "I'd like to think it is."

They said their good-byes, and she finished out her classes for the day. She then met Cat for an early dinner because she wanted to be in their room when it got dark.

"Is your *lover* coming over again tonight?" Cat taunted.

Aria smiled warmly as the butterflies stirred in her stomach. "Yes, I'm sure he'll be dropping in."

Cat held a hand up and raised her brows. "Well, don't you worry your pretty head because I'll make myself scarce and leave you two lovebirds alone."

Aria was about to tell her that she didn't have to, but then she thought about the awkward conversation that would take place and the fact that she wanted to make love to him, so she bit her tongue.

"Thank you, I appreciate it," she said with a wink. "Don't forget about the curfew though."

Cat looked at her nails and smirked. "Oh, I'll be safe—in Jason's bed."

"Good. Someone needs to keep an eye on you."

"Ha-ha. Now when will your lover boy be coming around?" she asked in a haughty tone.

Aria shook her head at Cat's nonsense. "He'll be there around 5:00 I think."

"Oh, just in time for dinner. Tell me, will you be dining at the Y?" she broke out into a peal of giggles at her innuendo.

Aria stood, gathered her mess onto her tray, and smiled sweetly. "Yes, I'm sure we will be." With a dramatic wink, she spun around and left her friend, who was still giggling.

She went back to the room and anxiously waited for sundown. She found herself pacing and looking out the window every two minutes, so she decided to dive into her homework that she was still catching up on.

As soon as it got dark, there was a loud caw outside. She jumped from her bed, with her books falling to the floor, ran to the window, and flung it open to let him flutter in. He quickly shifted and pulled her in for a long hypnotic kiss with her body molded firmly against his.

"Oh," he breathed into her hair, "I've been waiting for this moment all day."

Aria hugged him back and snuggled her cheek against his broad chest. "Me too, darling."

He lightly touched her chin and tilted it up to look at him. "We need to discuss some things."

She flashed him a coy smile in response and said, "We need to get naked."

He smiled sheepishly but shook his head. "Not yet, my love. There are some very important things I need to talk to you about."

Now he had her attention. "Like what?"

Kellan sighed, and a flicker of anguish crossed his face. "Gabriella—we need to talk about Gabriella."

Aria didn't want to talk about his former lover. "The woman from your past? Why do we need to go into that?" she pouted.

He looked serious, though, so her sultry smile faded. "Because she's here," he stated with grave concern thickening his voice. "She's here, and she'll try to get to me through you."

Aria let go of him and turned away, but he just wrapped his arms around her from behind.

"I will protect you, my love. She won't get close enough to hurt you."

She clasped her amulet and thought aloud, "She'll come for me, maybe along with the others, but I have this evil eye and my power to protect me. I won't be standing alone either. The Gypsy clans have banded together to fight with me"— she spun on her heel to face him again—"and I want you to side with us, even though that means going against your kind."

He tilted her chin up and leaned in until their lips were almost touching. "You are my love, and that makes you my kind. You are my mate, so there is no other that matters, and anyone against you is against me too," he assured her. "I'll take my last immortal breath if it means protecting you."

Aria smiled before he kissed her and murmured against his lips, "And they say chivalry is dead."

He kissed her once before telling her, "I promise you, my love, it will never be dead between us. I do come from a different era if you recall." He was about to kiss her again, but she started laughing.

"You are a *much* older man, so I'm not sure if my parents would approve."

He joined her in the laughter. "And the fact that I'm a vampire has nothing to do with it?"

"Well, it might affect their opinion a little." She held up two pinched fingers and burst into a new fit of giggles.

After the laughs died down, he scooped her up and carried her to her bed. He took his time stripping her clothing off, memorizing every part of her body as he went and kissing every inch he exposed.

Aria saw her heart reflected in his tender yet smoldering gaze and wondered about their future. They were lovers by night but only dreamers by day. What kind of life would that be? He was such a beautiful man, and he never pretended to be anything more than what he was, which is a rare trait. Every time he looked at her, her heart thudded in her chest—even on that first night—and she knew she wanted that feeling to last forever. The excitement, the expectation, the lust, and now the love, all mingled with the fear of the unknown, made them who they are. They belonged together—he'd finally proven it to her heart. Theirs was a passion that went beyond life and beyond death.

Now, as he kissed her soft flesh, blood throbbed in her veins with a scarlet web of desire, and he was all that she wanted. Every inch of her lit up from the burning, urgent need to feel as physically close to him as possible. When he made love to her, it wasn't just love they were sharing, it was madness.

He rose over her, and the length of his body burned hers with a shared and searing passion as his mouth made its way to her dusky peaks. His breath was a hot caress before he took the nipple between his warm, wet lips.

Aria's breasts were ripe, succulent mouthfuls for him, and he nuzzled them, savagely licking and sucking at the tips. He continued his play until they were diamond-hard and full of her desire. Then he kissed a scorching path down the flat of her abdomen to just beyond her clean-shaven mound.

His clever tongue tantalized and teased her until it set off a blinding heat inside her. She felt herself drowning in a pool of desire as he dipped in and out of her body with it. Every lash felt better than the last, and she lost herself in the bliss. He slid his finger inside and caressed to make her go mad for him, and she writhed against his hand, lost to pleasure. While his tongue flicked her bud, he pushed a second finger inside her, and she saw explosions of light behind her eyes. She could feel her moisture pooling around his expert hand.

"Are you ready for me?" he purred against her satiny wet flesh.

"Yes! Oh, yes," she cried out.

She looked down at his erection, which appeared thicker, harder, and longer than ever before, and she licked her lips for it.

"Will you take me in your mouth again?" he asked.

"Mm-hmm. Let me taste you," she murmured.

He brought himself up to her mouth, and she flattened her tongue under the sensitive tip before it glided over his length in rasping strokes. He growled in response, loving the feel of her mouth on him—he craved it like a drug. She moaned while she licked and sucked at his shaft before taking it inside her mouth, and the vibrations from her throat made him dig his nails into the bed.

He groaned as he slid the tautness inside her welcoming warmth, and his body bucked while she worked his length until it reached the back of her throat. Every time she came up, she used her tongue to stroke the underside of his girth, and he felt himself losing control rather quickly, so he pulled himself out and slid down her body.

She spread her thighs to receive him, and her opening throbbed with anticipation of the gift it was about to accept. His thick, swollen head teased her opening without entering before he teased her folds, coating himself in her wetness. He briefly paused and studied her face before parting her gates of heaven wide open and guiding himself inside. His rigid shaft stoked the furnace of her loins as it filled her, stripping away everything but her need. He pressed her into the pillows as he pressed himself into her, and it wasn't long before he felt her clenching him in a heated climax. The extra lubrication made his movements easier, and he picked up the tempo, thrusting harder and faster.

Her cries of ecstasy mingled with his and filled the room as they moved together like the parts of a well-oiled machine. Arching her hips, she met him thrust for thrust and led herself down the glorious path to ultimate pleasure as convulsive waves gripped her.

Her ripples of ecstasy gripped him again and again until he was teetering on the edge of his own splendid bliss. Friction on friction, they pummeled each other to the edge and then spilled over together into oblivion.

They panted in pleasure, lost in sexual heat, as he fell off to her side. She curled up into him, perfectly molded against his frame and looked into his sleepy sky-blue eyes. There were no words to describe the wondrous glow she was feeling, but she knew he was feeling it too.

Kellan ran his finger down her cheek and neck, lost in a dreamy passionate haze. There was no feeling in the world close to what they shared—they were beyond cloud nine.

He whispered huskily, "God, I love you so much," as he ran his hand through her silken tendrils.

Aria nestled her cheek to his pec and sighed, lost in a deep and wistful relaxed state. "I love you, Kellan, my hero."

"Your true love?"

"Mmm, without a doubt," she whispered before falling into a deep sleep.

Kellan turned the lamp off and relaxed to the sound of her soft snoring. He was happier than he'd been in his entire existence, and he wanted to ensure many more moments just like it. But, with Gabriella on the loose...

Eighty-eight

Gabriella burned with hatred for the human as she watched Kellan making love to her. She'd tasted that sweet surrender multiple times before, and she longed for it to be hers again and only hers. Seeing his naked hardness almost made her heart beat again, and she desperately wanted to feel it. Her longing for him equaled her lust for blood. Her love was the reason he'd died, and it was the reason he'd been reborn immortal.

She regretted having left him then. She couldn't even recall why she had, but to find him again had seemed impossible over the years. However, here he was just a few feet away. If only the damned human wasn't involved—well, she'd deal with her soon enough. She had already started gathering an army to kill the girl and wipe out her Gypsy comrades at the same time. She couldn't imagine Kellan going against his breed to side with the Gypsies, and that would break the bonds of love between him and the half-breed for sure. Her razor-sharp fangs glistened in the moonlight as she thought about the tragic break-up. She had no doubt her plan would work—she was as maddeningly arrogant as any woman who could cheat death.

It was time to feed, so she went on the prowl. Her revenge could wait another night. It would be battle time soon enough anyway. Both she and Mikel were turning more vampires—she knew for a fact he was recruiting the nine cult

members who had summoned her. She had bitten
a couple of men herself last night after her main
feeding, and she only needed to return to them
two more times, which meant tomorrow, Friday,
they would fight.

Eighty-nine
Friday

Aria woke up on her twenty-first birthday in the arms of the man she loved and adored. Her stirring woke him too, and like the day before, she covered the window for his safety.

"Good morning, my angel," he purred and cocked his head while squinting at her. "There's something different about you."

She beamed and extended her arms in front of her with her hands clasped. "It's my birthday," she cooed.

Kellan's smile lit up the room, and recognition crossed his face. "You're twenty-one, right? Happy birthday, my love!" His joy-filled voice boomed and filled the small room.

Aria's eyebrows shot up in surprise. "How'd you know how old I am?"

His joy was quickly replaced by another emotion—fear. "Because it's part of the prophecy," he reminded her. "That means it will be any time now."

Aria's face dropped too, and her eyes were shadowed with sadness. "Oh," she mouthed without any sound coming out.

Kellan climbed out of bed and went to her to take her protectively into his strong embrace. "I'm sorry, my love. I didn't mean to bring you down. I want you to celebrate your birthday with me and every one after it too."

Aria gave him a sweet smile and softly mewed, "I will."

His look of concern quickly changed to one of mischief. "Is it still customary to spank one on their birthday?"

Aria smiled again and nodded. "Yes, it certainly is."

He picked her up with her legs wrapped around his waist and carried her to the bed. After he sat down, she willingly unlocked her legs and lay across his lap with her bare bottom in position. He palmed her ass with his broad warm hand before giving her a light smack that sent a shivery thrill up her spine. Her moans of encouragement earned her twenty more.

Aria loved the hot slap of his hand on her bare rump, and when he was done, she was red-bottomed and sore, but regretted nothing. Conversely, she thought it might be a fun addition to their future love play. Presently, she could feel his burgeoning erection on her belly. She felt him swelling thicker and harder with every slap, and when he was done, she clasped her hand around the base of him and slowly moved it up and down his length, enjoying how rock-hard he became against her palm and fingers.

He grunted and groaned under the expertise of her hand. "Now that I've warmed your ass, my pet, perhaps you'd like to straddle me," he taunted.

"Mmm, indeed I would," she replied while facing him and wrapping her legs tightly around his waist.

As his tongue entered her hot mouth, his thickness penetrated her hotter core. She rode him slowly at first, grinding her hips back and forth. He had gone wondrously deep inside her, pressing against her most intimate corners while his hands played with her taut nipples, lightly pinching each one. He drew each breast up to his mouth to flick the peaks, only making them harder, before suckling.

Aria's climaxes came easily as she bounced up and down his thick shaft, and soon they were coming together.

"I wish I didn't have to go to class this morning," she sighed while her head rested against his shoulder.

"Well, I could write you a note," he teased.

She laughed and kissed his cheek. "I wish it was that easy." She met his lips in a passionate kiss, but her phone interrupted. It was Zelda, so she knew she had to take it.

"Happy birthday, Aria," her mentor greeted her cheerfully, but then her voice became serious. "The reason I called, though, is to prepare you."

"For what?" Aria interrupted, and a shiver went down her spine.

"For today, my child. I had a vision last night and the other council members did too. Tonight, is the night."

"Tonight? So soon?" Aria couldn't believe what she was hearing, and she shot a look of panic to Kellan, who was listening in.

Kellan had felt it in his bones when he woke up, too, so this was not much of a surprise to him. He gently caressed Aria's free arm to soothe her.

"Yes, it will be tonight, so you need to do more training today. I understand you have college classes, but this is a matter of life and death."

"Of course, it is. My classes will just have to go on without me," Aria responded without hesitation. "I'll work on controlling my new power and tapping into the amulet, but what else is there?"

"We need to show you how to connect your amulet to ours, so the council will be here at noon," Zelda informed her.

Aria nodded while she spoke, "Okay, I'll be there at noon, and I'll work on my powers in the meantime."

"You'll train with me," Kellan's voice boomed.

Zelda heard him and stated, "That's a great idea, but um, how is he there in the daytime?"

Aria felt her face flush. "I have the window covered, so it's perfectly dark in here."

A key in the lock made both Aria and Kellan jump. Cat was home.

"Zelda, I have to go now, but I'll be there at noon. You can count on it. Bye for now."

She hung up as Cat turned on the lights.

"Oh!" She jumped back in surprise. "I'm sorry. I don't mean to interrupt you lovebirds"— her eyes darted to the window—"Um, why is my blanket over the window?"

She started to walk toward the window to remove it, but Aria jumped in front of it protectively.

"No! Leave it up, and I'll explain later."

Cat looked at her friend like she was crazy. "Okay," she drawled. "By the way, happy birthday! Let's all go drinking tonight." She clasped her hands in joy, and her smile was full of mischief.

Aria looked at Kellan whose face was blank, but she could see the worry in his eyes. She began twirling her hair from her own nerves and glanced back at Cat, who was waiting for an answer.

"We already have plans for tonight, but perhaps tomorrow night we can." She went from playing with her hair to wringing her hands.

Cat noticed her nervous behavior, but she attributed it to them just wanting to be alone. "All right, you lovers can do your thing tonight, and we'll get together tomorrow night. I want to get to know your beau." She smiled warmly at Kellan, who returned the gesture. "But now I need to clean up for class. Are you skipping again today?" she smirked.

Aria felt tongue tied, but Kellan took over for her and answered with a wink, "I have convinced her to stay in bed with me all day."

Cat looked him up and down, twice, and grinned. "I'm sure it didn't take too much convincing." Her eyes shifted to Aria, who was pacing the room. "Just let me grab my things, and I'll be out of your hair. I'll get ready in the bathroom."

As soon as she was in the other room, Aria snuggled back up in Kellan's embrace. "How can I train with you?" she asked while looking up at him. "What do you have in mind?"

Kellan stroked the hair that had fallen on her cheek before brushing it aside to hold her face. "Well, besides ravishing you a couple more times, I can help prepare you for tonight. I know how to kill a vampire after all."

She grimaced at his words. *He's a vampire, and I'm half-vampire.*

He must've sensed her unease because he pulled her in tighter and stroked her hair. "I know, my love, but don't worry. It'll be okay. I'm going to take good care of you. Now, tell me about the powers I heard you speak of. What can you do?"

Aria was about to answer, but Cat came out of the bathroom, so she snapped her mouth shut and just smiled.

"I'm not here," she sang out while she put her toiletries away and threw her dirty laundry in the hamper. She quickly scooped up her books and bag and headed toward the door. Throwing a look over her shoulder, she teased, "You kids have a good time."

Kellan burst into laughter when she left. "She seems fun."

Aria smiled before confirming, "Yes, she definitely is. She is a good friend to me"—she looked up at him—"I believe you asked about my powers, so let me tell you. I have the evil eye, of course, but I can also control the elements," she explained with a smile. "Let me show you." She took a candle from Cat's nightstand and placed it on the desk. "Watch this." Aria clasped her amulet and concentrated the way Zelda had taught her. She imagined a roaring fire burning, and soon the wick had an ember glow to it. She kept concentrating until the glow turned into a flame.

"That's very impressive," he exclaimed with admiration. "And it will be useful too."

Her brows furrowed together. "How so?"

"Fire is one of the ways to kill vampires," he explained, and his smile showed off his fangs.

"Oh, groovy." She nodded with a smile of her own. "What else?"

Kellan began pacing the room while he rubbed his hands together in thought. It was strange to be discussing ways to kill his kind.

"Well, there is decapitation, sunlight, as you know already, and salt water. Also, a wooden stake through the heart will work in a pinch." He stopped pacing and took her hands in his. "We'll get through this."

She opened her mouth to speak, but her stomach interrupted with a loud growl. "Pardon my stomach," she said with a giggle.

"Go get some food. I'll wait here unless you want me to shift and follow you. I could always shift into a mouse and go in your pocket," he teased.

"Hmm"—she put her finger to her chin—"rodents in the cafeteria. I think not. You can wait here for me, and I'll just be a minute to grab something. Then we can talk more about you ravishing me." She licked her lips and leaned in for a kiss. Kellan obliged and then grabbed her ass and held her close for a couple of minutes before letting her leave for her meal.

After the door closed, he sat on her bed and inhaled the scent of her from her pillow. He was missing her already. He, too, wondered how their lives together would work if she remained mortal. Of course, all he had to do was impregnate her to complete her conversion, but now that they were mutually in love, he didn't want to take the choice away from her. It wouldn't be fair if he didn't let her decide.

Lost in his thoughts, he didn't hear the unlocked window opening. He also didn't hear the chimp climbing through it. Suddenly, though, he smelled the fragrance of roses and ambrosia, and that got his attention.

Ninety

Gail and the other members of the Daughters of Bathory met early in the morning and were filled with excitement. They had been bitten twice, and tonight would be the third time just as soon as the sun went down. Then they would begin their new immortal lives by serving Countess Elizabeth Bathory in the fight against the Gypsies.

Gail raised her hand to silence the group. "Sisters, please quiet down, so we can make our plans." As soon as the group hushed, she continued, "I'm as excited as you all are, but we must maintain order during the meeting. There is much to discuss."

Alicia interrupted as soon as she heard the pause, "What about Kellan? Has Gabriella done anything to sway his love for the enchanted girl?"

Gail leaned her head slightly to the side. "I'm honestly not sure, but I hope so. If not, we'll have to take care of him ourselves."

Betty raised her hand, and after getting a nod of approval, said, "I suggest we worry more about killing the girl. That, in turn, will take care of Kellan."

More chatter erupted within the group, so Gail used her gavel to gain their attention. "There is some logic to that idea, Betty. Thank you for your contribution."

"But he'll be protecting her," Alicia brought up.

"Of course, he will," Gail said exasperated, "but the other vampires are going to be there, too, to help fight him. There will be Mikel, and the others he's turned, and Gabriella, along with the men she has turned. Maybe even the Gypsies will want to see him destroyed. He is a vampire trying to turn one of their own after all." Her explanation seemed feasible to the others, so they remained calm and listened for further instructions.

"So, after we are changed, we'll follow Mikel to the battle grounds, wherever that may be, and try to get to the girl. If you get ahold of her, kill her, and then we'll worry about Kellan, who will be broken down and vulnerable"—she looked around the group—"Now, who has what weapons to use against the Gypsies? Personally, I've got a gun and some knives from my son's collection."

At the mention of Chris, a tear streamed down her face. She knew Gabriella had killed him, and it broke her heart, but it was all for the good of the vampire—what she wanted to become.

They discussed the weapons they would bring and then adjourned the meeting.

Ninety-one

Kellan stared at the vampire, unable to speak. He had nothing but contempt and disdain for her now, but he'd loved her deeply once, and the emotions were all muddled together in the back of his throat.

As she stared into Kellan's face, a gruesome feeling of regret washed over Gabriella. There was pain in her heart caused by the scorn in his eyes, and once again, she wished she'd not abandoned him centuries ago. But, what was done was done.

"Kellan, it's good to see you again, love," she said in a voice thick with seduction. He averted his eyes and leaned against the wall, though.

"I can't say the same, Gabriella. You don't belong here," he spat at her, and hate came off him in waves.

"Look at me," she demanded, "Look at me, and tell me you don't miss me."

Kellan looked at her, but a black curtain of disgust fell over his graveyard eyes. He had given in to his hate, and there was no turning back.

"I don't miss a single solitary thing about you," he snarled.

She cocked her head, feigning confusion and hurt feelings, and replied, "How can you say that? You loved me once, remember?"

He chuckled, but it was out of sarcasm. "I remember. I remember you leaving me dead, discarded, and unaware of what to do next"—he took steps toward her—"I remember waking up as this monster, this thing, and not knowing where you went or why you turned me. I remember being on the verge of proposing when you abandoned me. That is what I remember!" he snapped at her and got close enough to touch her, but he didn't.

"I did love you, but I had my reasons for leaving," she told him with a pout. "I had no choice but to go. A powerful Gypsy was after me, and I had to go into hiding." The last part was a lie.

Kellan felt four hundred years of rage boiling in his blood, and he was reaching up to strangle the bitch when he heard the door open, and it distracted him.

Gabriella saw her opening, and she took it. She pulled him in for a kiss—a deep, heated, immortal kiss—and heard the girl gasp in surprise. That was all she needed to do for now—plant seeds of doubt between the lovers. She turned to the window, shifted into a chimp, so she could pull the curtain back, and then a bluebird to fly away.

Kellan spun around to face Aria, who stood in the doorframe with her mouth open, and told her, "I'm sorry, but that wasn't me, that was all her."

Aria opened her mouth to say something, but no words would come out. She just found her love kissing another vampire—a gorgeous, exquisite vampire. Jealousy, naked and cruel, gnawed at her thoughts. Gabriella could have attacked her then, too, but she didn't. She was too busy making out with Aria's fiancé—*her* former mate.

Kellan walked up to her and pulled her stiff body into his embrace. "Please understand, my love, that wasn't me kissing her. She kissed me to hurt you."

Aria finally moved from her frozen state of shock, but only enough to look up at him. "Well it worked," she softly cried.

Kellan wiped away her salty tear and felt his eyes misting up too, which was odd because he didn't know he could still cry—he hadn't since he was human. His heart was aching, and he didn't know if he could get through to her.

"I hate seeing you hurt, my sweet. I wish I could wash away your pain. I promise I didn't mean to let her do that, and I promise I will never do anything to intentionally hurt you. Even if she wanted to rekindle what we had four hundred years ago, there's no way I'd do it. I love you and only you. I can't see my existence without you."

Aria could see the pain in his eyes, and she could see the anger he was feeling toward Gabriella, and she suddenly felt silly.

"Well," she began with a shaky smile, "let's teach that bitch a lesson, shall we? No one, and I mean no one, puts their paws on my man."

Kellan beamed as he picked her up and swung her around in circles. "I'm so glad to hear that!"

He leaned in to kiss her, but it didn't stop there. Soon, they were naked in each other's arms again. Afterward, instead of falling asleep like they had been, she was full of energy and ready to learn some fighting techniques. There was no time to waste, and she was expected at Zelda's at noon.

Kellan practiced hand to hand combat with her. He used a straightened-out hanger as a makeshift sword to show her how to get close enough to decapitate. He also showed her how to get out of a vampire's grip in case one gets close enough to grab her in a stronghold.

Aria felt vigorous during her training. She felt strong and agile, which was new for her, so she assumed her vampire half was surfacing and taking over. The hours passed quickly, and it was soon time to go to Zelda's house.

Ninety-two

Aria arrived at Zelda's house precisely at noon and had a hard time finding a place to park. Cars filled her driveway and the street adjacent to it, so she had a long walk. When she got to the front door, she could hear the laughter on the other side, and it put a picture in her mind of several older women sitting around drinking tea and talking about days long past.

Zelda answered immediately and ushered her inside. Several women and men of different ages greeted her and encouraged to take a seat. As soon as she did, they began talking to her like they were old friends. Once all the introductions had been made, it was time to talk business.

They discussed their individual gifts and tried to figure out how they would work with hers to their advantage. Most, like Zelda, could see the future using tarot cards and crystal balls, while a couple relied on spells from books. No one else, though, had the gift to control the elements, and Aria took pride in having that ability all to herself. The group was excited to see how her amulet would interact with their own, so they wanted to take things for a test drive. They put them all together and tried a couple of simple spells, which yielded expected results, and then they asked her to use her power to call the elements. Those results were better than expected—as soon as she thought of a storm, it brewed, and she almost lit the house on fire.

They regaled her with stories of victories against vampires and witches in the Old World, and they spoke words of encouragement to boost her confidence for the battle ahead.

Then the subject of Kellan came up. The final consensus was to let him fight by her side, but not all agreed. A few thought she shouldn't have anything to do with him despite being half-vampire. It was their idea that they work together to find a spell to kill the vampire side of her, so the Gypsy side could take over.

"No! No matter how you feel about vampires, he loves me, and I love him just as much. He wouldn't be going against his kind if it wasn't true," she argued.

"I think you'll learn to believe otherwise, and this is just a trap he has set," a woman named Maria claimed.

"If those are your true feelings, then you are a fool," Zelda scolded the other woman. "I have seen her future, and it is promised to be filled with love—his love."

Maria said nothing more, and neither did the others. After an hour of chatting, Aria decided it was time to go back to Kellan, so she said good-bye for now.

It was agreed that they would all convene in a secluded region near the bay. That way, no humans would be involved. Aria asked how they'd find the vampires, and she was told the vampires would find them.

She drove back to Kellan tumbled in a mixture of emotions. She was afraid of the battle, naturally, and of Gabriella, but she was excited by her love for Kellan, and she couldn't wait to be next to him again.

Kellan was waiting in her room yet, like he'd said he would be, and he immediately pulled her in for a kiss.

She chuckled when the kiss broke off. "I missed you too, big boy. That bitch didn't come back around, did she?"

"No, she stayed away. I think she's afraid she has met her match with you," he replied with a hearty wink.

Aria smiled up at him. "I think so too," she stated confidently. "After all, we're fighting over you."

Kellan began to quickly undress her. "Well that, my love, is no contest."

They enjoyed their lovemaking for the next several minutes and then fell asleep in each other's arms until the alarm went off at 4:15 p.m.

Ninety-three

Aria, along with a black crow, pulled up to the battle grounds where some of the Gypsies, including Zelda, were already waiting. Sundown was only a handful of minutes away.

Kellan flew off, but he didn't go far. The plan was for him to scope out the animals in the area to see how big the vampire army is. Surely, they'd followed the Gypsies, Aria included, to the grounds or had sensed their whereabouts. He was having a difficult time discerning shapeshifters from real animals, though, so Gabriella must have taught them well. It was also a possibility they weren't there yet. In any case, it would all be happening soon enough.

The sun finally hid behind the mountains, and it was safe for him to make his change back. When he appeared before the Gypsies, buzzing went out through the crowd. He had to laugh at some of the comments he heard.

"I didn't expect him to be so big or that handsome," a woman said.

"Holy shit, just look at him. He's magnificent, so no wonder the girl fell in love."

Aria heard the comments, too, and put her arm tighter around his waist. She didn't need the horny old ladies getting any ideas.

It wasn't long before a rustling through the trees caught their attention, and several blood-thirsty vampires, led by Gabriella, appeared. With a vicious smile, she stepped forth.

"It doesn't have to come to all of this, my darling Kellan. We can be together again, and I know you want that too. Just remember all the fun we had when we were together laughing, dancing"—she focused her gaze on Aria—"and making love."

He opened his mouth to say something in return, but Aria surprised him by pulling him into a deep and passionate kiss.

Kellan opened his eyes to see Gabriella's reaction, and he found it to be priceless. Her face was scrunched up in rage, and her eyes were blood- red. Then they opened wider, and she spat out a string of curses more vulgar than he'd heard even the swarthiest of pirates say—she had noticed the ring on Aria's finger.

She charged forth with Mikel right behind her. "Give me *my* ring!" she spat.

Mikel ran around her and lunged at Kellan, tackling him to the ground. Kellan quickly rolled over to be on top, and he punched the fractured cheek causing a loud cry to escape his enemy.

Gabriella stopped to watch briefly before continuing her path to Aria, who was braced and ready. "So, you're the special creature everyone has been making such a fuss over. Well, give me my ring, little girl, and maybe I won't hurt you," she hissed.

Aria's tongue darted quickly over her dry lips before she growled back, "Come and take it, bitch!"

Gabriella smirked as she slowly made her approach with her fangs brandished.

Kellan struggled with Mikel yet, and the other vampire got in a couple of cheap blows while Kellan observed the showdown between his love and Gabriella. He got to his feet just in time to see the glint off something metal that was coming toward him—Mikel had pulled out a large hunting knife. Kellan dodged, but Mikel quickly brought the blade back around, and it contacted Kellan's arm—the one that had sustained prior damage.

Aria saw the assault and cried out while grabbing her amulet and concentrating as hard as she could. Suddenly, a bright flare of light lit up the darkness as the vampire became an inferno. His blood-curdling cry caught the attention of everyone as the hungry flames devoured him.

"That's a cute trick," Gabriella hissed in her ear while snaking an arm around her waist.

Aria could feel the saliva dripping on her neck from the vampire's fangs, so she reacted quickly by bringing her fist up to punch Gabriella's forehead. It surprised the vampire and knocked her back far enough that Aria had some wiggle room to elbow her in the stomach next. Then she spun around to face the menacing creature, while Kellan was fighting off three of the newborn vampires—one of which was Chris's mother.

"Enough!" Gabriella spat. "You die now."

She lunged forward, but Aria side-stepped out of the way. Aria was about to make her own move when she saw another vampire headed for her, so she touched her amulet, and summoned a strong SW wind. It came on rather suddenly and blew the vampire backward over the cliff and into the bay, consuming her in salt water.

Gabriella growled and lunged again, this time gaining enough real estate to take Aria down. She went in for the kill, but just as her fangs pierced Aria's pale neck, Kellan was there to pull her off. He sent the vampire flying across the grass while another lunged at him. He caught him in mid-air, though, and wrapped his hand around the monster's head before cranking it far enough to break the neck.

"Breaking the neck also works," he explained with a wink just as Gabriella made her reappearance.

"Kellan, don't let her hurt me," she purred and batted her long lashes. "Remember how much you loved me."

Kellan took in a deep breath and pretended to think things over. "I can't," he smirked with a shrug while Aria took advantage and lunged with a knife she had tucked in her cargo pants pocket. She swiped in the air but barely caught enough flesh to do damage.

Gabriella laughed. "Is that the best you've got, pup?"

Aria shook her head. "No, try this on for size."

She firmly grasped her amulet and imagined the worst thunderstorm she could. Rain began to pour down on them, but Gabriella just laughed.

"I'm melting. I'm melting," she shrieked with a cackle. "Oh, wait, I'm not a witch—I'm a vampire!"

She began to charge, and Kellan jumped in front of Aria, but she pushed him aside.

"No, the bitch is mine," she ground out between gritted teeth.

She dug into her mind's eye and saw her mother's letter, and she began to chant.

"I am light, where the darkness dwells. I will fight those brought from hell. In the gloom of the night, I am too strong for you to fight. Romani blood sets me free. Ayres name protects me from thee. I am safe from the plight that comes from your immortal bite."

Then she imagined a white-hot bolt of lightning, and it suddenly creased the sky, lighting everything up around them. She pictured it moving and pulled it out of the sky to strike down where Gabriella stood. The electricity coursed up and down her body in a magnificent display of white and blue lights before it and she were both gone.

Aria walked with Kellan to where the vampire had been and found a pile of dust. "You can add electrocution to your list," she said with a big grin.

"I'll do that," he replied while pulling her close to him.

They surveyed the area and saw vampires retreating while others were still being slain by the Gypsies. Then, a loud cheer erupted, and they knew it was over. They ran hand in hand to the others, and many hugs were passed around. Even Kellan received some handshakes and pats on the back. He didn't care about that, though, he cared about the kiss he got from Aria. It was the most powerful kiss they'd shared yet.

Aria looked for Zelda among the others but couldn't find her mentor. Then, just as she was about to make an inquiry, she saw her friend crumpled up on the ground. She bent down with tears clouding her eyes and felt for a pulse, but none was to be found—her throat had been ripped out.

Bawling, she buried her face into Kellan's chest. He held her protectively and stroked her back while she let loose of all her emotions. After several minutes, she looked up into his own weepy eyes and forced a weak half-smile.

"Promise me something," she said in a quivering voice.

"Anything for you, my love." He wiped away her latest stream of tears from her puffy cheek.

"Promise me that we can name our daughter Zelda."

He smiled warmly at her. "If we ever have a daughter, we can certainly name her Zelda."

Aria took a shuddering breath. "Okay. Well, we will know if it's a girl in about eight months."

The End